ADVANCE PRAISE FOR
BEAR ME AWAY TO A BETTER WORLD

Ginna BB Gordon's 11th book, *Bear Me Away to a Better World*, is her first murder mystery, a scintillating tale that takes place in a professional theater setting in California's wine country. Her characters are delightful, colorful, and full of surprises, drawn from her lifetime surrounded by visual and performing artists. Readers of *Bear Me Away to a Better World* will want a sequel.

> – Barbara Rose Shuler
> Arts Writer on the Monterey Peninsula,
> California

Not all drama in a theater company happens on the stage, as anyone involved with theater can attest, and Villa Zanetta in Ginna BB Gordon's *Bear Me Away to a Better World* is no exception.

Ms. Gordon handles the suspected murder of a company member and all of its wild emotional consequences with an eerie ability that makes the reader feel part of the action. So much so, one can imagine hearing the seductive strains of Mozart that bind this tale together.

If this is not enough to bear you away, Gordon writes characters with such an uncanny skill that the cast and crew become living, breathing people you know and with whom you are spending time. They truly transport you "to a better world."

> – Dennis Britten
> Founder of Light Opera of Portland
> and author of *Men Shake Hands,*
> *a creative reminiscence*

BEAR ME
AWAY
TO A BETTER
WORLD

Other books by Ginna BB Gordon

Once a Baker
  100 favorite Recipes and Reminiscences
  A DIY in the Kitchen Collection

The Soup Kit
  A comprehensive map for creating good soups from scratch

The Lavandula Series
  Based on the fictional journals of Stefani Michel
  Book One: *Looking for John Steinbeck*
  Book Two: *Deke Interrupted*
  Book Three: *Humming in Spanish*

The Honey Baby Darlin' Series
  A serial memoir about cooking, love, & the love of cooking
  Book One: *Bonnebrook*
  Book Two: *The Gingerbread Farm*

Sunny Mae & Bird in Alaska
  A read-aloud book with illustrations by Dai Thomas

First You Grow the Pumpkin
  100 Cool Things to Make and Preserve
  A DIY in the Kitchen Collection

A Simple Celebration
  The Nutritional Program from the Chopra Center for Well Being
  Written as Ginna Bell Bragg, with David Simon, MD
  Foreword by Deepak Chopra (pub. by Random House)

Visit www.luckyvalleypress.com

BEAR ME *AWAY* TO A BETTER *WORLD*

THE TALE OF A DUO, THE POWER OF MUSIC, AND A CHANDELIER

Ginna Gordon

A NOVEL BY

GINNA BB GORDON

WITH DAVID GORDON

LUCKY VALLEY PRESS
2022

Designed and published
by Lucky Valley Press
www.luckyvalleypress.com

Cover photo: dashapetrenko/shutterstock.com

Printed on acid-free paper

Dedication

An die Musik

To Music

Du holde Kunst, in wieviel grauen Stunden,
Wo mich des Lebens wilder Kreis umstrickt,
Hast du mein Herz zu warmer Lieb' entzunden,
Hast mich in eine beßre Welt entrückt!

Oft hat ein Seufzer, deiner Harf' entflossen,
Ein süßer, heiliger Akkord von dir,
Den Himmel beßrer Zeiten mir erschlossen,
Du holde Kunst, ich danke dir dafür.

You lovely art, in so many gloomy hours,
While the turmoil of life swirled around me,
Have you kindled the warmth of love in my heart
And borne me away to a better world.

Often a sigh, flowing from your harp,
A sweet and holy harmony from you,
Has revealed to me a heaven of happier times.
You lovely art, I thank you for this.

Franz von Schober (1796–1882)
Vienna, 1817

English version by David Gordon

The Illustrious History of Villa Zanetta: 1900–2008

by John Eagle, Director of Development and Public Relations
The Theaters at Villa Zanetta
Sonoma Valley, California

In the rolling hills of the Sonoma Valley, there is an estate known as Villa Zanetta. Local lore suggests that Forrest Hendrickson, wealthy merchant and the builder of Villa Zanetta in 1900, perished in the wreck of the steamship Columbia heading from San Francisco to Portland in 1907. The tragedy also took the life of Mr. Hendrickson's traveling companion, Marcella Wheeler, listed in the passenger manifest as Hendrickson's "secretary."

Mr. Hendrickson's other "associate," known simply as Zanetta, was busy at the 8,000 square foot villa named after her, tending to her tidy little pleasure business. Fortunately, with the help of a crafty attorney, upon Forrest's death Zanetta was bequeathed the villa, and Mrs. Hendrickson, over in Napa, was none the wiser. Mr. Hendrickson was a busy fellow.

Villa Zanetta sits on 60 acres nestled into a gentle hillside. The original mansion began as a Tudor construction, and was then added onto, one too many times. There is a lily pond dubbed Lake Zanetta, fed by a trickling stream. Deer, ducks, geese, frogs, bobcats and all manner of birds call the 60 acres around Villa Zanetta "home." The occasional bear visits the pond to lap lily water, and the mountain lions come for sips, too. Not often.

Back in Zanetta's time, the Villa overlooked rolling meadows of grasslands and all sorts of trees, including manzanita, madrone, oak, pine, cedar, fir and willow. But soon, the expansive view was carpeted with vineyards and lined with yellow mustard. The breezes of Sonoma whistle through the Villa, wave through the trees and touch the tops of the curling, winding vines.

Villa Zanetta has experienced a few changes and a couple of face lifts over the years. When she died in 1935, Zanetta's will passed over her five children, whom she hardly knew, their having been palmed off on The Boys and Girls Catholic Aid Society for safe keeping. Besides, her ladies of the night needed the rooms.

With a fine sense of irony, Zanetta left her estate to the Catholic church, who changed the name and turned Villa Zanetta into a summer camp for troublesome boys; an early version of the Catholic Youth Organization camps. A dormitory was built, and a chapel.

In 1949, the Catholics sold the camp to three investors who called themselves The Highwaymen Conference Group. They put a million dollars (a lot of money in 1949) into a renovation and had several small conferences at Sulfur Steam Conference Center before falling three-heads-first into bankruptcy. That might have been because there was no sulfur steam.

The founders of The Theaters at Villa Zanetta, Robert DeWayne "Diesel" Edwards and Hayne Endicott Williams, returned the original name to the estate when, in 1957, they picked up the languishing property for a relative song.

Their goal? To follow their creative dreams.

Hayne Williams and "Diesel" Edwards took the old and beautiful but awkwardly remodeled Tudor mansion, its dorm, barn and tiny chapel, and created a prize-winning performing arts center, where thespians and musicians of all persuasions come together to create beauty, to embrace their watchers and listeners within the arms of the nine muses; fill waiting ears with the joys of music; delight the eye and warm the heart. This was the goal and the success.

Each season, each month, each week, in fact, there is something happening in the vortex of The Theaters at Villa Zanetta: plays are acted out, symphonies and operas performed, dancers twirl and leap across the stage of the 400 seat Well Lit Theater. Puppets create humor, pathos and general havoc in The Tiny Little Theater in the Barn. On the stage of the Old Hall, the local chorus, the Sonoma-based Bella Voce Chorale, and others share their harmonies with appreciative audiences. Banquets are held, marriages solemnized, ceremonies performed.

This Season marks the 50th anniversary of The Theaters at Villa Zanetta.

***

From the Program Book of the
50th Anniversary Spring-Summer Season, May 2008

Prologue
1955

H ayne Endicott Williams stood at the main entrance to the San Francisco Institute of Art for the first time. Gilmor Brown's scribbled instructions were penciled into the margin of his paperwork; show up at class with "paper, pencils, charcoal and a rag" and "don't be late."

Hayne wasn't late. He looked at his watch. *Ha. Half an hour early.* Didn't Gilmor remember after all Hayne's time at the College of Theatre Arts (six years, but who's counting?) that he was never late? And this! This was a cool opportunity; a drawing and design summer workshop that will complete his theater arts degree obligations. "You're missing some drawing techniques, so go," Gilmor had said with a grin. "We don't know everything in Pasadena."

Hayne made his way to #116 and peered into the empty room. He let go of the door frame and tiptoed in. Three days in San Francisco was not enough time to shake the Santa Monica Beach trailer trash out of Hayne Williams's consciousness, although Gilmor and the other Pasadena Playhouse mentors had certainly tried.

Hayne pressed his hands straight down by his sides, gripped his thighs, held himself steady. This room, this institute, this city, this whole new world; he had been thrown into it almost kicking and screaming. How on earth did he get here? Street kid, beach rat, quirky artistic loner. Not to mention his mother.

Better start thinking of Fatty as Charlotte Penelope Williams. Who else calls his mother "Fatty"? I shouldn't be here, he thought. *I should be back at the Pier, at the beach in the Ice Queen with Fatty, filling plastic mustard and ketchup bottles and frying onion rings and drawing caricatures of chubby sightseers in bad bathing suits. Or flapping the mouths of twenty sock puppets at the side door.*

Whatever was Gilmor thinking, setting up this scholarship? Am I too old? At 24, will I be the oldest student in the class? Is this awkward?

Gilmor says it's for my "expansion," whatever that means. Between work and helping Fatty and trying to concentrate on "book learning," as Fatty says, I am full up to capacity. Well, when I'm done, I'm finally and thoroughly and completely done with school. Done, done, done. It's taken long enough.

I'll go back to LA and...what?

DIESEL

At the same moment, Robert DeWayne "Diesel" Edwards leapt off the bus like a gazelle at the corner of Chestnut and Jones, his scarf fluttering behind him and dragging on the sidewalk. He couldn't help it if his Aunt Hazel knitted scarves too long even for a gazelle.

One might wonder why anyone with the grace of a wild animal would be carting around a name such as Diesel, but suffice it to say, unbeknownst to his father, Diesel was not destined to carry the Edwards Diesel Engine Co. and the Edwards family name into the future.

While Hayne struggled to grow up in a ratty "Covered Wagon" trailer by the beach in Santa Monica, Diesel attended private schools and thrived like a gardenia in a mansion in Winnetka, Illinois. But when Diesel's father discovered his teenaged son dancing in his bedroom wrapped in nothing but a bed sheet and waving his arms, the next conversation did not go well.

Diesel, more interested in theater arts than in the engines after which he was nicknamed, happened to be a bit bored by the six million dollars dropped into his bank account upon his father's death. After four years at Northwestern studying theater arts, he deserted Winnetka, Illinois, Edwards Diesel Engine Co., and his mother, Queen Elizabeth Edwards, and fled to San Francisco, taking his six million dollars with him. There he immersed himself in a lifestyle to his own liking and discovered the city's thriving theater and opera world.

Now that Diesel had his routine all worked out (exploring the arts in San Francisco, acting classes in the evenings with Madame Sorrento, and doing his thing as an opera supernumerary on weekends) he agreed to sit for the advanced drawing class taught on eight Saturday mornings by his friend, Gabby Lewis, at the San Francisco Institute of Art.

She said, "One hour sessions, three Saturdays in a row. That's all. 25 bucks."

He accepted the gig but turned down the money. He didn't need the money. He did it for the joy of grinning at a class full of ogling institute housewives and incoming freshmen. Diesel was proud of his physique.

HAYNE

San Francisco fog frizzed Hayne's hair and wrinkled his natty seersucker suit. He felt mildly unglued. It started on the bus to the Institute from his boarding house. His lightweight, 5'8" frame began to shake right about the time they stopped at the red light on Chestnut and Jones. He looked out the window and saw a bum curled up on a bench with his coat pulled over his head. At first Hayne laughed; it made him homesick for the Santa Monica Pier. Then he got depressed because he felt as if he could be that man. He could be broke.

Well, technically, he was broke. The fifty dollars a week spending money came from this outrageous scholarship, dinner on a tray arrived by magic every evening at 6 provided by Mrs. Mathews, his landlady, and Hayne bought books second hand at the school hub. Hayne Williams, about to make it in the world on his wits, understood his situation. The next item on his list: to look for a part-time job.

Hayne scurried to the back of the classroom and took possession of the last seat nearest the left wall behind a split leaf philodendron that filled up six square feet. He could witness the arrival of the teacher and the other students from here, without being noticed.

Did Hayne truly expect to go unnoticed wearing a rumpled seersucker suit and checked socks? The first person to walk into the class, none other than Diesel Edwards himself, noticed the seersucker and the checks right off and said, "Oh my, my..." as he sauntered through the room to the back and moved behind a screen to get practically naked.

Well. Hayne didn't know quite what to think of this. Was that the teacher? G. Lewis? If so, he'll be pretty to look at, at least. That calmed Hayne down a bit. Tall handsome teacher in white shirt and khaki pants. Lovely. He twisted his hanky into a corkscrew.

3

DIESEL

Behind the screen, Diesel carefully removed his khakis and placed them over the back of the chair. He hung his shirt on the hook and placed his shoes, underwear and socks under the chair in a neat little stack and wrapped a flowered sarong around his tall and lanky torso. He admired his profile in the mirror, slicked back his hair and, completely aware of the picture he presented, but cool as the ol' cucumber, strode like a king through his court to the front of the room through a forming throng of students. Just as he stepped onto the platform, Gabby Lewis arrived and said, "Ah. Class. Good morning. This is your advanced life drawing class part of your eight week summer workshop. If you're in the wrong room, go to the hall to see the new map. My name is Gabby Lewis. Meet Diesel Edwards, your first model. Today you'll be studying his stupendous behind. Let's get to it."

Hayne, in shock, as in "knock me over with a feather," could not take his eyes off this marvel. *OK. Not the teacher. A man. Oh my, what a man. Look at him, a work of art, not a mere man. Oh dear, oh dear.*

Diesel knew he attracted people like hummingbirds to red, and that everyone in the class, boy and girl, man and woman, would admire his derrière and other attributes. But, at this moment, Diesel did *not* know that a man in the back of the room, the one in the checked socks, had just fallen for him, head over heels.

Diesel's life took a surprising left turn.

HAYNE

Hayne could hardly hold onto his pencil. If he thought he was nervous when he came in, he knew he'd be a wreck on the way out.

It took ten minutes to calm down enough to even remember how to hold the pencil between his fingers, much less push it around on the paper. *Just concentrate,* he mumbled to himself. He shook his head like a dog getting out of a pool. He blinked. He cleaned his glasses for the tenth time. He put pencil to paper and snapped the tip off the pencil lead.

He sharpened his pencil. *Breath in. Breath out. It's ok. It's ok.* He chanced a look at the model, Diesel. *Really?* The man stood with his back to the room, facing slightly left, so better for all to view the flexed and beautiful cheeks of his exposed bottom. Hayne didn't even notice the rest of him—he was too busy blinking his eyes at that perfect butt.

Hayne slipped into the groove, though. Drawing could do that for him. He always forgot that. Once he got going, the drawing took care of itself. He worked it meticulously, made himself focus on the contours, the lines.

Holy Mary, the Dominican nuns never told me there'd be days like this. Oh No!

Gabby Lewis rang her little hand bell, signifying the change of position for Diesel, the model. Diesel jumped around a bit to loosen his muscles, then turned toward the room, fantastically uninhibited. Gabby, wandering around the room commenting on the various replications of Diesel's "stupendous behind," asked him to sit on one of the cubes, in any comfortable position.

Diesel sat down on a big cube and put one foot on a smaller cube in front of him and one hand on each thigh, arranging his sarong with the perfect drape.

Hayne finished his rendering of Diesel's cheeks. *Pretty good, if I do say so.* He was much more in tune when he was drawing. He kept saying to himself, *Look at him as a work of art. A work of art.* He looked up to see the next position.

Every bit of Diesel's skin was exposed to the light except what was under that daring drape. Hayne had a perfect view of Diesel's entire body: every contour, every line, every toe, the cleft in his beautiful chin, the curve of his calf. Even his kneecaps were beautiful. Hayne had never seen a more perfect specimen of a man in his life. His experience with men was limited. OK. Non-existent. But, this was a dreamboat in no clothes.

Diesel felt someone's gaze like a penetrating laser beam of energy directed straight at his chest, an arrow out of Cupid's pink quiver. He looked up from his own toes and caught the eye of the man in the checked socks. They locked eyes for exactly three seconds, before Hayne looked away, embarrassed.

Three seconds was long enough, though, for the arrow to hit its mark. Diesel felt its strike. It was light, like a feather, but deep, like a sound, and sharp, like a needle, but smooth, like skating on a icy pond. Diesel

5

wanted the man in the checked socks and seersucker suit to look at him again. It felt so warm, like a hug, like a scarf on a cold day.

Hayne concentrated on his drawing. He knew he'd have to look up eventually. He couldn't draw that body from memory, not yet. And so, he looked up and into Diesel's eyes. For the next five minutes, Diesel did not move, Hayne did not draw, and they did not take their eyes off each other. Hayne kept trying, but his eyes seemed to be tied by a golden thread to the eyes of Diesel Edwards.

They say that when two people fall in love, wild horses can't keep them apart; that there is a non-verbal, "Oh, it's you. Let's get on with it!" quality to the moment, when all five senses are on alert, and all roads lead in only one direction.

For Hayne, who knew it first, it was a doubly golden moment. He would vividly recall, to his dying day, even after his fertile brain slowed down in old age, he would never forget those first moments of being in love. And when he saw in Diesel's eyes the same life-altering joy of recognition, he dropped his pencil, put his head in his hands and cried.

After class, Diesel dashed behind that screen and dashed out in three minutes, heading straight toward the stunned Hayne Williams holding only half the assignment to turn in to Gabby Lewis. Diesel Edwards's kneecaps would have to wait.

Diesel thought, *There's nothing for it but to get straight on!* He made his way through the roomful of students over to Hayne, still poleaxed in the chair at his not-so-secret spot in the room. Diesel put out his elegant hand to shake Hayne's. "Robert Edwards. Everyone calls me Diesel."

Hayne, never articulate on the spur of the moment, stood up, took Diesel's hand in both of his and said, "Then I'll call you Robert. I'm Hayne Williams, and no one's ever called me anything but Hayne." He reluctantly let go of Diesel's hand.

The two men looked at each other for eons. In *real time*, probably three seconds, but in *falling in love time*, eons would be right.

Hayne finally croaked out, "Are you a student here?"

"No, I'm just doing this for a friend. C'mon. Let's go to the fountain."

"The fountain?"

"Never mind. C'mon."

The men walked to the brick courtyard. Hayne heard the splashing water from the fountain and remembered the sound from before class, when he was wandering around looking for Room 116, but due to his complete distraction at the time, he didn't track it or care. Now, he cared, because this specimen of wonder wanted to get know him! *Me! Hayne Williams.*

Hayne looked up and into the man's eyes, feeling insignificant and puny. *I wonder why he wants to talk to* me? said the negative voice in his head.

"So, like I said," said the god, "I'm Diesel Edwards. You looked wonderfully arty in there, against the wall, behind your plant, in seclusion. In a seersucker suit, no less. Compared to those bored housewives in Gabby's class, you're a breath of fresh air."

Hayne blinked.

"Tell me about yourself. Do you have time? Another class? Shall we sit here a moment?"

"I have a design class in twenty minutes," Hayne managed to say. He couldn't think what to do with his face. He tried to form a smile, but his face was frozen, a deer-in-the-headlights face. The headlights were the beaming eyes of Robert Edwards, otherwise known as Diesel.

To deflect the questions about himself, Hayne asked, "Why Diesel?"

"What? Oh, that. My father nicknamed me Diesel after patenting this little thingamajiggy to reduce the noxious fumes of diesel engines. He thought he was so clever. Well, he did make big money that day. He also started me on the road to ruin with my first whiskey in celebration of the fumeless diesel engine." Diesel laughed. "I was twelve. He died when I was in high school. Thank God, or I'd be a lush and in the Army now. Long story. I fled the scene for the theater when I was 22. What's *your* reason for being here in this spot at this very moment?"

"Er… I'm here on a scholarship."

"Well, that's not the reason. That's the means. How'd you get here on this day from…where did you say you were from?"

"Santa Monica."

"Ah. Santa Monica, then. What drew you from the sunny beaches of Santa Monica to the San Francisco fog?"

"A relentless teacher."

Diesel laughed. "You mean you didn't want to come?"

"Not exactly," said Hayne. "My guardian and Fa…my mother kind of made me. It's a long story, too."

"I'd like to hear it. I have time. Where are you living? We should meet for lunch. Tomorrow?"

"I just arrived in town three days ago, so I don't know my way around. I can meet you if you keep it simple. I'm in a boarding house at 111 Beach, near Fillmore."

"Perfect. I'm in the Marina. I'll walk over. We'll take a bus to Chinatown. I'll pick you up at 1."

And then, Diesel did the most charming thing, like some angel or oversoul tapped him on the shoulder. Call it intuition, call it the sight, call it Cupid! Give it whatever name you like, it's that other voice in one's head besides the everyday voice of reason. The one that owns the moment, seizes the day, makes it count. That voice said, "This. Now." He took a step back, looked Hayne in the eye, and gently put his hand on Hayne's shoulder blade. Just for a few seconds. Just a flash, in the great scheme of things, but long enough to relay the message: "At last."

And, poof, he was gone, gliding down the walkway, trailing a scarf. He was smiling…and his feet barely touched the tiles. Hayne, left at the fountain, felt like he'd just been whirled around in a typhoon.

With his mind and imagination full of Robert aka Diesel Edwards, Hayne found his counselor, his locker, and the right classrooms. He was so agitated by the end of the day, he walked all the way from Chestnut Street to the boarding house on Beach. He longed for a lay down and a cup of strong tea. And time. Time to just think about what happened.

CHAPTER ONE

FRIDAY, JUNE 6, 2008

If we shadows have offended, think but this, and all is mended,
that you have but slumber'd here while these visions did appear.
A Midsummer Night's Dream
~ Wm. Shakespeare

KABOOM

Villa Zanetta's Executive Director, Marcus Brown, called out, "Good night!" to his administrative team, Priscilla, MeiMei and LuLu, involved in a last-minute inventory of festival supplies. He wasn't sure they heard him back there in the storage room, but they knew his general plan; to zip out of the Villa on the dot of 5. All was well.

Marcus made his way down the circular steps from his office to the Lobby. He longed to be home, with his feet up on the coffee table and a glass of chardonnay within reach.

However, just as he stepped down to the Lobby floor, a thunderous crash stopped him dead. Shock waves riddled through his body right down to his socks. He sucked in his breath. Marcus's natty tan jacket, suddenly coated with dust and bits of glass, also twinkled with several crystal prisms. Just like that!

Wait. I'm not dead. Marcus exhaled, amazed he was still upright, because the theater's Stage Director, Falcon Jennings, who moments before had been walking across the Lobby toward Marcus, lay at his feet. *Falcon?* Falcon's long brown hair spread out like a fan. Thin glass shards littered the floor. The five-foot-wide, 400-pound chandelier had missed Marcus's head by inches and one of its gilded leaves grazed through his right jacket sleeve on the way down.

Falcon looks dead. He looks…crushed. Flat. Unreal. His head! Oh my God, his head is…smashed. Am I dreaming? This is nuts. Where is everyone? What just happened? Why did it happen? And more to the point, why can't I move? I am glued to this spot. Son of a motherless goat! I've got to sit down.

Marcus slapped his cheeks. *I'm talking to myself like a madman. Of course I am! I almost died there! And Falcon! Falcon! Fark!*

Marcus still couldn't move. A thousand pictures scrambled his brain, but he couldn't find an image to fit the scene. Had he really just witnessed the chandelier smashing his friend's head? He looked at his own torn sleeve. His eyes moved again to Falcon, the obviously lifeless Falcon. *There's not a chance he's still alive. Weird that there's no blood. Shouldn't there be blood? Why am I even thinking about this?*

After a minute that seemed like an hour, the first person on the scene was Willard Franklin, the conductor of this season's opera, *Cosi fan tutte*, and Marcus Brown's least favorite person in the land. Perhaps not in the land. There may be more disagreeable fellows in Marcus's sphere of occupation, but he couldn't think of one right now.

Ever conciliatory, although fake as all get-out, Willard strode (mind you, he did not rush) through the theater hallway to the Lobby and glanced at the mess, the broken body of Falcon Jennings and the chandelier. He stepped around the bits of glass, came to Marcus and took his arm to lead him to a bench. Marcus's eyes glazed over.

"What happened, Marcus?" Willard's 6'5" body and unruly shoulder length dark hair loomed over the stunned executive director. *Ew. I could light his breath with a match! How could he be so calm?*

Marcus pointed at the chandelier, bent and still wobbling over the body of Falcon Jennings.

"*That* happened," his voice quivered. "Go check on Falcon. My God, I'm sure he's dead. Oh, Lord. Of course, he's dead." *Now I'll never know what he wanted to talk to me about. What did Falcon say on the phone? That he was "deeply distressed"? Heavens, always so dramatic. Well... mum's the word on that. My mind is a jumble. Keep breathing, Marcus. Just breathe. Fark! If I hold my hands together, will they stop shaking?*

What did happen? We were walking toward each other. Falcon looked down. So I looked down, and, Wham! I heard...what? A little bit of racket from above and then...whoosh? What word can describe what happened? It was so fast. One moment, eye contact, the next moment, gone. Down on the floor and gone. It could have been me. My sleeve was torn right through. And Falcon is gone!

Marcus started to cry.

Kendra Masters rushed in next, tossing her cigarette in the bowl of sand by the front door. Racing toward Marcus, she glanced at Willard, checked at the sight of Falcon crushed on the floor and continued toward her friend slumped on a bench.

"What's this, Marcus? I heard the kaboom! What happened to Falcon?" She started to go to Falcon, her boss and mentor, but Marcus grabbed her hand and pulled her down on the bench next to him. "Don't," is all he managed to get out of his mouth. He squeezed her hand. She looked at him like, "What? What?" He shook his head. "Just don't."

He thought, *Kaboom. That's right out of Marvel comics. But completely on point.* "Someone should call an ambulance," he croaked out to Willard, who, true to form, slipped a found penny into his shoe as he stood up.

Willard turned his back on Falcon Jennings. He walked over to Marcus and with spooky calm said, "It's too late for an ambulance. He's quite dead." He said the word "dead" liked he had just ground a poisonous spider to bits with his foot.

"Holy Mother," said Marcus, shaking his head as if to wick rain out of his brain. Tears slid down his cheeks. He felt light-headed, fuzzy. His fingers were cold. His knees shook, even though he was sitting down.

Marcus looked at Kendra Masters; she held his hand, and she, too, started to cry.

Everyone loved Falcon, Marcus thought. *Most everyone. And she was his assistant! They were together every day. And this! The chandelier just hurtled through space and killed Falcon Jennings!*

He forced himself to put his invisible Executive Director hat on and sat up. He wiped the tears from his cheeks with his hand.

"Kendra, I know you're upset, and I am, too. But, we have to get it together here. I need you to go upstairs and get Priscilla, she'll know what to do. I can't seem to move yet. My legs are like noodles. Priscilla obviously didn't hear that crash. They must still be in the back room. Tell her that Falcon is…Falcon is…likely dead under the chandelier. She should call an ambulance. Someone will have to declare…someone will have to…take him way. Oh, Mother of Pearl." *Am I thinking straight?*

Kendra wiped her tears but did not let go of Marcus's hand. She looked over at her teacher and constant work buddy, Falcon, lying on the floor. She stared at the lifeless body. She let go of Marcus's hand and made herself go toward the circular stairs to the office level. She stopped and turned and said, "I think we should call the sheriff, Marcus."

"Yes. Yes. You're right. OK. Tell Priscilla to get MeiMei and LuLu and come down immediately! And find John Eagle!" Marcus called to his friend.

Marcus looked around the Lobby. On Sunday, three weeks of creative chaos would commence. The day had been so quiet—the calm before the storm. He had looked forward all day to a fireside chat and a glass of wine and some cheese and crackers and a bedtime story. As he walked down the steps from his office, his mind had considered this exciting season and Villa Zanetta's 50th anniversary and all that it entailed and at the same time how ready he was to retire from it all and go to his cabin in Point Reyes and get a dog.

Marcus carried the weight of so much responsibility on his shoulders. *Maybe that's why I'm fat*, he thought, apropos of nothing going on here.

"I can't believe this, Willard," he said to the silent Willard Franklin.

"No. No. It's an unfortunate thing." Willard looked as cold as ice and as grey as a ghostly specter. His usual baritone delivery came out in a whisper. Marcus studied Willard's grey face.

Marcus had nothing personal against Willard, although he knew plenty of people who did. Take the man's own ex-wife, Smooch McGuinn. The divorce rumors buzzed that he'd had ten one-nighters right under her nose. She heard the news from one of the disgruntled husbands. Didn't help Willard's career any. But, that was a while ago. And he's supposedly reformed. *Sigh, he is a good conductor*, Marcus understood, *but really. And I think he's supposed to be on the wagon.*

Marcus weaved in and out of shock. *Your mind is wandering, Marcus. Stay in the present.* Marcus had nothing to do but consider his dead friend and wait for the staff and the sheriff and for whatever one does next after a kaboom-related death because his legs were like cooked spaghetti and he had just barely escaped his own death by a few hairs. He contemplated more odd elements coming together in his world.

Willard, for one, pacing around like he actually cared about Falcon Jennings when everyone knows different. He's unusually dark and pensive,

Marcus thought. *Well, he never wanted Falcon for this show in the first place. He should be happy. His nemesis is dead. And that chandelier. Did it just…fall down? Unravel? Did it hang by a thread for ages, like a loose tooth? We could be sued. Who would sue us? Martha? A wholly unpredictable person, so perhaps. She will predictably flip out, though. Oh, poor Martha. This is all she needs after all their romantic drama. Is that what he wanted to talk to me about? Where is Martha, I wonder? Both his parents are gone to their maker. Thank God, there are no children. Well. Focus on the moment, Marcus Brown. Your friend is dead with a chandelier on his head.*

Artistic Administrator, Priscilla Pendleton, and the two office assistants, twins LuLu and MeiMei Chinn, were coming out of the back room, arms filled with boxes. Kendra Masters burst into the office and said, "What are you doing? Falcon is dead! Marcus is unraveling! Come! Now!"

Dead! They dropped their boxes on the nearest surface.

Kendra tried to explain in a few words. "Yes! Dead. The Chandelier! Fell on Falcon. He's down there, on the floor! Oh, horrible mess! And… Oh, God, he's…like…smashed!" She leaned out the open window for some air.

Priscilla dashed back to her desk and made a few calls. Then, Priscilla, LuLu, MeiMei and Kendra moved out to the mezzanine and leaned over the railing as a group. They looked up, but saw nothing but the tiny hole out of which once hung the chandelier cable.

Kendra looked down and saw yet another view of the lifeless, dear Falcon. It made her dizzy and ill. She touched Priscilla's arm. She sat down on the steps for a moment and put her head between her knees. Priscilla sat down beside her. MeiMei and LuLu watched in twin disbelief.

After a moment in silent contemplation, the women moved down the spiral staircase and there to greet them was Willard, who came in close to people and exhaled that boozy lightable breath all over everyone. He wrapped his cold arm around Priscilla, who recoiled and moved away. Willard repelled some women just as he attracted others.

LuLu and MeiMei sat down on the bottom step and held hands. They'd never seen anything like this before, and they had observed their share of deaths. They couldn't take their eyes off the lifeless, flattened body of that cute director. They watched things unfold from the safe distance of just outside the circle of action.

Kendra knelt down beside the chandelier and contemplated Falcon. An hour ago they were backstage, admiring the fake Albanian Cowboys' fake fur coats for the *Cosi fan tutte* first act finale. Now, she sat on the floor, keeping watch over the dead man in the chandelier cage. She couldn't reach him, but she knew she probably shouldn't touch him, anyway. She couldn't look at him, but she felt no life emanating from Falcon's body. No aura glimmered. The body was inert, spiritless and cold. Not Falcon anymore. A dead body in the Lobby. Her tears fell in earnest.

Marcus gathered himself back together like a ball of yarn, stood up and said, "Everyone to the bar."

THE SHERIFF

Sheriff Grady Mulligan arrived ten minutes later in his official tan Jeep Wrangler. After he unhooked his seatbelt, he noticed the Johnny-on-the-Spot Sheriff Detective, Patrick Delaney, getting out of his red truck.

Dang it, thought Grady. *How does he do that? Not even time to put up crime tape without his interference. We don't even know yet if there's been a crime. Doesn't even give me a chance to call. Out of uniform, of course. And look at his boots. Did he just muck a stall?*

To his young sidekick, Joe Budd, Grady said, "Go check around the grounds." Joe did as he was told.

Sheriff Mulligan admired his own starched and creased pants. As he stepped out of the spotless Jeep, he brushed imaginary crumbs from his uniform shirt. He ran his fingers through his thinning hair and placed his regulation sheriff cowboy hat just so. The sheriff straightened his spine.

Detective Patrick Delaney slouched against his red '49 Ford pickup, fondly known as Molly McGuire, waiting for Mulligan to sort out his appearance. He smoked his Camel down to his fingers and stubbed it out on the bottom of his boot.

Patrick Delaney *was* in the barn when he got the call. Not mucking stalls, but his Red Wings had traveled many miles of farm dirt, and his

14

jeans pretty well took the prize for "beat up." He flashed his winning grin at his old buddy, Grady Mulligan.

"Grady, baby. How are ya?"

Grady Mulligan growled. "How'd you get here so fast, Delaney? I haven't even been in."

"Me neither. I was just waitin' for ya. Let's go."

"OK, Just let me do my job."

"Sure, pal. Just doin' mine."

"Too early, man. Just leave me to it."

Patrick rolled his eyes.

They moved in silence toward the Lobby. Grady Mulligan raced through the facts as he had heard them on his cell phone. One man lay in the Lobby under the chandelier, presumed dead. One witness, maybe hurt. Perhaps an accident. Perhaps not. A bunch of staff on site. *Classic*, he thought. *Wonder where the old fellows are...?*

Patrick, always amused by Grady's general demeanor, knew he was early. He was supposed to wait for Grady's call but, well, that sweet daytime dispatcher at the sheriff's office had a crush on him, he knew it, and she loved to pass along juicy news. Besides, Patrick just loved to needle Grady Mulligan.

The two men skipped up the brick steps to the front patio of the Villa and, just before they opened the door to the Lobby, Grady said, "OK, so, why are you here, Patrick?"

"I just couldn't stay away. I had a feeling. Don't worry. I'll wait."

Grady just stared at his annoying cousin. Then he sighed, opened the door and stepped into the velvet-lined, high ceilinged room. Patrick stepped inside and stayed by the open door. *All the better to see y'all*, said the detective/wolf in Patrick's eyes.

Shards of, not ordinary glass, but that thin and delicate light-bulby kind special ordered for the antique lamp, lay in shatters all over the red-carpeted Lobby floor. Bits of glass stuck to the spilled white silk flowers that once graced the big table in the foyer and little crystal teardrops scattered across the carpet. The Chinoiserie vase was toppled to the floor, and it, too, lay in pieces. *Lucky that big fancy mirror didn't come down*, thought Grady. *Looks like an earthquake happened in here.*

The body under the chandelier had begun to leak fluids. He did look thoroughly dead, the head told the whole story. Grady bent down and put his hand over the mouth of the presumably late stage director. *OK. He's not going anywhere.*

Grady stood up and scanned the big open room. A gaggle of theater people (*You can always tell theater people,* he thought. *They dress like the cat dragged them in. They give root to that line, "Are you an artist or did you just get dressed in the dark?"*)...anyway, a group of people stood at the bar at the other end of the room. They all had drinks in their hands.

Two men leaned against the highly polished bar. One, the Executive Director, Marcus Brown, held a wet cloth to his forehead and looked frazzled. His lightweight sport coat had a rip down the sleeve and his red tie skewed to the left—*Ah, the "maybe hurt witness."* A woman with jeans she had to lie down on her bed to zip up perched on the edge of a stool. Behind the bar another woman poured the little woman in tight jeans a glass of white wine and then a glass of red for herself. He could see in the back bar mirror that her hair was slowly unraveling from a French Twist. She wore a tan suit. *Probably linen,* he thought. *Very wrinkled.* Two small Asian girls sat together at the bar, holding drinks with straws. *Their clothes are from the theater lost and found, for sure.*

Grady approached the group; a silent bunch, in shock, watching his every deliberate move. He settled down to business, said hello to Marcus.

"Before we start here," Grady said, "is there anyone else in this building? On the property? Hector? The old gents?"

Marcus sent MeiMei and LuLu to look for Hector in the garden and then looked at Priscilla, who said, "The soloists arrive tomorrow. Magnolia, the housekeeper, is offsite until Monday. Same with Jake Ortman, groundskeeper and maintenance. John Eagle is expected sometime tonight. On his way home from Utah. And, I think Chef Henry plans his usual prep all-nighter, so he'll be along. The tech crew left about half an hour ago—just before the...crash."

Grady watched the Asian girls run out the door like they were on their way to recess. They were both about 4'10", and twins. They looked like teenagers, but they were older than their diminutive sizes suggested.

"Where are the old gentlemen?" Grady asked Marcus, as he took his eyes off MeiMei and LuLu. Grady, from the fossilized school of gender and equality, looked to the guy, even though Priscilla had called the sheriff, alerted everyone and gathered all together. *She* had ordered up the ambulance, called John Eagle. She knew Hector's whereabouts. *She* knew where the old gentlemen were.

Priscilla checked her watch. *On their way. Thanks to me.* Priscilla also knew that Falcon's wife, Martha, was coming at 6:30 to pick up her husband for a dinner date.

Marcus was busy being poleaxed in shock, so of course Priscilla took charge. *Well, he* was *almost killed by a chandelier.* She fumed a bit and gave Grady the look. Then she let it go while she debated whether or not to tell them of Martha's imminent arrival.

"At home up on the hill, I presume," said Marcus to Grady, taking the wet cloth from his brow. Grady was writing "W & E at home" when Hayne Williams and Diesel Edwards, octogenarian founders of The Theaters at Villa Zanetta, walked in the door.

Hayne and Diesel, the length of their lifetimes behind them now, had stepped outside the circle of Villa Zanetta, to let the 21st-century players and singers and dancers and musicians—and, of course, puppeteers—do their thing. It was time.

But they were not far away. Just up the hill, in the home they built on their land. From their perch by Lake Zanetta, surrounded by madrones and oaks and manzanita and separated from the general goings-on down at the Villa, they planned to glory in their creation and wind down their frantic, constant, wildly productive and satisfying careers as entertainers and, in the very best sense of the word, retire. Hang up their hats. Rest their bones. Sit in rockers.

Priscilla chose to just keep her mouth shut and let the chips fall.

DEAD

Grady watched the founders come in through the glass door to the Lobby, saw their raised eyebrows, and moved toward them immediately.

"Mr. Williams. Mr. Edwards. There's been an accident here."

"So we heard from Priscilla, Sheriff," said Diesel Edwards. "Is Mr. Jennings hurt? He looks hurt. He's bleeding. Why has he been left under the chandelier?"

"He's…dead, sir. We're taping off the area now. We hope there will be little disturbance."

"Dead. Oh my," said Hayne.

"Yes, sir. We're going into the little atrium room there. Will you join us? We'll see what we can find out."

He ushered the group into what was affectionately known around the Villa as the "Not-so," short for the "Not-so-Private (all-glass) Dining Room."

Many interior walls of the 8,000 square foot Tudor mansion at Villa Zanetta were removed to create the Lobby for The Well Lit Theater, added "onto" the Villa in 1970. The Well Lit Theater seated 400 and poked out the back of the Villa like a submarine, an appendage, a new arm on an old body; a bit barn-like, it fanned wide open, with red-padded raked seats, a low stage, nice orchestra pit, surrounded by exterior fake Tudor and interior redwood panels.

One entered the Villa Mansion via the Not-so. When opening the glass doors, a straight mosaic walkway led into the Lobby. Turn right and the mosaic pattern took you into a lush, atrium/dining room, with tables and chairs for about twenty. It could be closed off with sliding glass doors; a good place to gather all these people while a little Q&A took place.

Grady saw Joe Budd come in the side door, shake his head and shrug his shoulders. In Joe's wake came the twins, MeiMei and LuLu, on either side of Hector, all of whom Grady gestured toward seats in the Not-so. He motioned around the Lobby and pointed up the stairs. Joe took the hint, nodded, put on his cotton gloves and proceeded to inspect the immediate premises; the back-up squad would be along shortly to dust for fingerprints, clean up the chandelier and remove the body. Now, time to look over the late and leaking Falcon Jennings.

Meanwhile, Patrick Delaney inspected in his own way, by watching the people. Grady invited him into the atrium, put his finger to his lips as if to say, "Shhhh," and pointed to a chair. Patrick sat in the chair and leaned it to the wall, tipping up the two front legs.

Grady called his meeting to order.

Each of the attendees gave their name and where they were at the time of the "incident." Grady liked to go by the book.

Hector sat next to Hayne. Hayne took his hand. Hayne whispered to Diesel on his other side, "Well. Hate to sound cold, but we've just lost our stage director, Martha will, of course, unzip, and she's worked so hard to …stabilize, we've got a possible scandal on our hands and the ensemble begins arriving tomorrow."

Hector tugged at Hayne's sleeve and asked, "What ith going on, Haynie? Who'th that on the floor? Who'th thith perthon with a shiny badge? I 'member him. I like hith shoes…all shiny like that, like hith badge. Oh, Yeth! The sheriff!"

Hayne leaned into Hector, whose eyes were as big as saucers, and whispered, "Yes, it's Sheriff Mulligan, Hector. There's been an accident. Someone is hurt. It's all right. Just stay right here by me."

Hector didn't do well in close gatherings. He did not take to drama of any kind, unless he was in the front row of an audience, or "doing the puppetth" with Haynie. "OK," he said to his friend. "If you thay tho, Haynie."

Hayne smiled. His perennial child, Hector. *He's been saying that since the day we met. Lordy, when was that? 50 years ago.*

Grady was saying, "…and you're not hurt at all, Mr. Brown? Your sleeve is torn."

"No, I'm not hurt. Just shaken up like a maraca. As I said, it went right by me so fast, I didn't have time to react, much less move out of the way. Falcon looked down, so I looked down and all of a sudden, I felt a…whoosh and…whiffed a kind of metallic wind passing by me, and then I heard and felt a…a *kaboom* at my feet, which shook the floor and all of a sudden my clothes and hair were covered in bits of glass and crystals and then dust was poofing up from the red carpet and Falcon…Falcon was…" Marcus's eyes again filled up with tears.

"Any other witnesses?"

"No," said the beleaguered executive director, wiping his eyes with his handkerchief.

"Next of kin?"

"His wife, Martha." Marcus looked at Priscilla.

"I called her cell and left a message to call me," Priscilla said.

"It was wise of you not to move the body, or the chandelier," said Grady Mulligan.

"Wisdom had nothing to do with it, Sheriff," said Marcus. "We could barely move our own bodies, much less a dead person. Or 400 pounds of chandelier."

"Did anyone go upstairs? Since the incident?"

"No. The girls were in the office, but no one went up to the cupola, if that's what you mean."

"The girls?"

"Priscilla, LuLu and MeiMei."

"Why were you in the Lobby at the time?"

"I was leaving, Sheriff."

"Going home for the night?"

"Well, hopefully for the weekend."

Grady noticed Joe Budd by the door. He motioned for him to come in, heard his whispered report, nodded and sent him back to the Lobby. The back up team was arriving.

"I think you'd best stay put for now, Mr. Brown. All of you." Grady looked at Patrick Delaney.

Marcus, sitting two feet away, heard Joe Budd's whispered report. "Looks cut, Sir." *Son of a biscuit. Who in the world? And why now? Great Lord. This is not happening.*

Marcus raked his fingers through his thick hair, a calming technique learned from a men's group buddy. His thoughts went wild with real- izations and implications. *They'll think it's one of us. And, it very well could be. Willard, most likely, of course. But, no, he got here too fast. Or did he? I was in shock. I don't remember!*

He looked over at Willard, sitting at a table alone, with his elbows on his knees, his face pointed at the fern fronds. Willard held an unlit cigarette between his forefingers and thumbs, rolling it back and forth, back and forth. He just stared at those ferns.

Next Marcus's eyes rested on Priscilla, sitting toward the back with her feet up on a chair and her shoes dropped to the floor. She was awfully quiet. But, no. Obviously not Priscilla. She had been with the Chinns in the office. The sheriffs might not believe that, either. She did say she was in the bathroom around that time. But, no. Priscilla?

John Eagle had nothing against Falcon, and besides, he was on his way home from Utah. *Chef Henry? No. Henry hasn't an enemy in the world. Will I have to call the Tech Crew back in? Does that make them on overtime? Gads, do I have to think about that right now?*

JOE'S REPORT

Everyone babbled at once. Willard looked wan and bleak. Marcus put the cloth back to his brow. The reliable Kendra ignored the sign on the wall, as well as her various resolutions, and lit a Virginia Slim.

What did Kendra care for the rules at the moment? Falcon was dead, and not only was she sorry he was dead, she was sorry for the dominoes about to fall because of his death. First, Martha's a widow. Second, There's no director for this show. Third, she might lose her job and fourth, she has definitely lost a mentor.

The two front legs of Detective Patrick Delaney's chair came back to the floor in a thud. He exchanged a nod with Grady that said, "Meet me in the Lobby."

The two men walked a few feet away from the Not-so door. Joe Budd was there to greet them.

"What's on your mind, Joe?" asked Grady. "Tell us what you found."

"The cable, sir. It's been cut. There must be a winch, but I don't see a way up to it."

Grady went to the door of the dining room, looked at Marcus Brown and said, "Is there a winch up there? In the cupola? Do you have a key to a stairway door?"

MeiMei and LuLu said in unison, "We'll go." Marcus nodded. The girls hopped out of their chairs. MeiMei took the Villa keys out of her pocket.

Patrick said, "I think I'll just tag along."

Grady looked at the others, nodded, sighed, and said, "I'll be here."

THE CUPOLA

MeiMei and LuLu led the way. Just for fun, the sisters chattered in Chinese about the Jingchá, the policemen following behind them and that other one, debating who was cutest, and which one they would each marry, if they were the marrying kind. Joe Budd and Patrick Delaney listened, amused by the lilting foreign sounds with no comprehension of the words. Patrick smiled, nonetheless.

The foursome stopped at the mezzanine and looked down on the fallen chandelier, now surrounded by EMTs and a group of finger-print-dusting young sheriffs-in-training. Patrick considered the height, the fall, the size of the chandelier, the cut cable.

MeiMei took her group of followers to the end of the hallway where the small, ancient door to the cupola stairs hid itself in an alcove. She fiddled with the skeleton key, wiggling it around in the old slot. Patrick moved to the door and turned the knob with a cloth. When there was no sound, MeiMei said, "Oh! Someone's oiled the squeak." Joe Budd and Patrick Delaney exchanged a look. Patrick's eyebrows raised.

Of course, the small Chinese women scurried up the stairs like they'd done it a hundred times. They started out as housekeepers at the Villa back in the days when they spoke no English. After 15 years, they knew the place well, assisted the office staff and helped wherever needed, and they could tell some tales. But, long ago they agreed to not tell other people's stories unless they were necessary. And so, they kept their mouths shut.

At the top of the stairs, they entered the tiny room. The hand crank winch was the only occupant. The neatly chopped but fraying other end of the cable hung there for all to see.

D.E.A.D.

Ah, Hayne's favorite part of the day, when the sun began its disappearance, slowly dropping behind the hills. The light gentled and settled into its evening repose, casting long shadows of oak and pine and madrone trees across the fields. The poppies were in bloom, and the lupine, creating blurred Monet patterns in heart-piercing deep blues and sharp oranges. The birds twittered to the threesome as they walked up to their home on the hill.

Today, Hector gripped viselike on Hayne's fingers. *A cup of tea and a couple of biscuits. For all three of us,* Hayne thought.

Diesel said, "So, what do you think, Haynie?"

"Well. We can focus on the theater needs, I think. Looks like Sheriffs Mulligan and Delaney are focused on the scene of the crime."

"We don't know yet that there's been a crime, dear."

"There's been a crime. I saw the cable on the way out; clearly been cut. Someone wanted Falcon hurt or canceled. He couldn't be more D.E.A.D."

"Falcon Jenningth ith D.E.A.D.?" asked Hector. "What made him D.E.A.D.? I juth thaw him A…..L…..I…uhm…V. E."

"Hector," said Hayne, as they entered the kitchen, "we have to tell you the truth." He put his hands on Hector's shoulders. "Falcon is dead, the chandelier fell on him. The sheriffs want to know if someone dropped it on purpose."

"Ohh, That ith bad. Vewwy bad, for sure. Who would do that to a perthon?"

"Indeed, Hector. Indeed," said Diesel.

The three were quiet for a few moments while, as usual, Hayne put some English Breakfast Tea in the pot, Diesel got out a tin of McVitie's Biscuits and Hector set the table with small spoons and butter knives. Mundane tasks to settle the nerves.

> "Good night, good night! Parting is such sweet sorrow,
> That I shall say good night till it be morrow.
> *Romeo and Juliet*
> ~ Wm. Shakespeare

MARTHA

At 6:30, full of life, ready to roll, Martha Jennings flew open the front door and twirled into the Lobby. Her red and white polka dotted cocktail swing dress twirled in with her, stiff petticoats and all. Martha's penchant for a 50s look went all the way through—she had coiffed the top of her dark hair into a roll and wrapped the rest with a red silk scarf tied in a big bow; her ruby-red lipstick glossed her perfect lips. The white high-heeled Mary Janes fairly twinkled on Martha's dainty feet. Sheer white stockings ended in lace above the knees, and the little white seam-like dots traveling up the backs of her calves made one look twice as she floated through a room.

Martha, her own canvas, went all out for her dinner date with Falcon. Hours were spent in front of the mirror, primping at her dressing table.

23

Martha painted her nails a glossy red and had applied her lipstick just so, just as neatly and surely as Grady Mulligan donned his hat each day. Martha's relationship with Falcon troubled her and she wanted to make up for it, wanted to please him, not leave him. She couldn't handle leaving him. Oh, no. She'd do anything, even dress up in red and white polka dots, Falcon's favorite. Just to make him happy.

Martha didn't see Falcon on the floor of the Lobby, surrounded as he was by forensic explorers in yellow coats. She looked around the Lobby, saw Marcus talking to a deputy and tottered over to them for the scoop before clickety-clacking those white high heels backstage to meet Falcon.

"What's all this?" she asked Marcus. Marcus rolled his eyes at Grady Mulligan. "Come over here, dear," he said. "We need to talk."

Marcus led Martha into the Not-so, empty of all the possible murderers at the moment. Willard emerged from behind the bar with a vodka tonic and stopped short at the eye-catching vision of Martha. When Martha noticed Willard, her heart jerked in her chest. She froze. She winced and turned away.

Through the glass walls one could see, if not hear, her conversation with Marcus Brown. Marcus put his hand on her arm, Martha looked at his face. She exclaimed. She looked horrified. Her hand flew to her mouth, like she might throw up. She held onto the back of a chair. Marcus did not let go of her arm as he talked. She made a move toward the Lobby; Marcus held her back. He had to tell her everything before he let her go. You could see him trying to tell her as gently as he knew how.

Martha wrenched herself out of Marcus's grip and ran to the door, slid it open and tripped over her own shoes as she stumbled out into the Lobby. Falcon's handlers were about to slip him into a plastic body bag and lift him onto a gurney. A deputy sheriff stopped Martha when she approached the scene. Marcus moved right behind her. "It's his wife," he said to Joe Budd. "Let her see."

Joe Budd stepped back, but still held Martha Jennings out of reach of her very dead husband. Martha stared the body for a long time. "He's dead. He's dead. He's dead. After all this, my Falcon is dead." Marcus led her away and back to a chair in the Not-so. Martha put her be-ribboned head down on the table and cried.

Marcus was not all that steady himself. Seeing Martha cry made him weepy and want to lie down with his face in a pillow. But, he had no time for sadness, for grief. Something terrible had happened. And on his watch!

Not only on my watch. I had to watch it. I can see it so clearly now. He heard the sounds: the kaboom of the chandelier itself as it plummeted to the floor; the shattering of the glass; the toppling over and then the crash of the Chinoiserie vase; the crack of Falcon's head. He heard the gilded leaf rip through his jacket and whisper past the hairs on his arm. He remembered a door shut—that must have been Priscilla on the way down. Or Falcon's spirit, leaving the building. Oooh, too weird to contemplate.

Marcus found that if he didn't keep himself busy, he processed the "incident" over and over and over again. And, a whole gaggle of people and changing events demanded that he manage it all. This was definitely no time to break down.

Marcus wrestled himself together and went to the Old Hall kitchen to make tea.

WHO DONE IT?

One at a time, Grady Mulligan and Patrick Delaney interviewed those staff members just lucky enough to be at or near the Villa when a presumed murder occurred. The interviews took place in the Not-so, and the others drifted off into the Old Hall.

A much more comfortable environment, the Old Hall was once known as the Great Hall before the Well Lit Theater was built. The Old Hall remained much as it had been for 50 years; a high-ceilinged, casual but elegant theater/dining room, with a clubby atmosphere.

There, one could relax in comfy love seats or Queen Anne chairs, or sit at a table for four. Dinner Theater events in the Old Hall always sold out. The 100 seats of great variety filled the room at floor level, the floor covered in a rich dark multicolored carpet. The stage, raised about four feet, had seen myriad performances. The commissary-style kitchen usually hummed with human endeavor. The Old Hall remained a popular venue, a dining hall and comfortable gathering place for the Villa participants, and no less popular tonight, while the present company prepared for an all-nighter.

Respecting her grief, Martha was excused from questioning for the moment. She stopped crying long enough to call her mother, now on the way from San Francisco. Martha, wrapped in a Hayne-knitted dorm blanket, curled up in a love seat. Her shoes toppled on the carpet, the rolled hair cascaded to the right side of her head, the red bow slipped to the left. Martha's makeup rubbed off on her hankie, that bright red lipstick smeared across her perfect lips.

Poor girl. Poor Martha. Suddenly rudderless without her man and all her defenses down. Even her petticoats sagged in sorrow. One could almost hear Martha's inner voice. Over and over, it said, "What will I do? What will I do?"

Kendra wanted to comfort Martha, but she didn't know her that well, although she'd gathered a little bit about their ups and downs just from a few words Falcon had said. That was one of the things Kendra admired about Falcon Jennings. He was super professional and didn't bring his relationship to the worktable.

When it came time for Kendra's interview with the sheriffs, she was able to say she knew very little about Falcon Jennings's personal life. "We had only been working together a few months," she said. "He kept his cards close to his chest."

"And where were you, Miss Masters, when this incident occurred?" asked Grady.

"Out to my car to get some chips. I was just outside the front door, smoking a cigarette. I heard the crash and came into the Lobby and found Willard leaning over Falcon's body, like testing for a breath, and Marcus sitting on a bench, quaking like an Aspen."

Patrick and Marcus sat at the bar.

"Mr. Brown, are your people here for the night?"

"Yes, yes, everyone here has a dorm room assignment for the next three weeks."

"You understand there has been foul play?"

"Well, that cable didn't cut itself," said Marcus.

"Yes, Mr. Brown," said Detective Delaney.

"Please, call me Marcus. Perhaps Martha can go home with her mother?" he asked. "I understand Mrs. Watts is on her way. I think a sedative is in order. Martha is…a bit…dramatic."

"We'll let her go with her mother. I'll get her address and visit her in the morning. She'll need some time."

"As for the rest of us," said Marcus, "I imagine we'll hang out together for a while. No one wants to leave the group."

"We'll have to make this area off-limits. And the rest of the Villa. Perhaps the theater, too. We'll see. The team is exploring now, but consider this a crime scene from this moment. We'll let you know when you can get back into your offices. You can use the Old Hall, but stay out of the rest of the building and the theater."

Marcus said, "You should know that the six soloists and a couple of orchestra members arrive tomorrow morning—in fact, we have a rehearsal scheduled for 3pm."

"In the theater?"

"Sort of—down the stairs, in the conductor's room, with a piano."

"Well, I'll let you know when you can get back into the theater. Best to consider another location with a piano. What else is scheduled for tomorrow?"

"Fortunately, nothing. The rest of the ensemble arrives on Sunday, there is an open rehearsal at 3pm and an orchestra runthrough at 7."

Patrick asked, "'Open rehearsal' meaning what, exactly?"

"Well, what it says. Open to the public. Anyone can come."

Patrick thought about it. "Hm. You might want to cancel that. At least the *open to the public* part."

Detective Patrick Delaney took off his hat for the first time that day. His hairline, flattened by the pressure of the cowboy hat rim, immediately began to spring back; all those tight curls had to go somewhere. The handsome, casual and irreverent Patrick was all business now. He thought through Marcus's information and said, "We'll do our best to get you back to normal by then. But don't hold your breath."

Hmph, thought the still mildly rattled Marcus. *I've already done that once today.*

The group of colleagues spread out and ensconced themselves and their belongings in the Old Hall. All were happy to be released from the Not-so. First, Kendra Masters *would* smoke in there; and Martha sucked up the rest of the available oxygen with her emotions. Everything was fraught; with danger, with fear, with sadness.

Priscilla picked up a bottle of the bar's best pinot noir and settled into a table near the kitchen, by herself with the upcoming week's schedule, recently tossed in the air by a big blanket of disaster. She could hear Chef Henry clattering around and she was starving. She poured some wine in her glass, took more than a sip, and looked at the rest of the room.

MeiMei & LuLu sat together at their favorite table by the door. They said they wanted to be available to the staff, but the truth was, they just didn't want to miss anything. They could see the Lobby, the stage in the Old Hall, the door to the kitchen. MeiMei and LuLu were like the Encyclopedia Villa Zanetta; they knew it all.

Kendra stood by the side entry of the Old Hall, blowing smoke out the door. She had a thin ciggy in one hand, a glass of wine in the other and a bubble of pink gum popping out of her mouth. Her wrists were covered in silver bangles and, the retired dancer now Falcon's assistant had the hips of a nine year old boy slipped into the tightest of jeans.

If I looked like that, I'd be in painted-on jeans, too, thought Priscilla. *Well, not Falcon's assistant anymore. That must be a blow.*

Willard sat in a corner alone. *Weird, too, how we all want to be near each other, but not really together. I have nothing to say to Willard. The man doesn't know how to have a conversation. With a woman. With Willard, unless it's about music, his conversations are all about seduction. Even if he doesn't want you, he'll still try, just to see if he can. And I'll bet Martha would just like Marcus to leave her alone. He's fussing like an old lady. 'Do you need a bigger box of tissue? Water? Tea? A pill?'*

John Eagle went to the kitchen to bring Henry up to speed.

Thank God for John Eagle, Priscilla sighed as she watched her friend move through the room.

The voice of reason has arrived. He'll sooth all the feathers and comfort all those flying emotions. I want to yell at people, "Calm the EFF down!" He'll be all warm and fuzzy.

Marcus brought Martha a cup of tea and went back to the Not-so for the next get-together with the sheriffs. Marcus wasn't sure whether he was happy or unhappy that Hayne and Diesel were in this meeting. The discussion went something like this.

Patrick said, "Mr Williams, we understand Hector was in the garden when the incident occurred. May we ask him what he might have seen?"

Hayne, expecting this, said, "Of course, Sheriff, but I need to be at his side. This is all upsetting to Hector. But, yes. Come up to the house later. He'll be more comfortable there."

"Ok. All right. Well, we'd better talk about Willard Franklin, now. It appears Mr. Franklin didn't much like the late Mr. Jennings. His name popped up several times with your staff and tech crew. Can you give us a little insight?"

Marcus said, "Ah. Well, it's true. They weren't…fond of each other. They never made peace."

Patrick asked, "What was the issue?"

"Oh, there were many," Marcus replied, "but let's just say, creatively as well as functionally, they were on different roads. One went south, the other, north."

Grady: "Any real issues?"

Always a diplomat, Marcus hesitated.

Hayne had no such compunctions. "They simply hated each other." he said. "It's true. It goes back a long way. Some kind of a deep and dark rivalry. They take…took the conductor/stage director archetypal feud thing too far."

A few moments passed while Patrick fiddled with his notes. Patrick said, "Is it true Willard didn't want Falcon as his stage director for this show?"

Marcus sighed.

Hayne said, "Yes, he wasn't thrilled by it, but it's what had to be."

Patrick said, "Mr. Franklin is not a favorite."

"He's…he can be difficult," Hayne said.

"In what way?"

Too many moments of silence ensued. Then, Diesel blurted out, "Because he's a womanizing drunk under a cloud of disrepute and is often more trouble than he is worth."

Hayne looked at Diesel like, "Are you happy now?"

Patrick's left eyebrow rose in question. "Why is he here?"

Hayne said, "He knows the show."

Diesel resisted rolling his eyes or making any sarcastic remarks.

Patrick changed his tactics. "Do you think Willard Franklin disliked Falcon Jennings enough to kill him?"

A few more seconds passed.

Hayne said, "Detective Delaney, just because Willard is a jerk, doesn't mean he's a murderer."

MARCUS

Marcus sat under a tree on a little bench dedicated to Gabriel Michaels, the Music Director of Villa Zanetta for the first thirty years.

A particularly sweet spot for Marcus, this bench; in the back of the Villa, up the little hill a ways, "…so Gabe could enjoy the view," Hayne once said.

Marcus pondered the view in 2008, wondering what it must have been like 50 years ago, when Hayne, Diesel and Gabe were just getting started. *So much in the world had changed, and yet,* Marcus thought, *this scene remains pretty much the same; the roofs of the Villa, the barn, the dorm, and much of Hector's garden. The Well Lit Theater wasn't there, and the pictures show how much of the thicket of trees and bushes had been cleared to make room for the 20,000 square foot addition. The long view had expanded into grand vistas of vineyards. Sonoma was nothing if not its vineyards.*

Most of the photos from 50 years ago are black and white Polaroids, fading in their albums, Marcus thought, while snapping pics with his brand new 2008 3G iPhone. *We should probably start scanning those old photos.*

At 7:25pm, on this Friday night at the Villa, all seemed so peaceful and quiet from this perspective. Walking by, one would not suspect a dead body had just been removed from the Lobby and all hell had disrupted a very normal festival preparation. But, Marcus knew. And Marcus was the leader of this company. He sighed. *I need more than five minutes of quiet time in a day.*

Marcus joined Hayne and Diesel at a table in the Old Hall.

"You didn't have to come back down," Marcus said.

"Of course we did. We're here to support you. And, you know, we'll stick our fingers into the Villa Zanetta pie as long as we can. We apparently haven't made a clean break. We'll try not to annoy you."

Marcus laughed.

"First of all," Hayne said, "how are you doing?"

"I'm OK," Marcus said. "It's hard, having been in the middle of it and yet needing to stay on top of everything, but I'm beginning to calm down a little."

"Good, good," said Hayne.

Diesel said, "We're sure you've thought of all the pertinent things, but we are here to offer our help. There are questions, such as: do we or do we not continue? Falcon is dead; perhaps murdered. Martha will certainly need help. We suppose there should be some sort of gathering for Falcon."

Marcus said, "Oh, I hadn't even thought of that."

"And of course, you'll have to find a replacement for him," said Hayne.

"I *did think* of that."

Diesel said, "OK, so first things first: are you planning to continue?"

"Well, yes, of course. The show must go on. Falcon would be the first to say so."

"We thought you'd say that," said Hayne. "Then we'd like to memorialize him, up on the hill. We'll have the entire company. Let us know the best time to fit it into your schedule and if Henry could manage it. If not, we'll call a caterer. We'll check in with Martha and Mrs. Watts tomorrow."

"And what more can we do to help you, Marcus? You must be on overwhelm with all this."

After some logistics and changes were discussed, Hayne and Diesel left, and Marcus had to admit they were a couple of fine, old fashioned gentlemen. They don't make people like that anymore; well-bred, classy, kind, thoughtful. They seemed to know things, like when to step in and when to step out, which can't be easy, their living, basically, in the backyard of the Villa and its being their creation for their

entire adult lives. Which made him think about his being *this* close
to telling them he wanted to retire. Ten years ago he promised to take
the reigns when Hayne and Diesel retired, and he didn't want to let
them down. But...

HAYNE AND DIESEL CHAT

Hector, a little discombobulated by the events of the day, chose to stay
in his downstairs room at Hayne and Diesel's "new house," as he called
it, although it had been built in 1975. Going down the hill to his little
cabin seemed too lonely to Hector when life wasn't right.

Things in Hector's life were mostly right, but his mind held onto
some of the "baddieth" from "befo'," when life didn't fit so well, and at
those times, the closer to Haynie the better.

When baddies came into play, Hector became more childlike, a little
less resilient.

Hector drifted down the stairs to his room.

Hayne, sitting down in his chair in the living room, spoke to Diesel,
"Did you hear that? Hector just said, 'The thky ith falling.' Poor dear.
This is too much for him. Glad we're still alive to hold his hand."

Diesel looked up from his book. "'Glad we're still alive'? Has it been
on your mind? Death, I mean?"

"A little. Today, of course. And when Hector gets fragile. I start worrying about whether or not Rosie will outlive us and if not, who will
get custody of Hector."

"Rosie's children. Reyna and Felix."

"Oh, you know what I mean. Will they be good to him?"

"Oh, Haynie. Of course they will."

"And—bless my living soul—who hated Falcon Jennings enough to
kill him? I don't really think Willard would do such a thing. Detective
Delaney is leaning in that direction but, I don't know. Hate is one thing.
But to *off* a person with a chandelier...that's just too extreme."

"And what if Falcon wasn't the target? Marcus was there, too."

"Oh! That's a new twist, D."

"Just a thought. To muddle things up."

"Hm. Probably best you keep those thoughts to yourself. And who
would want to hurt Marcus, either? What do you think about the stage

director issue? Marcus asked for suggestions, but I wouldn't want anyone I can think of who would be available on such short notice."

"Goodness, Haynie. We never thought about these issues 50 years ago."

"We never thought of a lot of things 50 years ago."

Chapter Two
1956

Hayne Unpacks His Puppets

On a beautiful Sunday morning, Diesel sat in the chair in Hayne's sunny bedroom at 111 Beach watching Hayne fiddle with the trunk latch. He observed his friend for a few minutes, but couldn't figure out if Hayne was excited about or dreaded opening that trunk.

Diesel said, "I'd like to hear about your puppets."

"It's silly," Hayne replied. "You'll laugh at me, and I couldn't stand that."

"I won't laugh," said his new best friend.

"You will," insisted Hayne. "People always do."

"But, they're puppets. They are supposed to make us laugh."

"That's not my point, and you know it. You'll laugh at *me*, not the puppets."

"You mean I'll laugh at you because you *have* the puppets? Because you obviously *love* the puppets? Why would I do that?"

"Ah. I don't know. Because I'm a 25 year old child hiding behind finger and hand puppets? Because you think I'm nerdy or a pansy or too old to be doing this. Because I knit. There. I said it. I knit."

"Oh, bother that. Your male Celtic ancestors have been knitting for eons. Who cares? I care more about the fact that you even think for a moment I would laugh at you. Or at you with puppets! I love puppets. I want to see what you've made and what you've done with puppets. Your mother sent that trunk three months ago. And that box which I believe holds your traveling stage. You've never even opened that."

"I'm afraid."

"I'm afraid, darling, that you are afraid of everything. I'm not your shrink. However, I am your, yes, I'll say it, I am your devoted companion and I have a right and responsibility to know the contents of that trunk."

"Right and responsibility?"

"Indeed. The right to know your deepest longings and the responsibility to see that you are free to explore them."

"Oooh la la, you certainly know how to woo a man. OK. You can see them. But only if you let me unpack the Bleeps and set up."

"The Bleeps?"

"Yes. The puppets are collectively known as the Bleeps."

"Who knows them?" Diesel asked, stifling a smile.

"Well, pretty much all of the Santa Monica Pier contingent from 1937 to 1950, and anyone who came to the Ice Queen. And I performed a few shows at the Pasadena Playhouse."

HAYNE REMEMBERS...

Whenever Hayne thought about Fatty Wills, his butterfly stomach kicked in, his eyebrows steamed and tears welled in his eyes. He didn't know how to tell Diesel about his mother and his world. Her world. He could never take Diesel to the Santa Monica Pier.

How could that happen? How could he ever, ever show up at the trailer behind the Ice Queen with Diesel in tow?

There Fatty would be, her corpulent self squeezing through the side door of the Queen, fingers greasy, hair in a rag. She possessed maybe three outfits—ancient sweatpants and gigantic T shirt in Spring, a fantastically inappropriate Summer sundress, where all her exposed fat wobbled and she couldn't keep her boobs inside the top, and a muu muu the size of a pup tent for "at home" in the trailer.

Oh how Hayne loved and hated his mother. God love her, everything she owned smelled like sweat and rancid oil and popcorn. Her breath came out all foggy with cigarette smoke and coughs and phlegm. Fatty's eyebrows glistened with sweat and her bright red lipstick traveled up the thin cracks above her lips.

How could Hayne ever say, "Diesel, this is my mother, Charlotte Penelope Williams, but she's known as Fatty Wills around the hood."

Could I show him the trailer with the rusted metal walls and the curtain made from an old towel? The rumpled unmade bed? The back room of the Ice Queen?

Nope. Can't. It'll never happen in a million years.

By the time Hayne was 12 years old, Fatty slept in the recliner and had given the trailer's only bed to the sickly boy. *You'd be sickly, too,*

Hayne thought as an old man, *if you lived on milkshakes and burgers with unending ketchup.* Hayne came down with every cold and flu that stormed the winter nation. He suffered through the measles and chicken pox, too, both so badly he couldn't move on the bed for weeks and drank milkshakes and root beer in paper cups with straws.

From birth to his flight to Pasadena at age 14 in 1942, he called the back room of the Ice Queen and then some time later, the trailer, home. And his mother remained steady at her job for 75 cents an hour, plus tips and all the burgers and fries she/they could eat. At night, she played euchre and pinochle with the boys in the lean-to.

He could see her in the lean-to with the boys. First, the tall and ungainly Pete the Pilgrim (whose specialty was proselytizing to small groups on the beach, "Praise the Lord and pass the hat," an old fashioned cap, in his case). And there was Sandbox Sam, whose Odds and Ends of the Beach table held, well, just that—detritus Sam deemed worth selling; shells, sea glass, rusted metal spoons. And, of course, Fatty's long time buddy, Jerry the Juggler, seen every afternoon by the water, juggling bottles, or oranges, and sometimes even raw eggs, his beloved top hat turned upside down, hoping for tips. Those were Fatty's friends and the Santa Monica Pier her life, in a trailer parked behind the Ice Queen Concession on the Santa Monica Pier.

THE BLEEPS

The Bleeps emerged out of Hayne's abject boredom in 1937. There he was, this precocious but undernourished nine-year-old boy, lying in bed for the umpteenth time that year, fiddling with his socks while battling the latest communicable disease. He'd read the two books in his possession for the bazillionth time (tattered copies of *The Adventures of Huckleberry Finn* and *The Wizard of Oz*, proudly presented to Hayne by Jerry the Juggler on Hayne's sickly 9th birthday—someone had left them wrapped in a towel on the beach).

Hayne was bored with the radio, and he had colored in all the pages of his Tarzan coloring book, about which he told no one, lest they make fun of him.

People often made fun of Hayne. Especially other kids. He only had one friend, Mabela Gabriella, who lived with her father, Tony

Gabriella, known as Tony the Toned, a regular at the Santa Monica Beach. When too old to lift a plate much less 250 pounds, Tony would be remembered as one of the Muscle Beach Boys. For now, he tended bar at the Pier, raised his daughter alone in a two room apartment above Winchell's Donuts on Santa Monica Blvd, and consumed prodigious amounts of beer on the sly, since he was supposed to be a teetotaling athlete.

Mabela didn't make fun of Hayne, but she wasn't allowed in the trailer when Hayne was sick, which was most of the time, so Hayne had to be creative to fill his hours.

This day, he fiddled with the rumpled sheets for a while. He tore a piece of paper into tiny bits and threw them in the air. He folded another piece of paper tiny and tinier until he could fold no more and then unfolded it and counted all the little squares and triangles. He colored in all the squares and triangles with his colored pencils.

Hayne wondered what sick kids in hospitals did with their time. Would he ever have any friends because he lived in a trailer with his fat mother and he was a sick, scrawny, stupid kid from the Santa Monica beach?

Well, at least I have the beach, he thought. *Not everyone has the beach.* And so he filled his mind with the beach and all its wonder.

While Hayne imagined all the sandcastles he'd built, and the moats, and the shells, and coral, and rocks and sea glass he'd found for Sandbox Sam to sell, and the elaborate sandcastles he and Mabela Gabriela created last summer, he fiddled with his striped socks.

While pondering the Ferris wheel and the carousel at the Hippodrome, he put a sock on his right hand and liked the feel of it so he poked the fabric in and made a sort of space between his fingers and his thumb. *Neat. Look at that. I made a little mouth. I could make a face on this. It just needs eyes. Ha ha. I can make it speak. I just made a puppet!*

Hayne cut two circles out of white construction paper. He didn't know how to make eyes, but for the moment, he colored in two black dots in the middle of each circle and glued them to the top of the sock. The look was other-worldly.

Suddenly, the sock introduced himself, his voice a metallic monotone. "Hello. I'm Mr. Bleep."

In his nine year old wisdom, Hayne thought, *I'm onto something here. I just made friends with a man from another planet.*

"Where is the rest of my family?" said the monotonic Mr. Bleep to the boy.

"The rest?" the boy asked.

"Yes," said Mr. Bleep. "Mrs. Bleep. And the little Bleeps, Bongo and Bingo. And the furry Parleysnart and the feathered Ibstot. And of course, my great grandfather, Boodie. Where are the Bleeps?"

I guess I'd better get busy, said Hayne to himself.

THE DUTCH DOOR

"That was wonderful. Haynie, just hearing you talk about it and seeing this, well, it's something special. The whole Bleep family. I'm in it already," said the young and enthusiastic-about-anything-theatrical Diesel.

"That's mighty fine, because I have more. Much more. The family goes off in space on an adventure and they meet earthmen."

"Do you have a real show?"

"A real show? The rest of the trunk is filled with other puppets and props. I've done approximately 1,000 puppet shows since I was nine."

Hayne's mind could go to that time so quickly. He'd be doing the dishes or sewing on a button, or, heck, be in the middle of a rehearsal, and start thinking about the beach...and the puppets...

By the end of that fateful sickness in 1937, six of Hayne's socks were magically repurposed into rudimentary Bleep Family puppets.

When Hayne realized he could only play with two puppets at a time by himself, he added finger puppet Bleeps. At first, he made them out of cones of paper and different little paper hats or ears until Jerry, the Juggler said, "Git Glenda to knit ya some tiny finger socks." Glenda was Jerry the Juggler's girlfriend, who knitted scarves and pot holders to sell at Sandbox Sam's little table.

Glenda didn't make Hayne any finger socks. Instead, she taught him to knit. He made little socks for his fingers and thumbs and sewed on ears and eyes and noses and made colored hair out of pieces of his mother's new mop.

Pretty soon, Hayne had an entire Bleep Family to play with. The Bleeps' heads were covered with flaming bright hair and they played music on flowers and lit candles with stars. Hayne made a tiny, colorful spaceship out of a PF Flyers shoebox and had all the Bleeps traveling fast through their space adventures.

Hayne got so excited by the Bleeps that it made him want to get out of bed. He was tired of the bed and the trailer. He only had a few spots, he argued with his mother, so why couldn't he get up and go to school? He hated school, but it was better than being cooped up in the trailer all day every day forever. Fatty said because the nuns say, ya don't come back til those spots're gone!

Fatty was right, of course, but that didn't satisfy our Hayne. He said, "But it's dark in here, and lonely. Why can't I go outside?"

"Come into the Queen," said his mother. "You can play in the back room. Yer not goin' til Monday."

"Monday! Four days? This is torture."

Fatty rolled her eyes and heaved herself out of her chair to go whip up a milkshake for her boy.

Hayne left the sad and rumpled bed, gathered his puppet family into the PF Flyers shoe box and, trailing a blanket, traipsed across the dirt lane to the Ice Queen's side entrance. At least his mother had opened the top of the Dutch door to let in some air.

Hayne lay on the Army Surplus cot in the back room of the Queen. *Same scene*, he thought. *Just different walls, and a way worse bed.* He used his knees as props and the Bleeps blundered through a space flight from The Land of Boo to Tallahassee, an exotic place Hayne had heard about from his mother, who always wanted to go to Tallahassee. It sounded like it could be another planet.

Hayne's knees were tired. He squirmed around. He looked up when he saw a shadow by the Dutch door. A man glanced in the room as he passed by. He saw Hayne and waved. Hayne waved back with his puppet-filled fingers and said "Hi" in four tiny unique voices. The man laughed and continued on. Hayne laughed, too.

Later, Hayne sat on a stool by the Dutch door eating a bowl of Wheaties and cream. He had a spoon in one hand and three finger puppets on the other, practicing metallic monotonic voices for Bingo,

Bongo and their Great Great Grandfather Boodie Bleep. He put the PF Flyers Shoe Box Space Ship on the Dutch door shelf and pretended the Bleeps were singing Old MacDonald Had a Farm, which was all he could think of, not knowing any songs from the Land of Boo. He made up Land of Boo farm animal names like badoodle and hisperalto and kachoonie, and the sounds he thought they might make, trying to keep everything in the same tinny monotones.

"Squeak!" "Honk!" "MwaMwa!"

Three girls, each around seven years old, stood on the sidewalk, mesmerized by the little colorful puppets flying through space in the hands of that boy from the Ice Queen. When Hayne looked up and saw them, he put his hands down to his sides, embarrassed, and looked at his shoes. The girls all yelped and said, "No, please. Don't stop! Do that some more! Do more funny talk with your little people!"

A TINY PROSCENIUM

Unwilling to ask the Dominican nuns about how to build a stage set for his Bleep family and their growing entourage, Hayne found his way to the public library. What would nuns know about building things? (Later, Hayne would discover that some nuns knew quite a bit about building things.)

The librarian, Clover Carpenter, listened to Hayne's dilemma. When they found no books about building puppet theaters, Clover took Hayne to the Federal Theater Project in LA to see *Snow White*, performed with puppets.

This changed Hayne's life; all he had to do was see an actual proscenium and puppet theater and he knew what to do with all those cardboard boxes his mother made him break down every week.

Clover often came to the Queen for a cone and visited Hayne while he prepared his proscenium. They set up a table outside the back room of the Queen and cut boxes into curlicues and pillars and borders to be glued and taped together and painted. One day, Clover brought Hayne a book on Greek mythology so he could draw copies of the nine muses to grace his stage's proscenium.

And so, the Bleeps grew. The friends of the Bleeps developed and when Hayne ran out of socks, his well-meaning mom brought home

40

six pairs of used white socks from the resale shop down the way. She dragged an old steamer trunk behind her, too, the kind with little drawers, to give to her boy for his tiny Bleeps.

When he got older, old enough to have a past and a so-called "childhood" behind him, Hayne rarely talked about himself. Because of the Bleeps, and the millions of cardboard boxes, he became a master of the moment, enticing people into his creative world, or worlds, to join him on a journey. And he got to stay behind the curtain and make people laugh and cry and clap.

A DUTCH DOOR, A TRUNK, AND A THEATER FOR THE BLEEPS

Hayne's cup overflowed with new bounty. Like magic, a few things happened at the same time. Or, close enough to the same time for Hayne to save them together in his memory bank.

The first thing was Hayne's puppet discovery via a single sock on a boring day while lying on a cot, recovering from the measles.

Next, came the Dutch door. Earlier that morning, it was just an ordinary door; you opened it, you walked through it, you let it shut behind you. Sometimes the top of the Dutch door was open during the day, but Fatty said that was like an invitation to the beach bums to help themselves to buns or ketchup on the shelves.

When Hayne rolled out of his sick bed and into the back room, Fatty left the top of the Dutch door open for him, and that changed everything.

By the time Fatty Wills came home dragging that old steamer trunk behind her, Hayne had created an entire family of Bleeps, who lived in a pile in a, yes, cardboard box.

The steamer trunk contained eight drawers on the left and a tiny closet space on the right. The outside, covered with travel stamps and stickers, told stories all over itself. That trunk had traveled to Paris, and London, and Istanbul, to Athens, and Crete, and Lisbon, and at least twenty other places.

It smelled like old leather and books and vaguely of a thousand perfumes, and Chinese dumplings, and sweat, and old socks, and sand, and sea.

The Bleeps, being only sock puppets, all fit in one drawer. Hayne gathered all his supplies and stashed them in the rest of the drawers; glue, and paper, paint and rulers and scissors and box cutters. In one drawer he put all the finger puppets and his yarn and needles and knitting supplies. In the space on the right, he collected pieces of cardboard and rolls of paper and fabric.

Hayne didn't really know what to say to Fatty Wills about the trunk. He couldn't think of anything she ever brought home to him before, besides the necessary items of clothing from the Goodwill shop or perhaps a grilled cheese sandwich from her griddle. She wasn't much for gifts, and never had any money to spare. But this. This was…this was a miracle.

He didn't have a lot of experience with the words, "Thank you."

"Fatty, I…This is really cool. I mean. Everything fits. I mean…thank you."

Fatty was a woman of even fewer words than her only child. But, Hayne had learned to read his mother's commentary with some skill.

"Aw, just do somethin' fine with it. Make yer puppets. Yer an artist."

That meant she was proud of him.

AND THEN CAME GILMOR BROWN

Gilmor Brown invented the Pasadena Playhouse in 1917. When he wasn't in the midst of theatrical or personal drama, or squiring new talent to theatrical events, he frequented the Santa Monica Pier. The regulars, the people who hung out at the Pier, inspired Gilmor. They built unique and separate, alternative lives; they were creative; he felt at home among them. He watched the muscle beach boys pressing pounds and stretching their powerful physiques; he'd have a gin fizz at the bar; he wandered from stall to stall, checking out the beads or the shells or the fishing gear or the food and the people who made or cooked or sold all the things that made the Pier the Pier.

One warm Wednesday afternoon he happened upon the Ice Queen as he left the Pier. He saw the tall glittering Crown nestled in sparkling ice on top of the little flat-roofed building and thought, "It's time for a cone."

As he approached the Ice Queen, he noticed a commotion at the side door—a throng of children watching something. Gilmor moved on to the front window and was confronted by Fatty's backside while she made a root beer float for a customer. He just about fainted when she turned around and unconsciously flashed him a side view of her sundress and all it hoped to envelope. *Whoa*, thought Gilmor Brown.

Gilmor ordered a chocolate cone, took it from Fatty's fat hand, gave her the coins and wandered to the side of the building to consider the Ice Queen. While thus pondering, he looked again at the children hanging out by the side door. Cone in hand, he joined them.

At that moment, the Bleeps had just landed on the Planet of Janet, who met them at the door of their PF Flyers space ship.

Gilmor watched as the Bleeps offered Janet a Rannytap Sapp, their favorite "rainbow" beverage. Bongo played her a tune on a giant flower from the Land of Boo. Bingo scored a rainbow across the sky with her rainbow broom.

Gilmor loved the tiny broom, made of strips of colored paper attached to a little stick. He wanted some Rannytapp Sapp! He wondered who was managing these funny little puppets on the other side of the door.

The 14 year old Hayne had developed the Bleeps into a Pier phenomenon. His trunk overflowed into the back room of the Ice Queen with sets and puppets, extra socks, ribbons, fake eyeballs he'd made out of halved ping pong balls, yarn, etc. The Dutch door had become the base for a regular puppet theater, built out of big boxes and scraps of wood and tin and shells and whatnot, discovered on or around the beach. The backroom of the Ice Queen became backstage to Hayne's Tiny Little Theater.

Never a good student, Hayne put his considerable artistic talent entirely into his puppet shows. Oh, he went to school but mostly resented it—he never seemed to learn anything he really needed to know from the nuns (like how to make a tiny stage) and was relatively content in the back room, or sitting outside next to the Queen with his supplies, making puppets. Hayne gave puppets to the local kids, who followed him around the beach like he was the Pied Piper of Puppets. They begged him for more tiny plays with the tiny Bleeps. And so, after school on Wednesdays and on Saturday and Sunday mornings, Hayne became a regular attraction at the Santa Monica Pier. And guess what? Even Hayne's health got better.

This being a Wednesday, Gilmor Brown's Pasadena Playhouse was dark. He had time to consider this puppeteer.

The kids and the adults laughed and laughed at the Bleeps and Gilmor Brown laughed, too. He loved the part where the furry Parlysnart chased the flapping red Ibstot around the stage. The feathers and the fur flew!

Ever inspired by talent, Gilmor waited until the end of the show to speak to his new discovery. When all the kids had put their coins in the tip basket and gone home, Hayne took the last puppets off his fingers.

Behind him, covering the walls of the back room of the Ice Queen were superbly executed caricatures of the beach people—the regulars, the tourists, the beachcombers, the bums, the kids, the hookers and the workers. When Hayne wasn't puppeteering in his Tiny Little Theater, he drew unflattering but realistic images of what his mother dared to call "the Great Unwashed."

If Fatty Wills had a redeeming feature, it was her good heart. It was said she had a "fat heart," and she took it as a compliment and believed it. She fed stray cats, dogs and kids; she slipped coffee to the bum with perpetual DTs; she once used her entire jar of tips to buy a pair of shoes for Mabela Gabriella.

Gilmor Brown approached the Dutch door while Hayne took down the puppet theater. Hayne set it on the table and went back to the door to greet the person there.

"Hello," said Hayne, unaware that he spoke to his future. "You can orders burgers and stuff in front."

"Are you the puppeteer?" asked Gilmor, looking at the back room and the miles of art all over its walls.

"Yessir, I am." Hayne immediately worried he was being shut down—*this natty dressed guy in his brown suit and tie, he's here from the beach patrol or something. Ugh.*

"Who made these puppets?"

"Uhm… I did."

Who made the stage? That elaborate proscenium?"

"Me, again."

"And, well, who wrote your script?"

"All me," said Hayne, and looked at his shoes.

Gilmor Brown was silent. Hayne got worried. "Am I in trouble?" he asked, always prepared for the worst.

"Not to my knowledge," replied our friend, Gilmor. "But I think we should talk."

HOPE AND PURPOSE

Gilmor, a kind of godfather to many rising male stars in Southern California, knew talent when he saw it. He had a great reputation for being the man behind the success story.

After some lengthy discussions with Hayne Williams, a few touching conversations with Fatty, and a quick but eye-opening look inside the trailer, Gilmor knew he'd found his next cause—getting this genius off the beach and into the right hands.

No offense to Fatty, of course. She did the best she could. But, did she know her son was a creative genius who just needed an education? Could she provide him with the necessary chops to make his way in the world? Gilmor didn't think so. He could see Hayne loved his funny fat mama, and she, Fatty, always referred to Hayne as "her boy" and showed him much affection in her own sort of sloth-like way. But, let's just say, her bar wasn't very high. Hayne skated by at school just because the nuns were tired of chasing after him and he was an elusive and irregular student at best.

He'd gotten less sickly, though, and Hayne himself believed it was because he had better air at the Dutch door, and bought better food with his tip money.

He was in love with the Dutch door—he saw it as the door to his future. He wasn't exactly sure what that meant, but he knew he just felt better when he performed his plays and made people laugh, especially kids. The kids gave him hope. The Bleeps gave him purpose. He'd never experienced either one of those things before.

And then, Gilmor helped him find the way.

DIESEL EDWARDS

Robert DeWayne "Diesel" Edwards was the kid who made everything into a show. He draped the wall behind his bed with a red velvet curtain. In the morning, he tootled a soprano whistle from his upstairs bedroom window to the robins and finches in the trees. He ate *his* Wheaties with his left hand while, with his right, he conducted his way through favorite moments of classical music history. When he got to the dining room every morning, Robert DeWayne greeted his parents as if he were Fred Astaire on the lookout for his Ginger Rogers. Robert DeWayne never simply walked into a room. His concerned father thought he rather pranced.

And, the boy sang like a lark. His young voice carried the church choir to some local fame and sooner or later Episcopalians from all over the Chicago area showed up at the Church on the Hill in Winnetka, to hear that "tall blonde boy in the choir."

That went well, until Robert DeWayne turned twelve. He freaked out about the overnight change in his voice (and body, yikes!) and for quite some time could hardly utter a monosyllabic word, much less a warble. He cried over the thought of never singing that magical soprano line again. He was mortified, ashamed to admit he suddenly, and quite definitively, had become a baritone. And, unfortunately, his baritone just wasn't as beautiful as his soprano. He took up dance and acting.

Diesel knew he was really in trouble with his dad. That fateful night, he was draped in a sheet leaping around his room with his favorite invisible dance partner, Isadora Duncan, who taught him everything she knew from the other side of the veil. He was about to leap off the bed with the imagined Isadora in his arms when his bedroom door opened. The scarf Diesel had flung out in front of him flitted right over his father's surprised face.

Uh oh. Not good, Diesel rightly thought. *Pater will be pissed, for sure.*

"What is the meaning of this, Diesel? What are you doing here?" He ripped the errant cloth off his face in a fury.

"Uh...practicing?"

"Practicing for what? Being a pansy? Take off that silly garment. And meet me in the parlor in five minutes."

And this is where Robert DeMontfort Edwards tried to block nature's course. The man wasn't about to let his son become another Oscar Wilde, that degenerate creep. Monty Edwards had a reputation to uphold.

In the hope it would make his only son Robert DeWayne a man, Monty had already nicknamed him Diesel, and supplied his first of many whiskeys. Now, he prepared to send the boy to Culver Military Academy, to polish him up good, to take some of those effeminate proclivities out of him—theater, dancing, singing! *For God's sake, put a saber in his hand. That'll make a man out of him.*

Old Monty Edwards was a man's man.

DIESEL GOES TO SUMMER MILITARY CAMP

Diesel reluctantly packed for a summer at military camp. He had a feeling this wasn't going to be weaving lanyards and taking swimming lessons and eating piles of pancakes for breakfast. He saw the brochures.

No one but Robert DeWayne knew the inside of Robert DeWayne's mind, and that was how he would keep it, forever, if possible. On the outside, why, he was bright and brilliant, like a shiny copper penny; witty and educated, well-dressed and generally a good all around American boy. Well, if boys were allowed to love the color pink and secretly longed to wear frothy ostrich boas.

Diesel cried himself to sleep every night, determined to not let those naysayers, those teasers and tormentors, know how he really felt—like he was a sinner and a liar and no good. Diesel's perfect life had a thin veneer, like a porcelain cup. Every morning, when he got out of bed, he reasoned with himself to be perky and alert and ready for whatever happened out there. Being Robert DeWayne "Diesel" Edwards was a lonely business.

CULVER MILITARY ACADEMY

Robert DeWayne arrived for his eight weeks of Culver Military Summer Camp prepared for the worst, and he was not disappointed.

"Line up, in alphabetical order, now! Fast! Move it!" bawled the Company Commander, an eighteen year old senior camp counselor loving every minute of his power.

"Strip down to your birthday suits, boys, and lemme see what God gave ya."

First of all, Diesel and ten others in "Company B" were sent to the communal showers, where much towel snapping and general bad boy behavior ensued.

Diesel, embarrassed, knew already that he wasn't like these boys. He had absolutely no interest in football or hockey or hunting and shied away from any personal contact. When he heard they were going to be riding horses, he almost threw up. Diesel hated horses.

6'2" tall and handsome as he was, though, he could not hide out in the corner for long. First he got teased for his hair, slightly long and blonde and curly and they said he looked like a girl. Then he got teased when he said he was a dancer. A singer. An actor. Ho boy.

When they all got routed into the campus barber shop and watched each other lose their locks to the razor, Diesel still stood out in the crowd because he was so beautiful, from his toes to his nose. He couldn't help it. He was a specimen and he, shyly, knew it. He wrapped a towel around his middle, scratched at his nonexistent hair and took himself back to the dorm.

When Diesel walked in, there, spread out on the bottom bunk was a behemoth by the name of Victor Magenta, Diesel's roomie for the next eight weeks. Victor already did not like his roommate based on the elegant monogrammed maroon luggage, and they hadn't even met. Now, they took one look at each other and thought, *No. Not this.*

Victor was built like a Viking, replete with flaming red hair. He obviously hadn't paid a visit to the campus barber yet. *Your moment will come, big boy,* Diesel thought. *I can hardly wait to see you shorn.*

Victor, born for battle about 600 years too late, groaned at the thought of eight weeks in the company of this wimp. He couldn't wait to get out on the field, to practice military maneuvers and mock battles, to march in the weekly military honors parade. While Diesel was dancing around his room at home, Victor stomped down his mother's polished hallway pretending he was Attila the Hun. He planned to eat people like Diesel Edwards for breakfast.

Diesel climbed his way to the upper bunk and flopped down without even speaking to the behemoth. He buried his face in his pillow.

DODGING A BULLET

The good news is that Diesel only had to endure a week of this cruel folly. The bad news? It was because his father suddenly died. It is significant that Monty Edwards's head fell on his desk during a fatal heart

48

attack. Significant because it happened to be just moments before the pen in his hand signed the papers to commit his only son to that illustrious military boarding school for four years.

Queen Elizabeth may have been haughty, but she knew her son better than her husband had. When Diesel came home from Culver to attend his father's funeral, Mater told her son that 1) he could stay home and 2) he had inherited quite a lot of money, but he couldn't have it until he was 21 and/or had completed college.

It must also be noted that when Diesel's hair grew back, it was steel gray and straight as a stick.

He was fourteen!

Diesel didn't miss his father, Old Monty, much. The money was nice, but the best part was that Queen Elizabeth let him go to New Trier Township High School, like a normal person. No military academy, no boarding school, just a good and simple high school. And after two summers as a "Cherub" at Northwestern's summer program for outstanding high school students, where he dove into theater arts like an all-star swimmer, he enrolled in their university four year program and set out to learn everything he could about theater. He already knew what he would do with all that money.

QUEEN ELIZABETH EDWARDS

Elizabeth Edwards, known to all as the Queen, or sometimes, Queenie, had her own reputation to uphold as the widow of the diesel engine tycoon. She planned to continue his philanthropic ways, and stay in control, and never, ever would her son know her true feelings. Never would she confess how she felt about the man to whom she was married for 20 years, for whom she bore a son, and with whom she reared that son as best she could to take over Edwards Diesel Engine Company.

But that time had come, the man was dead, and she knew Diesel would never have anything to do with EDEC. He was lost to her in that way, in any way that could carry on the plans. To go forward, she had to go without him.

No. She didn't miss Monty Edwards.

She dialed Hazel's number.

"Hon?" she said into the phone. "I'll be right over."

AUNT HAZEL

Hazel Winthrop seriously disliked her brother, Monty, and didn't miss him, either. In fact, there is not much evidence that Monty had any fans in his own family. The Edwards household went on as if nothing had happened.

Oh, to have grown that company from a nugget to a goldmine just to be dead at 42 years old. All the fun was left to Monty's widow, his son and his sister and he is dust and forgotten already.

There was an element of guilty glee in Hazel's heart.

DIESEL LEAVES THE NEST

Northwestern was to Diesel what the Pasadena Playhouse was to Hayne. Whereas Hayne had a mentor and a guide in Gilmor Brown, Diesel had lots of available cash, and he could already see his visions before him. He lived at home while attending Northwestern, happy to share many of his meals (cooked by the ever-faithful Daisy) with his mother and Aunt Hazel, stalwart companion and knitter of famously long scarves.

Aunt Hazel asked her nephew one night why he didn't start calling himself Robert, or Bob, now that his father was no longer with them. Why keep "Diesel" as any kind of name? Diesel was spooning tomato soup into his mouth at the time. He paused. He put his soup spoon on the saucer. He looked at Aunt Hazel and said, "Well. You've got to admit it's more interesting than 'Bob.'"

After Diesel had squeezed all the knowledge and training he could out of Northwestern, he made his plans to fly the coop. He sat in his room at night and studied his big atlas. He spent hours at the library during the day and looked up cities with theater life, trying to capture an idea of the lifestyle and character of the towns and their people. He spent three week after graduation mapping his moves and finally announced to his mother, and Aunt Hazel, of course, that he was moving to San Francisco.

"Why San Francisco?" his mother asked. "It's so far away."

"Not that far. And, I think I'll like the scene there. I want to get to know San Francisco."

"Why?" asked Aunt Hazel.

"Because I'm going to build a theater."

CHAPTER THREE
SATURDAY, JUNE 7, 2008

With mirth and laughter let old wrinkles come.
The Merchant of Venice
~ Wm. Shakespeare

NOW WHAT?

Midnight. Darkness surrounded the Villa in every way, although at the Old Hall, the lights still burned.

Hayne and Diesel, all talked out, were ready to rest.

"So unsettling," Hayne finally said, as he turned off the light.

"So dark," said Diesel.

"I can just see the headlines: A Murder at Villa Zanetta!"

"Hopefully, the only."

"Goodnight, D."

"Goodnight, Haynie."

Everyone onsite, including all the folks in the Villa at the time of the incident, and all coming and going crew and staff, spent time in the Not-so with Grady and Patrick. They were all questioned at least once, the body removed to the morgue, the nit-picking forensics almost complete.

The sheriffs' team explored and fingerprinted every corner of Villa Zanetta. Everywhere? Hundreds of stories in fingerprints? A dictionary of whorls? An encyclopedia of babble! Ah, well. They must have a plan.

Martha Jennings's mother arrived with the medication. Mama calmed Martha down and took her home, promising to stay put at Martha's home in Petaluma.

It wasn't hard to get Martha to go home. She yielded to whatever anyone told her to do: drink this, eat that, take this, here's a blanket, put on your shoes. Patrick let Martha go, following the two out the door with his eyes.

When she arrived at 6:30, Patrick thought how beautiful, young and perky Martha looked, like she had great fun being a 50s girl. She blew in the door, anxious to see her husband! But, in the last few hours, Martha's great appeal had begun to wear off and fifteen years had piled onto her age. Her hair hung down, petticoats drooped, those sexy white over-the-knee stockings rolled down as she left the building leaning on, practically sagging against, her mother. A person's life can change (or end) in an instant.

The All-Nighters could have gotten a few hours sleep in the dorm, they all had rooms, but, tired as they were, no one wanted to leave the Old Hall, leave each other.

MeiMei and LuLu went into the kitchen to scrape carrots for Chef Henry. Chef Henry, that magnet, put smiles on most faces. Actually, it was Henry's smile that won him the job, and his culinary skills served him well over the last six years. Marcus's judgment at the time of hiring was, "Anyone with good references and a smile like that can handle a ship of fools."

Willard, Marcus, Priscilla, John Eagle, Sampson Powers and Kendra Masters (the Artistic Team) sat in comfy chairs around a hand-carved low table in the Old Hall, discussing Falcon's replacement.

Sampson held the post of Associate Conductor for the production of *Cosi fan tutte* at the Well Lit this summer as well as the year-round directorship of the Bella Voce Chorale, the local ensemble, who would sing the *Cosi* chorus parts. Sampson had received a call from Marcus Brown, who filled him in on the happenings of the evening and said, "Please, come to the Villa to help decide what to do." Awakened from a dreamless sleep, Sampson yawned. Priscilla brought him coffee.

Priscilla posed the first question on everyone's mind: "Why won't Kendra take over for Falcon? As his assistant, she knows every element of this show."

Marcus said, "Kendra, I'll let you respond to that. You're the one with the issue, and a reasonable one it is."

Kendra Masters, a tough little dancer from the Bronx, hung up her dancing shoes on her 40th birthday in 2003. Her reasons were not merely physical, although her knees did ache in cold weather and her big toe on the left foot, the one she broke in a fall a few years ago, gave her trouble.

But, it was more than that. She felt…unable to stand up (literally and figuratively) with the competition. Her musical knowledge was extensive, Kendra played the piano with some skill, and she had won many accolades and not just a few prizes along the way of her dancing and performing career.

Could she say her heart wasn't in it? That it was too much trouble? Oh, never leave show business, of course not! But, she wanted to move into something new, where the greasepaint and fake boobs and wigs and costumes were left to someone else. Kendra wanted to join the creators on the other side of the curtain and play God and make things happen, try something new that used her brain and not her body. Her body would not hold up to the strain of being a dancer too much longer, anyway, so she quit a few years before expected.

Now, she said, "Please try to understand, I would like nothing more than to say I took over for Falcon Jennings as Stage Director for *Cosi*, but, you all know, I am in training be an assistant director, not a director. I am petrified. I am not ready. I'd know it if I were ready. And, Falcon was…Falcon was my…friend and mentor. And he's dead now."

"I'd think he'd want you to do it," said Priscilla. "In the spirit of *the show must go on*."

"Yes, I know," Kendra said, wiping her tears. "All the same, I get the hiccups whenever I think about it. Maybe I'm just not good enough for this."

"'Not good enough' and 'not ready' are two different things," said Marcus. "I'll try to support your decision, but you may be our last hope."

So they proceeded to ponder possibilities but every name considered for Falcon's replacement, and there were only three, got nixed on the spot.

"Sorry to throw more fuel on the fire," Marcus said, "but we'll also have to find a fill-in for Martha. She'll be in no shape to continue in Wardrobe."

When Kendra Masters suggested Smooch McGuinn, Willard shuddered and groaned. "Please, no-o-o," he said, but he was outnumbered. Everyone liked Smooch; she lived in the City; she loved Villa Zanetta; she'd be here in a heartbeat. Marcus didn't think Smooch would care one whit that her ex, Willard, was here, conducting *Cosi*. And, *she's worked with Diesel here a few times, she knows the ropes.*

Wait! Why didn't I think of this before? Diesel could direct this show! He's done Cosi *at least twice! So what if he's 81? He is the answer!*

Marcus suddenly woke up! *Diesel can get along with anyone, even Willard. And they offered to help. Would he do this?*

Marcus thought about Patrick's question: Why *is* Willard here?

He thought back to the meetings last summer when the *Cosi* decisions were on the table. Willard just seemed like the right choice at the time. *The board president likes him; he would. Willard is an excellent schmoozer, when he wants to be. Hayne had heard he was reformed after some sort of recovery thing. Anyway, the man is 50, too old to be chasing women and having his first drink of the day before breakfast.*

"Oh, Marcus Brown," he said aloud. *You have no idea if he drinks before breakfast. It just seems that way. His pores overflow with his excesses. I thought he was on the wagon, anyway.*

He's here because he excels at and loves Cosi. *What a blooming disaster.*

POOR WILLARD

At about 12:30am, Patrick left Grady at their meeting place in the Not-so and walked to the door of the Old Hall.

"Mr. Franklin, could you please come? We've got a few more questions."

Willard froze. After the disgruntling artistic meeting, Willard went back to "his" table and opened his *Cosi* score, blearily distracting himself from the dramatic events of the day. He glanced around the Hall. Everyone was looking at him. He put down his drink, picked up his cigarettes and put them in his shirt pocket. He stood up.

He'd been expecting this moment, of course; everyone knew of his and Falcon's ongoing general feud. But, he just couldn't help it. The guy drove Willard nuts. Yes, it went beyond the normal conductor vs. stage director thing. Way beyond. That was peanuts compared to all the other reasons. He wasn't sorry Falcon was dead.

But he, Willard, would maintain forever that he had nothing to do with it. Had no connection with Falcon Jennings other than what did or did not happen on the stage. Did not ever hang out with Falcon and his perfect little wife. They meant nothing to him. He was ready to swear to it.

They entered the Not-so. Grady was there at the table, Patrick asked Willard to sit down across from them. Willard asked if he could smoke and they relented. It was just the three of them; fine, if it made the most difficult person here more agreeable.

Patrick said, "Mr. Franklin, we'd like to know a little more about what you were doing at the time of the incident. Can you describe your movements?"

Willard took a drag, blew the smoke away from the table, wicked back his long hair, cleared his throat and said, "I did not kill Falcon Jennings."

"Just answer the questions for now, Willard. What were you doing at 5pm last evening?"

"I told you this. I left the tech meeting about 4:30. I went to the conductor's room. I was there for about 30 minutes. When I felt and heard the crash, I came upstairs to see what it was. I was afraid it was an earthquake and I didn't want to be stuck in the lower level."

"Was anyone with you?"

"I was alone."

"What did you do in those 30 minutes?"

"I had a drink. Two drinks."

"And…?"

"And, what?" He spit this out. Now his angry side emerged. One could hear it in his clipped, low-voiced answers.

"You had a drink or two and…"

"I just…sat down…and drank."

"Was Mr. Jennings at the tech meeting?"

"Yes. You already know that."

"When did he leave?"

"I don't know. He was still backstage when I left." Getting madder.

"The tech crew tells us you had an argument with Mr. Jennings."

"We had arguments whenever we were in the same room. I'm used to it."

"Why did you leave early?"

Willard thought about this for a moment. He closed his eyes. Willard rarely drank enough these days to get seriously drunk, but it was unusual to have an alcohol-free body. Right now? Not one of those moments.

The old Willard, a relatively functional alcoholic, could fake it, if necessary. He had to fake it often. But, Willard was tired. And fed up. When Willard got tired and fed up, he got reckless; let down his guard. And when Willard Franklin's guard was relaxed, he brooded more, drank more and events were known to spiral into some pretty dark regions.

Willard meandered around in his head before responding. He had visions of all the times Falcon Jennings got in his way, made him mad, or disrupted his careful musical planning. In his mind, he saw Falcon whirling Martha around the dance floor at a party, schmoozing with board members at events, acting out movements for soloists with the grace of a ballet dancer, smiling—just plain moving—like Gene Kelly, wrapping the world around his little finger. Yes, he vehemently hated Falcon Jennings.

Willard blurted out, "I left early because the little twit really pisses me off, and I thought I might just throttle him if he did not shut up."

Then he realized what he'd said.

"But I didn't kill Falcon Jennings."

"Willard," said Grady Mulligan, "is there someone who can verify that you were in the conductor's room last night at 5pm? Did anyone see you go in or come out?"

"No."

"Tell us what happened when you encountered the scene in the lobby. What did you do first?"

By 2am, Willard needed a drink. He was chain smoking and tossing the cigarette butts into the big potted palm to his right.

This act rankled Grady Mulligan, for two reasons. One, he was not a smoker, never had been, considered it a filthy habit and had been in an enclosed room with Kendra Masters and/or Willard Franklin all evening. Thankfully, they were the only smokers.

Two, his own fastidious behavior recoiled at the thought of cigarette butts in the potted palm. His opinion of Willard Franklin slipped lower by the minute. Grady came close to telling Willard Franklin to clean up after himself, but decided against it.

ALL NIGHT LONG

Chef Henry, pulling an all-nighter anyway to prepare the kitchen for the upcoming weeks, focused his attention on what was in front of him, mainly the constant act of feeding a semi-wild bunch of bohemians whose appetites never waned. It was intense work, being creative. Now, curiouser and curiouser, men in uniforms with badges roamed their halls and poked in every cupboard. *What a great combination*, Henry thought; *actors, artists, musicians and cops.*

Back from his little break outside, Henry pulled his long black dreads into a ponytail, donned a clean white coat embroidered with CHEF in red letters, turned up the music and slapped a Bob Marley-style Reggae beat on the countertop. A vast array of ingredients lay before him. He knew his job: fill their tummies, make lots of coffee.

MeiMei and LuLu were in the kitchen, too, standing on low stools, up to their armpits in flour, jabbering in their beautiful, colorful, sing-song way while rolling out Henry's dough to make pastries for breakfast.

Priscilla dozed with her forehead straight down on the table and her hands in her lap, that French Twist finally unraveled all the way. Her linen suit had wrinkles on its wrinkles and Priscilla had replaced her heels and stockings with flip-flops.

John Eagle sat at a table with a cup of tea and his laptop, writing a press release about death.

The sheriffs were not quite finished with Willard Franklin, whose curling cigarette smoke continued to toxify the Not-so.

Marcus and Kendra sat together on one of the little love seats against the back wall of the Old Hall. Two bottles of wine, one empty, one half full, sat on the little table before them.

Marcus's emotions were in full bloom now that he *could* let down. Until this moment, he had embodied the Executive Director of The Theaters at Villa Zanetta; he answered all the questions, tried to make the right decisions, and made sense of necessary schedule changes with Priscilla. He kept it together and showed up and did his job.

But he also wanted to comfort Martha, had to be civil to Willard, and was mourning the loss of his long-time friend, Falcon. Oh, and let's not forget he felt the hot wheeze of that chandelier as it dropped like a bomb to the floor.

He truly had been an inch away from his own death. He had time to think about that now.

"Thank God I have you to talk to, Kendra. Without you, I'd be drunk all by myself, and that is worse than what I'm doing right now. I'm sorry I'm such a mess. I can't stop crying. I feel empty and drained and so sad. And scared. Why am I scared?"

"Geez, Marcus, you don't think it might be that, but for a simple, tiny quirk of fate, you, too, would be lying under that chandelier right now? Give yourself a break, hon."

"You're right, you're right. But, I keep seeing that moment over and over. Why does it scare me? It didn't hit me, so I should be happy, elated, throw-my-hat-in-the-air-joyous. But I'm not. I'm scared. My knees feel like chopsticks knocking together one minute and noodles the next. My hands are still shaking. I feel, I don't know...violated."

"Well, your personal space *was* compromised. Just look at your sleeve. And you haven't had time to release all that shock. Someone, not some *thing*, by the way, not the chandelier, but *someone* wanted Falcon dead. Another inch and that person who wanted Falcon dead, would be saying, 'Oops! Sorry, Marcus. No hard feelings!'"

"Kendra, you make me laugh at the most inappropriate times."

"Think about it, Marc. Assuming Falcon was the target, you were almost killed, too."

"Do you think it was Willard?" Marcus asked. "I mean, who else here, just look around you, who else is capable of doing such a thing? Even of all the tech people, or Henry?"

"Well, this is my first experience of Willard up close and personal, but I'd say..." and here, not that anyone was listening, Kendra moved in close for a confidence... "I'd say he's a bit creepy and...I don't know. Volatile. Like a steaming volcano. He kind of...percolates."

"I'm always uneasy around Willard. Maybe it's because he's got too many secrets," said Marcus.

"Ha. Maybe it's because he's a narcissist and needs all the attention in the room."

"Ah. You're not seduced?"

"Not a bit," she said.

"Be sure to tell me if he tries."

"I will hand you his tender body parts on a golden plate."

By 2am, Patrick and Grady, who loved and hated working together, had come to a few conclusions. They loved and hated working together because they loved and hated each other, so it follows.

The love was there because they had no choice; they were first cousins, their mothers were sisters and Grady and Patrick had been thrown together ad nauseam their entire lives.

They hated each other because two more different men you could never find; the Oscar Madison and Felix Unger of the Irish/American culture living in the Sonoma Valley.

These two would never live in the same house, though. Oh, no. Grady is fastidious, spotless, extremely vain and mildly neurotic about it. He is not as smart as Patrick, nor quite as cute. Patrick is eccentric and kind of sloppy while Grady prides himself on correct behavior and dress. They've been snapping like turtles for thirty years, since their mothers first plopped them into the same playpen.

But when Patrick came home from college and joined the sheriff's department as a detective, they continued to be thrown together; this time around, on cases just like this. And for some inexplicable reason, they usually solved the puzzles.

"Let me see your list," Grady said to Patrick. His cousin handed over the slip of paper.

1. Some people know more than they let on.
2. Willard - almost too obvious a choice, but…
3. Willard said "Falcon pisses me off," like he forgot the man was dead.
4. Find out more about Kendra Masters. No alibi.
5. Talk to Martha Jennings – where was she, who had it in for Falcon?
6. What specific time was Priscilla in the bathroom on the mezzanine floor?
7. What does Hector know?
8. This place is a beehive of distractions.
9. I am tired and want to go home.

Grady nodded. "Yeah," was all he said.

Willard returned to the Old Hall. He could have gone to his beautiful, airy conductor's apartment at the south end of the dorm, just fall down on his nice bed and go blissfully to sleep. But, he was out of cigarettes and needed a drink. He was agitated, irritated and pissed. He knew they didn't believe his story. He had no alibi, and even if he did, they knew he hated Falcon Jennings. He went to the bar.

Grady and Patrick opened up the Not-so to air it out (Patrick did not smoke indoors and was usually offended when someone did). They walked out to the brick patio to have a discussion. Patrick lit a Camel.

Grady said, "Maybe if we take him in to the station he'll talk more. There's a lot going on here. He's got no alibi and he's the only one with a motive."

"I don't know," said Patrick. "Seems risky. He'll want a lawyer, who won't be happy to be called at 2am on a Saturday. And, if he did do it, how did he get back down to the theater so fast? The outside stairway starts on the mezzanine floor on the other side of the building. You have to go through the offices to get there. He couldn't do it in one minute, or without being seen. The three women were in the office. I don't think we have enough to take him in, certainly not to arrest him. All we can do is ask him nicely to stay at the Villa."

MARCUS GOES UP THE HILL

Kendra finally drifted off to her room in the dorm for a little sleep. Marcus, up all night, prepared himself for a meeting with Hayne and Diesel on the hill. He went into the Lobby bathroom and sluiced water over his gritty eyes and stubbly face, paid a visit to the kitchen for one of those pastries, poured himself some more coffee.

Was this a good idea? Should he broach this subject with Diesel? 81 is a little along in years to take on a show a week prior to opening. *But, the soloists are prepared after weeks of rehearsals with Willard in the City, we have Falcon's notes and marks, everything else is in place. Kendra will stay on as the AD if she has Diesel, I'm sure. She can do this. Would he be willing to be a hero and step in? Would he take on someone else's notes or have to change everything?*

Well, no time like now to find out, Marcus mused as he walked up the hill. *Let's go ask.*

The "new house" as Hector still referred to it after 33 years, was in full sun, and Hector puttered outside on the deck, filling the bird feeders. He saw Marcus coming up the pebbled driveway and waved. Marcus waved back and noticed fresh dirt piled by the squash mounds. A bucket of Hector's gourmet Chicken Manure Tea sat by his little gardening stool.

Hector put his hand out and said, "Good mo'ning, Mawcus Bwown," like he always did, and shook the hand of his "neighbo." Eleven years ago, when Marcus first visited Villa Zanetta and learned that Hector pretty much "came with the place," he didn't understand. But Hector had grown on him, and now, he couldn't imagine the Villa without him; his sweet energy, his quirky ways, his funny speech, that special view of the world. His garden!

Expected, Marcus knocked on the screen door and walked in. The old gentlemen sat at the big dining table in the Great Room, having toast, marmalade and tea. Marcus turned down the tea, jagged already from no sleep and three cups of Henry's strong black coffee, but he buttered a slice of toast.

Marcus gazed out the big picture window overlooking the glorified pond. Lake Zanetta, they called it. Carp dashed under lily pads, and hid under rocks. Jake Ortman regularly cleaned out the algae and other green, growing vegetation to allow the carp to thrive. The reeds and lilies attracted frogs and the water invited all the neighborhood critters over for a drink. Marcus tuned into the bullfrog sitting on a rock, belching out a song for his sweetie across the pond in the bushes. *Calm environs down there, pond-side,* he thought. *No fraught frogs or fish. No puzzles to solve.*

How's it going down at the Villa?" Hayne asked. "Any new developments?"

Marcus blinked back from his reverie to the present moment. "Mmmm, not really. They've cleaned up a bit, and we'll be able to use the conductor's room this afternoon for the soloists' rehearsal, after all, but the sheriffs have been focusing on Willard. They almost took him in for questioning but decided against it for some reason. He's pretty shaken up. Last I saw him, he was smoking Kendra's Virginia Slims and drinking tomato juice—probably spiked with vodka."

"Have you been up all night, Marcus?" asked Diesel. "You look a bit bleary."

"Yes. Yes, I have. It's been a long night. The All-Nighters, we've dubbed ourselves. But the sheriffs have left Joe Budd to continue to poke around, and Grady and Patrick will be back later. I'm hoping Willard will get some sleep before the rehearsal this afternoon. Priscilla is organizing breakfast, Kendra's asleep in her room. John Eagle dozed for a bit in the Old Hall. I'll take a nap before the rehearsal, if I can."

"Well," says Hayne, "you won't be any good to anyone or anything if you don't take that nap. Where will you go? Do you need a bed?"

"No, thanks. I have my usual dorm room. The sheriffs want us all to stick around, since we can. But I do need something from you. A very particular something. You may think I am mad when you hear it."

"Heavens, what on earth?" says Hayne.

"Well, this is for Diesel, but you'll both be affected by it." Marcus paused for dramatic effect.

"Yes?" said Diesel, who gazed out the big window at the same gold fish bowl in the ground. Suddenly, he knew. He turned and looked at Marcus. "Wait. Don't say it. Let me guess. You want me to direct *Cosi*! Am I right?"

"Yes. You're right. Were you expecting this?"

"No, actually. I was not. But, I should have known. Kendra said no?"

"She succinctly said no. She insists she's not ready. She said she's barely had time to be an AD much less a full blown stage director. But, there is no one out there. The artistic team is stymied. Although they did agree, well, except for Willard, about Smooch McGuinn filling in for Martha. I think she'll come."

Hayne and Diesel looked at each other with their eyes wide, like, *Good Lord. What next? Aren't we retired?*

But retiring from show business is just kind of an idea. Remember the joke about the trapeze artist who, when too old to swing in the air, wound up doing less and less and finally found himself cleaning up after the elephants? Someone asked, "Giorgio, why don't you just retire?" and Giorgio replied, "What? And leave show business?"

Marcus said, "I'll just say that the soloists are well rehearsed, we have Falcon's notes, and we have Kendra, and here is the stage rehearsal schedule. I figure that if anyone can get along with Willard, you can.

I know you didn't plan on doing this again in your life, but you have done it before and, well, we are in a bit of a jam."

Hayne waited to hear what Diesel would say. Diesel was very quiet. The pause gave Marcus time to chew his toast. He took a cup of tea after all and sipped it, just to have something warm in his hands. He fidgeted with a case of nerves, hoping Diesel wasn't going to get mad or be offended. Not that he'd ever seen Diesel mad *or* offended.

Hayne, coming to Diesel's rescue (Diesel looked a tad spacey across the table) said, "Marcus, do you mind if we talk about this as if you weren't here?"

"That's OK. I don't have to stay. I certainly have plenty of other issues on my mind. In fact, the soloists are beginning to arrive and they have to be told of the 'incident,' as Grady Mulligan would say. But this is tops on my list of Take Care of It Nows. It would be marvelous if you said yes. Just let me know when you want to talk."

Hayne and Diesel watched Marcus go out the door, heard him speak to Hector ("See ya, Hector," "See ya lato,' Mawcus Bwown"), listened to his steps on the gravel driveway. They were very quiet at the table. The room filled with ghosts and stories of the past.

MAYBE YES, BUT...

"Well, old man, what do you think?" Hayne asked his friend of a lifetime.

"Oh, don't call me 'old man.'"

"You know it's a term of endearment."

"Yes, but right now, it rings too true. I'm past my prime."

Hayne said, "You'll not be past your prime until you're dead."

"Well, this might just kill me off. Things are so charged and heavy, Haynie. Let's add it up. Falcon is dead, someone in the company likely killed him, although I can't imagine who, Martha's a widow, Willard's ex-wife might show up, and Willard is being his usual obnoxious self. Not the least bit redeemed, as we thought. I would actually have to be nice to Willard Franklin, and you know how I feel about that.

"Not to mention a broken chandelier in the Lobby. It all adds up to a carnival side show, if you ask me. And, at this late date, I'd be expected to take Falcon's notes and stick to a plan, never my strong suit."

63

"Well, you know you could put your own stamp on it. Those six soloists all know and love you. Plus, Opening Night is only one week away. How much change can there be? Once you got into it, you'd make it work." Hayne knew his man.

"It sounds like you want me to do it."

"I don't *want* you to do it. I want you to be happy. You're a happy man on the stage set. And besides, what are we doing up here right now except wondering what is going on down at the Villa?"

"It will probably always be that way, even when there are no likely murder suspects hanging about," Diesel said.

"True. But, we did say we'd help."

"We. Not me."

"OK."

Diesel snapped his finger. "I've got it! I'll do it if you perform the Old Play."

"Oh, no. You're kidding."

"No, I am not. This is a WE show, not me. You know I am better when you're there. Besides, if I took this on, what would you be doing? Knitting up here by yourself? No, you'd want to be in the middle of it. You would! I know it. If you did the puppet show, we'd both be helping. And the Old Play was the very first presentation at the Villa."

Hector walked in the door. "Did you thay puppetth? Do we get to do the puppetth? Yeth, yeth!!"

Hayne said, "Now you've done it, D. Hector, it wouldn't be the Bleeps Adventures. It would be the Old Play. We haven't done that since…well, I don't remember the date."

"I do," said the so-called Down Syndrome man. "1983 (thwee). When DD did the *Cothi* ope'wa thing, we did the puppetth. The oneth in the poofy clotheth. The Old Play! I 'membo', Haynie. 1983. And that time befo' that, the firtht time wath, uhm, when we firtht made the tiny thtage thingy."

They were discussing *Le donne ingannate* ("*The Deceived Women*") written by Alberto di Nuccio in 1591, a one-act Commedia dell'Arte play and a precursor to the *Cosi fan tutte* libretto of 1790. *The Old Play*, they always called it; a special piece to Hayne, something he discovered at the Pasadena Playhouse a long, long time ago.

64

Hayne shook his head with a smile and said, "Well, that's right. We did it in 1958. It was our very first show at Villa Zanetta, when we built The Tiny Little Theater in the Barn. You were seven years old. You're amazing, Hector."

"I know," said Hector.

THE SOLOISTS ARRIVE

In the Villa Zanetta 2008 *Cosi fan tutte* performance, the two ladies from Ferrara, sisters Fiordiligi and Dorabella, were sung by Patricia De Lhonge and Carlotta Concepcione, respectively. Lovely ladies, the best of friends, they arrived at Villa Zanetta together and shared the room in the dorm known as the Twosy, with twin beds facing the eastern sunrise.

Tenor Egbert Holloway sings Ferrando, Dorabella's soldier lover, and Baritone Horace Fenberger performs the role of Guglielmo, the soldier lover of Fiordiligi. The baritone in the role of Alfonso, the old philosopher who instigates all the shenanigans in this operatic story, is none other than Danny Bargetto, whom everyone loved as Figaro in *The Marriage of Figaro*, presented at Villa Zanetta last summer under the direction of Robert "Diesel" Edwards (Diesel's final opera directorship before retirement) and conducted by Willard Franklin.

Bette Belle, the more than lovely soprano who sings the role of Despina, the conniving maid, is a beauty, a songbird and a game changer.

Willard's eye had followed Bette Belle for some time; he had looked forward to this opportunity at Villa Zanetta. He thought she might be different, worth the chase and the effort. All the rest have been utter disappointments.

Now, though, it hurt his head to think about it. His clouded mind was too befuddled by fear and anxiety. He spent two hours being grilled by officers who obviously believed him guilty of murder. Willard knew his memory had lapses, but he'd know it if he'd murdered that little gnat. He'd remember every detail because it would give him great pleasure. No, he wasn't sorry Falcon Jennings, that little twerp, was dead. But he was sure he did not do it.

After the sheriffs released him with the "request" to stay on the Villa Zanetta compound, Willard sat by the open back door in the Old Hall and smoked his way through the rest of Kendra's Virginia Slims while consuming a liter of champagne right out of the bottle.

He somehow made his way to his apartment in the dorm at about 10am. He held onto his throbbing head with one hand while his other hand scrambled through his bags, feeling around for some aspirin and hopefully some cigarettes. He felt like that bucket of Chicken Manure Tea in Hector's garden. He washed down the one found aspirin with a shot of vodka. Ah! Six loose cigarettes lay in the bottom of his briefcase, slightly squashed. He checked his watch.

The Conductor's Apartment took up two original dorm bedrooms and viewed a stand of madrones. Willard's bed wilted with rumpled sheets, the bedspread tossed on the floor aside his piles of clothes.

Willard was upset. Not good. On a roller coaster ride of upsetness, he tossed back a few more shots of vodka and inhaled the smoke of a few more cigarettes before passing out on the bed.

A few hours later, he sat on the side of the bed and lit another cigarette. 2pm. He had time for a shot and a shower before the rehearsal. He actually tossed back three shots and had no shower and now was pretty far gone. He passed out again.

Meanwhile, blissfully ignorant of what might happen, the soloists and the pianist took in the information about the current situation and sallied off to their rooms to rest before the 3pm rehearsal. For them, so far all was well, if just little disturbing to be rehearsing where a murder recently occurred.

YES AND NO

Diesel said, "Yes," to Marcus Brown. What other course but to say, "Yes"? Diesel should have known it from the get-go—yesterday afternoon, almost 24 hours ago, he should have seen it coming. He gave it no thought until Marcus transmitted images to his brain by osmosis that morning.

But, Diesel had been viewing the picture from the outside in, thinking he really could put his feet up on the porch rail and just watch Hector in the garden for the rest of his life. Diesel liked this simple living, pondering the greatness and the silliness of the universe, playing scrabble with Haynie, strolling down the hill to see what they were up to at the Villa and catching a play or a concert once in a while.

However, Diesel was a true thespian and an artist to the bone, dedicated to the creation of art and beauty in every way. And, he missed it. Haynie was right. He was a happy man on a stage. He admitted here, in the quiet of his own mind, that the moment he said it out loud, he knew he would do it. 81 or not, he knew he *could* do it. He and Kendra together. She had the score and the notes and now him. He'd show her she *could* do it.

That Hayne agreed to "do the puppetth," well, that just sweetened the deal. If they were both involved, what a way to celebrate 50 years at Villa Zanetta! Bring those old duffers out of retirement!

At 3pm that Saturday in June, Diesel and Hayne walked down to the conductor's room in the theater, prepared to observe the rehearsal and keep tabs on Willard.

Diesel still wondered why they were dealing with Willard at all. In late 2006 they heard from their colleagues the story of Willard's recovery in Arizona. The Villa hired him for 2007 and again now because Hayne trusted that Willard Franklin was a changed man, abjectly sorry for the havoc he had caused in the past and eager to conduct. He wasn't that bad in 2007 during *The Marriage of Figaro*. Just his usual philandering self. No scenes.

The "conductor's room" in The Well Lit Theater at Villa Zanetta filled 600 square feet of quiet space down just a few stairs from the theater's backstage. It was a combination of private dressing room, complete with bathroom and shower, and a studio containing a grand piano, orchestra chairs and a large L-shaped white sofa for the soloists or rehearsers.

The attorney for the Villa Zanetta board of directors, Bill Palmer, and his wife Odella, sat off to the side with Diesel and Hayne. Also present for the occasion were Marcus Brown, the tech director, Pete Daltry, and his sidekick, Melissa Partridge, stage manager; all guests for the first on-site rehearsal for *Cosi fan tutte*, 2008.

The fact that Bill Palmer had arrived for the express purpose of assessing the death of a beloved company member and the collateral damage caused by a falling chandelier, well, that wasn't discussed for the moment. Later, when the Artistic Team and the "All-Nighters" (those present at the "incident") were invited over to the Palmers' for cocktails –that would be soon enough to discuss death and destruction. Right now they settled in to appreciate some beautiful music-making. To lift their spirits.

Sampson Powers sat on a stool in the back of the room, prepared to watch Willard do his thing. Sampson had received an earful of details from Marcus about the events of the evening before. He, too, had heard about Willard's shenanigans and was rather put off by the man. But, considering his own past, he was the loathe to make judgments. And besides, Willard was famous for conducting this piece.

But, Willard was late. The six singers sat on stools, ready to rehearse the *Cosi fan tutte* first act finale. They had all warmed up their voices in various places around the compound. Yes. They were ready.

But, Willard was now fifteen minutes late.

Diesel said to Sampson Powers, "Are you prepared to step in, Sampson?"

And, of course, the answer was, "Yes, Mr. Edwards. I am ready." One had to be ready. Sampson was the Associate Conductor, after all. He carried the title and responsibility, but he never thought he'd get the chance to conduct even the teeniest portion of *Cosi fan tutte*.

But, Willard was late.

Diesel stood up and said to the room, "Welcome to you all. We are all saddened and perplexed today by the death of a well-loved member of our company. In the spirit of our camaraderie, I would like to dedicate this rehearsal to the memory of Falcon Jennings, and truly, may he rest in peace and may the show go on." He nodded to Sampson.

Sampson stepped over to the music stand, turned and faced the group. The smile on his face showed his elation. He was conducting the first act finale of *Cosi fan tutte*, his favorite opera ever written; and this finale the most beloved of all. He knew it well.

When Sampson Powers, tall and elegant with grey hair and a silvery Amish-style beard with no mustache, and that slightly stooped but still regal presence of most tall men, looked at the score in front of him, he didn't need it. He kept it there as a prop, but he could do this with his eyes closed.

Since last fall, Sampson had been preparing for this. Ah, he'd been preparing his entire 53 years, but a few things got in the way.

Sampson acknowledged the pianist and saw that he had a copy of Willard's marked score. But, everyone was relaxed because Willard himself wasn't there.

There was a moment of silence in the room. And then, in a low sweet voice, Sampson simply said, "Let us begin."

No one was surprised by the gentle approach. Sampson was loved by the local *and* professional singers. They stepped into their roles.

And on the "stage," our story continues: the fake Albanian Cowboys have taken fake poison because the two sisters don't love them! The fake "doctor" arrives, that traitor, Despina in disguise, played by the lovely Bette Belle. All is crazy in this opera scene, but the participants worked together perfectly, happy to be under the guiding hand of Sampson Powers and without Willard Franklin, secretly known in their circle of operatic soloists and members of the orchestra as the Drama King. No one even thought to go looking for him.

But, alas. Diesel was the first to see him. Diesel felt a shadow move across his left side and looked up from his reverie to see Willard hanging onto the door frame. *Oh, botheration*, Diesel thought. *Now this.*

Willard is more than drunk. He is wild with anger and burdened by fear and hate and retribution. He is afraid of what comes next. He is confused. He doesn't know he is late and doesn't care or even get what it means. His chemistry is now completely out of whack. Later, Marcus thought it surprising that the man even made it to the door.

When Willard arrived at his conductor's room, *his* room (at least for the next few weeks), and saw that white-haired old hippie failure in front of his, Willard's music stand, well, if you couldn't see the steam coming out of his ears, you weren't looking in the right direction.

He yelled, "Noooooooooo!" and lurched into the room, stumbling across the floor toward the piano and the music stand, where Sampson stood, his back to Willard. Sampson noticed his singers had stopped singing. Their eyes were opened wide and their faces turned various shades of pink in shock.

Willard stomped into the room and practically shoved Sampson out of the way, as if to say, "My world. Get out." Sampson, not drunk, disorderly and maniacal, like Willard Franklin, calmly stepped aside, but did not go away.

Willard whipped out his conductor's baton from its little sleeve on the stand. He had no idea where anyone was in the music. He didn't care. He really didn't know what *he* was doing, because he was not currently in his body. Willard's body was controlled by a cocktail of madness and fury. He'd clean forgotten that alcohol was as toxic to him as the venom of an Australian Box Jellyfish.

The harmony of their rehearsal evaporated. As a group, the soloists stepped away. Stunned into silence, the six singers wondered if it was time to bolt. Willard yelled at them, "Pay attention to me! ME!" He looked at the music and told the pianist to play. Bette Belle, in particular, moved as far back as possible. Her crush on Willard Franklin blew away with the wind. Melissa Partridge, page turner of the moment, looked first at Willard, then Marcus, then Sampson, then Diesel, like, "Christ Almighty, do something!" If she hadn't been on the far side of the piano bench, she would have gotten up herself and smacked Willard's crazed face.

Diesel sighed and got up from the sofa. He approached Willard from the left. Sampson was on the right. Diesel took Willard's arm, with no small strength, and said, "No, Willard, you are unprepared for this rehearsal. It is time to step aside."

Willard didn't even see that it was Diesel Edwards. His eyes saw nothing but his demons, and they were large, and they loomed over the scene, and they controlled his moves and made him do things he didn't even remember, much less feel sorry for. A jumble of mixed memories crowded Willard's mind and he could not sort it out. He thought of all the times he wanted to kill Falcon Jennings and now the man was dead and Willard was nothing but glad for that and sad for everything else and sorry for nothing.

Sampson and Diesel tried reason but Willard was in the midst of a fit of pique so big, why, it was bigger than Godzilla. Willard fought Diesel and Sampson as if they were about to throw him off a roof, when they were really just trying to say NO to this disruption and show him the door. Bill Palmer stepped in to add his substantial size and weight to the situation, but Willard had picked up a lucite bookend with which to hit his current demon, Diesel, and missed. Instead, he knocked Bill Palmer to the floor.

Willard stopped in his tracks. In a snap moment of clarity, he stepped back in horror. He shook his head. He locked eyes with Bette Belle. She turned away. They have all turned away.

Diesel, panting, looked at Marcus Brown, who said to Willard, "You're fired."

Pete Daltry escorted Willard back to the conductor's dorm apartment, only because Marcus promised the sheriffs he'd keep him on-site. Otherwise, he'd say, "Pack your bags and leave Villa Zanetta now."

"Should we call the police?" Odella Palmer asked.

Marcus tried not to laugh. "No problem, Mrs. Palmer. They are already here."

Sampson Takes the Baton, Again

The soloists were prepared to flee, but they, too, saw the energy settle right down after the Drama King let himself be led from the room. After checking that Bill Palmer was fine and things were under control, Diesel gave Sampson the signal.

Sampson Powers literally didn't skip a beat. He turned to the music stand, gave a nod to the pianist, looked at the soloists and said, "Let's pick up where we left off. Despina, put on your doctor's mustache and wig and enter the scene."

And so they began again.

"What a hero," Melissa whispered to the accompanist as his fingers touched the keys.

Sampson was coming to the place in the music he loved best; a little ironic for Sam, remembering this part of a recording played over and over again for his lover.

You see, it was his lover or, more to the point, their love affair, that got the man in hot water, so a bit of baggage comes along with the memory. And the consequences of that affair (with a very young student where Sampson had been employed as a professor) got him fired and basically blackballed from any quality gigs. The story followed the man around like a Jack Russell Terrier, nipping at his heals. It's hard to get respect when a Jack Russell has attached his teeth to your pant leg.

Here, in the conductor's room at The Well Lit Theater, Sampson proved himself with ease; he conducted his favorite piece of music, with his bittersweet memories, and a baton right on the mark. The soloists picked up his calm, professional and inclusive vibration and decided to stay. After all, it was about the art.

Diesel, back in his chair and just a little bit ruffled, remarked to Hayne that at least something seemed to be going right. Sampson was downright marvelous.

SATURDAY EVENING

Smooch McGuinn arrived at 5pm, just in time to accompany Marcus and the All-Nighters (they were beginning to sound like a 50s rock band) to the Palmers' Sonoma home for cocktails and a discussion of the previous day's events. Smooch was invited as the newest member of the Artistic Team as well as her position as Willard's ex-wife. Marcus hoped she could cast some light on her ex-husband.

Smooch McGuinn carried herself like a star, although she dressed like a classic bohemian. Grady Mulligan would surely have an opinion about Smooch's clothing. Like most mavens of the wardrobe, Smooch possessed a closet-full of eclectic cast-offs, costume parts, headdresses, wigs, scarves and enough costume jewelry to open a booth at the Alameda Point Antiques Faire.

Going on 50, looking 35, Smooch had the shoulders of a mannequin, the stature of a true model and two college degrees, in art and theater design. The blonde wave for which she was well-known was pulled back in a loose pony and tied at the nape of her long and lovely neck. Her ears, pierced in several creative places, sparkled with CZs in studs. Her tie-dyed shirt (from a production of HAIR) and the mini skirt (from THE BOYFRIEND) showed her trim legs, encased in black tights. And, oh, those little booties. Smooch left Marcus a little breathless. He couldn't help but see that she was the antithesis of Martha, all cutesie compared to this goddess. To think Willard played around the entire ten years of their marriage.

Marcus hadn't understood the severity of Willard's affliction until he saw the wild man unleashed in the conductor's room. After the rehearsal and before leaving for the Palmers' home, Marcus visited Willard's apartment in the dorm to try for a civil conversation, unless Willard was passed out on the bed.

But, Willard had left the building. His clothes were gone, several unmatched socks lay on the unmade bed. The proof and detritus of Willard's bender/breakdown spread out on the floor like a Jack Kerouac poem. When Marcus checked the parking lot, Willard's car was there, but Willard and his stuff were gone.

MARCUS

Marcus dragged himself to his room in the dorm and, finally, got into the bed, although there was not much sleep in store for Marcus Brown.

The word "commitment" commanded his attention this night. Ten years ago (ten years!) he promised Hayne and Diesel he'd be here for them after their retirement. He and they agreed that things were always subject to change, but Hayne and Diesel had taught Marcus everything they knew about running an operation of this size, and expected that he would continue for some time. It wasn't his fault that they took ten years to do it.

When "the old duffers" retired last year after *The Marriage of Figaro*, they knighted Marcus with the title of Executive Director and hoped they could leave the Villa in his capable hands.

Sure, there were other worthy leaders out there, but Hayne and Diesel felt Marcus had what it took to survive the long haul. They observed other theater companies and music festivals go through new directors every three or four years, and the productions and overall health and well-being of the company suffered from that occurrence. One of the reasons for the success of The Theaters at Villa Zanetta was the continuity of leadership. And they should know—they had held the reigns for fifty years!

Not that they expected fifty years from Marcus. But, knowing that someone cared about their vision gave them the grace and peace to retire. Marcus knew how to work with the Board of Directors, understood the world of running a non-profit, had a good head for business, got along with most people and loved show business.

And now, thought Marcus, *here I am, in the midst of a crisis of great proportion, wanting to walk away. What do I say to them? What are my reasons?*

Before the chandelier incident, and Falcon's death, he wanted to leave because he was lonely. That alone mystified him. How could he be lonely in the midst of all these people, many of whom were his friends? Wouldn't he be even lonelier in Point Reyes in the cabin, even with a dog?

And now, post-chandelier incident, he wanted to leave because the job had suddenly become dangerous. He felt alone in the world, and afraid of the dark, afraid of surprises, and certainly had a new and healthy fear of chandeliers.

And, I'm tired. Not physically tired. Just tired of propping it all up.

There was suddenly no joy in it, no fervor. He felt depleted and bereft and, overall, kind of sad.

HAYNE AND DIESEL CHAT

Hayne and Diesel came home to a warm fire on a chilly night. Reyna Rosario, daughter of that faithful retainer, Rosalie, had not only built them a fire but made soup and bread while helping Hector with his miniature fort for his garden faerie community.

Hayne and Diesel settled by the fire, each with a cup of herbal tea. They watched Reyna and Hector at the table for a while, enjoying the calm and peaceful atmosphere after a very strange day. Hector had tweezers in his hand, carefully placing a tiny pitchfork into a tiny wagon which he would nest somewhere in his garden tomorrow.

The fire crackled. The lights were low except for the dining table, where Hector worked his mini magic most evenings.

"D?" Hayne said.

"Hm?"

"What do you make of all this? Doesn't Willard's disappearance make him look guilty? Why would he do that?"

"Why isn't relevant, hon. He's off his rocker, he's stepped into a zone we can't enter. No one can. If he doesn't end up in jail, he'll find himself in the psyche ward."

"That paints a pretty picture. But, Robert, really, I'm sorry I pushed for Willard this season. I take some responsibility for all this. I should have read the signs better. I believed hearsay. You have every right to say, 'I told you so.'"

Diesel took in the *this is serious* clue (Hayne had called him Robert) and said, "I do, but I won't. All I can say is, Willard's made me nervous since 1998. Of all the conductors we have shepherded through this place, maybe all the participants as far back as the very beginning, right to that first performance of the Old Play, I can't remember anyone so coarse who could create such beauty. No one has rubbed me so severely wrong as Willard Franklin. The man doesn't belong in polite society, much less in a world of respected music makers and artists. Plus, I am too old to be involved in a fist fight."

"Next time, just make me listen," said Hayne.

Diesel said, "Ha! Don't make me splutter my tea!"

Chapter Four
1956

Queen Elizabeth

Hayne squirmed in the big canopy bed on the third floor of the Edwards mansion in Winnetka, Illinois. He ran his hands over the off-white silken sheets, got up and poured a glass of water out of an antique porcelain pitcher, slipped into the scuff slippers left at the foot of his bed by the amazingly attentive maid, and went into the bathroom. He brushed his teeth with the fresh toothbrush placed for him on the counter and splashed his face with cool water from the brass tap. He looked at the white terrycloth bathrobe, hanging on the back of the door. "For me, too, I suppose," he marveled out loud, and put it on.

Hayne missed his boon companion. He didn't dare try to find Diesel's bedroom in the dark. Lonely tears ran down his face all night. *This wedding of, who is it? Diesel's third cousin once removed? I shouldn't have come*, he thought. *I still don't know which of the four forks to use at these elaborate formal occasions, and Queen Elizabeth Edwards gives me the heebies. She keeps looking at me. I bet she thinks I'm after D's money. Well, dear Queen, you are very wrong about that. Sometimes I wish the man was as poor as a church mouse.*

Hayne wondered what Diesel, well-bred, elegant and beautiful to boot, saw in the little beach rat who still troubled over keeping words like "ain't" out of his vocabulary.

Whenever Hayne threw his worry-wart questions about their relationship into the conversation, Diesel said things like, "Haynie, you just don't get that I love you, do you? I imagine I'll spend my lifetime trying to make you see how wonderful you are."

Tomorrow, Diesel will dance with all the well-dressed, haughty women and I…I will get quietly schnockered at the bar. I wish he hadn't taught me how to fox trot and waltz. If I didn't know, it might not bother me so much that we can't just dance our way through these affairs, together. It's a danged shame.

And, Get this! he said to the moon. *Both of our mothers are queens, in their own way. Good Lord. Bad enough to think about taking Diesel home to Fatty Wills.* He tried to imagine Queen Elizabeth Edwards ordering a chocolate shake from Fatty at the Ice Queen.

"Hey, Lady," Fatty would say at the order window. "What can I git for ya?"

And the queenly Elizabeth would squint and purse her lips in that "I'm so much better than you are" kind of way and put two clean, polished quarters down on the counter, so she wouldn't have to touch Fatty's fat hand. "A chocolate milkshake, please," she would drawl. "James, our driver, will bring it to the Cadillac." And she'd put her gloves back on, as if to protect her polished nails from this slovenly rabble, and tiptoe back to the car, as if touching the sandy ground might permanently stain her pretty high-heeled black patent leather shoes. James would open the back door for her, and she would slide into to the turquoise and chrome car and powder her nose. When the milkshake arrived, Queen Elizabeth would set it in the Cadillac's cup holder and throw it in a trashcan at the first opportunity.

"Dear Lord," said Hayne to his imagination, "just get me through this wedding and back home and I promise I won't whine for a week."

The wedding turned out to be the least of Hayne's surprises. On the dark side, he felt so completely out of place, he wanted to hide behind the palms (he was good at that). All these rich, full-of-themselves people, their shiny wardrobes, their bouffant hair and polished shoes, they made him as nervous as a whore in church, as Jerry the Juggler might say. He kept looking down at his new tux and felt like a fraud. He knew nothing about dressing up like this, whereas Diesel took to it like a swan to a lake.

The biggest surprise at the wedding turned out to be Queen Elizabeth herself. She and Aunt Hazel sat a table for four with a bottle of champagne and four glasses. They each held a glass of bubbly. The Queen gestured to Hayne, who was sitting alone by the palm he wished to hide behind. She raised a third glass of champagne in his direction and waved as if to say, "Join us," and so, of course, he did. What else could he do? Avoid the den of the dragon forever?

She sat him down between the two of them, which felt to Hayne as if he were about to be eaten alive, or at least eviscerated by their combined sets of long red pointy nails. *Jungle Red. They must have seen The Women lately. Rosalind Russell has nothing on these two.*

They made small talk for a few minutes, but Hayne knew something was coming. He could see it in the queen's eyes. She wanted to talk to him. A predatory glitter beamed ferociously his way. She was about to tell him to stay away from her precious son, that he was ruining her careful rearing of this most special person in their illustrious, well-known family. She would say, "Take your hands off my boy."

What she said blew Hayne out of the water. "Don't you wish you could be dancing with Diesel?"

Hayne blinked. "I beg your pardon?" he said, blushing down to his toes. *Oh my God,* he thought. *Where is she going with this? Does she have to get mean about it?*

"I'm serious Hayne. I know the truth," said Elizabeth.

Hayne groaned inside.

"It's OK, dear," said Hazel. "We're on your side."

Hayne blinked again. "Uhm," was all he could muster.

Hazel, who had brought her knitting, of course, put it down. She laughed and wagged her head.

"You don't have to be afraid of us, Hayne. We're members of your tribe. We're friends of Dorothy."

For a moment, Hayne was mystified. Asking "Dorothy who?" was out of the question. He knew what Hazel meant. He just…didn't know how to apply it to the situation.

"I…oh. Honestly, Mrs. Edwards. Aunt Hazel. I don't understand. I mean, yes, OK, Dorothy. But…how?"

"First," said Queen Elizabeth, "you'd better call me Elizabeth. I might grant you the privilege of calling me Queenie one day, but for now, Elizabeth will do."

"Ooooo…kay…" said the intrepid Hayne Williams. His mind was going in circles now. *What on earth is she telling me?*

The women, one on his right, one on his left, turned their heads toward him in one motion, as if they had choreographed this moment, timed it down to the sigh and the smile and the way, without taking their eyes off him, they reached across the table and, just for a moment, touched index fingers, the tips of their red nails meeting at the point.

"Oh. My. Word. Oh. I…" and then Hayne laughed out loud. He laughed so hard, Elizabeth thought she might have to look for a glass of water or smelling salts. Hayne put up his hand and said, "I'm OK. Just give me a minute."

Hayne smiled and closed his eyes. He inhaled deeply and took a short but meaningful journey into his consciousness to completely absorb this new information. *Mrs. Edwards…Elizabeth and Aunt Hazel are… they…oh, my.*

Hayne opened his eyes, smiled, picked up his glass and raised it to them. Elizabeth and Hazel lifted their glasses in response. And they all had tears in their eyes.

Diesel danced by with a dark haired girl in a long slithery red gown. Diesel caught Hayne's eye, and Hayne patted his heart.

"Does he know?" Hayne asked, adding, "Elizabeth? I can't imagine he does, or he would have told me by now."

"No. Not yet." She smiled. "Hazel is my sister-in-law and best friend who has come to live with me. We'd like to be friends, Hayne. We want to know you."

The threesome was quiet all around, until Hayne said, "Elizabeth, may I ask you a serious question?"

"Of course, Hayne. Anything."

Hayne looked at his place setting, picked up a utensil and polished it with his napkin.

"Is this a fish fork?"

HAYNE AND DIESEL CHAT

Later that night, Hayne and Diesel sat in two chairs next to a tiny table on the third-floor landing of the Edwards's mansion. The attentive maid remembered Hayne liked sherry and had left them a carafe with two little crystal glasses. Hayne poured them each a thimble-sized shot.

As he handed one to Diesel, he said, "D, I need to talk to you about your mother."

Diesel looked pained and almost hurt. He said, "Oh, Haynie, I'm so sorry she's such a formal old gal. It's only for a few more days."

"Oh, it's not that," said his pal. "I'm over that. I know she has a reputation to uphold, and it just doesn't look right, us holed up in your old room. This is fine."

Diesel stared at Hayne like he'd just gone over the edge. "You mean that? You don't mind?"

Hayne smiled. "No, I don't mind," he said.

"I thought you were lonely and uncomfortable up here in your loft."

"Well, I am lonely when I close the door and you go down the stairs and climb into your old bed with the satin sheets and the red velvet drape. I'm glad she's kept the red drape, by the way. Makes me feel even better about her."

"Goodness, Haynie, what changed your mind? Yesterday she was a dragon ready to rip out your heart."

"Well, that's what I wanted to talk to you about. We had a little chat."

"Uh oh," said Diesel.

Hayne said, "D, have you ever thought about your mother's friendship with Aunt Hazel?"

"What about it? They've been best friends since high school. Hazel introduced my parents at a football game. Hazel and Queenie were both cheerleaders. They go back a long way. Why?"

"I repeat," said Hayne, "have you ever thought about how close they are?"

"Hm. No. Aunt Hazel has always just…been there."

Hayne was quiet for a moment. "Well, I know something you don't know, then. Or at least, I don't think you know it. You should have figured this out by now."

"Lordy, hon. What do you mean?"

Hayne turned his lips into a very knowing smile. "Well, I have permission to tell you…no, actually, your mother *requested* I tell you that… uhm."

Here, he took a deep breath, "Hon, your mother and Aunt Hazel are…" he put the first and second fingers of his left hand together and wrapped one round the other. He just looked at Diesel.

Diesel blinked. His mind flew over the years. He saw vignettes and scenes with his mother and Hazel, curled up on a couch, or reading to each other, or sharing a bottle of wine, laughing. He took their friendship for granted, but he never thought about it as anything more than buddies, sisters-in-law.

But it all suddenly made sense. Queen Elizabeth and Hazel. All along. It was always the Queen and Hazel, holding it all together. Monty Edwards was hardly ever there, working long hours with lots of travel expounding and poeticizing the virtues of the diesel engine. Whenever he traveled, Hazel was there, at the dinner table, or playing cards, or watching a movie. Hazel. It was always Hazel.

Diesel was speechless. Then he said, "But, they have their own rooms."

"Well, said Hayne, "technically, so do we. We must. So must they. And, you know, your mother is a respectable widow who runs a giant company." And then Hayne told him about their elegant revelations at the reception, after which, Diesel asked, "Should I say anything?"

Hayne said, "No. I think just knowing is enough."

And so, they said good night. Each of the four persons in that house, lying in their own beds, sleeping alone, were thinking about each other and, each in their own bed thought, *And this is love.*

THE BRISK MANSION

One day, Diesel said, "Haynie, it's time for us to do something with our lives. You're out of school looking for jobs and I...I have floated long enough."

Floating to Diesel meant going to stage performances in every theater in San Francisco, being a supernumerary (an extra at the San Francisco Opera—"one of the most fun volunteer jobs ever," Diesel once said) and taking acting classes. Hayne's idea of floating had something to do with the indoor swimming pool at the YMCA in Culver City. He still wasn't used to being the companion of a rich kid from Winnetka, the most expensive town in America.

"What do you suggest?" he said to Diesel. "I have a degree and 25 cents in my pocket. And, you're doing all these theater things. How is that connected to floating?"

Diesel looked at him like, *Quit being such a wet rag! I'm talking about more than a job.* But he said, "What kind of job?" They processed

100 occupations from design firms to stage hands and everything in between with the slightest connection to art and theater. Nothing was decided that day.

One afternoon, after a few more months of romance, inseparable behavior, and more conversations like this, Diesel arrived at their walkup in the Marina with news. He'd found an apartment in the Brisk Mansion and he hoped Hayne would move there with him. Diesel said, "I think the place has creative possibilities."

Hayne wasn't sure, at first, but who was he to argue with D's enthusiasm? And after that amazing turn of events in Winnetka at the wedding of Diesel's third cousin once removed, Hayne had settled in, and even felt like part of the family. Elizabeth practically adopted him. He and Hazel were already exchanging knitting patterns.

He shook his head at the prospect of "creative possibilities" at the Brisk Mansion, smiled and said, "Let's go see."

The front double doors opened wide into a foyer flocked in red velvet. Of course, it was red velvet. The winding staircase, carpeted in marbled maroon, followed a highly polished walnut banister up to the top floor, where two doors fit their keys; one, into their "ballroom," for that is what the room was in the Brisk's heyday in the 20s. This day in 1956, it had been turned into a big, open, empty, high-ceilinged apartment, with vistas of the San Francisco Bay. Up a tiny flight of stairs, they came upon two bedrooms joined by a bathroom and down the hall, a small but perfect kitchen and a little room and bath for the "help." This beat any apartment Hayne had ever seen or even heard about.

Diesel took Hayne back out to the hall. With the key to the other door, Diesel led Hayne outdoors to a flat-roofed patio, where he presented him with the *crème de la crème*—Hayne's own conservatory studio, a little glass room on top of the world surrounded by plants.

"Just think," Diesel said, "think of the things we could do here."

THE LITTLE GEM

The duo moved into the Brisk Mansion Ballroom and soon found themselves in the middle of a team of actors and musicians, whom Diesel seemed to attract like bees to a pollinator garden. This afforded Hayne his first opportunity since leaving Pasadena to get the Bleeps into action. He opened his trunk, examined and made alterations to the Bleeps, dusted off the best of his puppet theaters, and dashed some gold paint on the proscenium columns. He even wrote a new play for the Bleep family, called *Flight to Italy*, wherein the Bleep family takes their friend Janet (remember Janet? She's the one with her own planet) on vacation to Italy. Janet falls down and breaks her leg, but when they take her to the Italian hospital, she falls in love with the Italian doctor and everything turns out well in the end and they, of course, live happily ever after.

In honor of the new play, Diesel and Hayne created a private, Italianate dinner party for eighteen. Three tables for six, covered in red checked tablecloths, filled one end of the Ballroom. On each table, a drippy candle flickered in its green chianti bottle, with cleverly folded fluffy white napkins beside each plate. Baskets of fresh breads and bread sticks and platters of antipasti, too.

A strolling tenor and his accompanying violinist serenaded the dinner guests with Italian love songs while the guests sipped their soup and tasted the flavors of the seven course Italian feast prepared by their associate and friend, Chef Todd. And so, the Bleeps debuted the *Flight to Italy* in San Francisco and received rave reviews.

After the show, Diesel said, "We have a little gem here, Haynie." And his companion had to agree. "Let's call it that," he said. "The Little Gem."

Hayne and Diesel soon became known among the bohemian set in the City as avant garde theatrical presenters, from puppets to one act play, musicals to poetry readings. Put your donation in the basket, set yourself down in a Queen Anne chair by the fire, sip sherry from a crystal glass, and enjoy a performance. The Little Gem was a hit.

On his own, Hayne would have been happy to have small, poorly budgeted gatherings of like-minded people forever. But, he had fallen in with a man with some entrepreneurial spirit, that is a fact, and Hayne decided to get into the spirit with him. He didn't have the visions, that was Diesel's bailiwick, but he discovered he loved implementing Diesel's big ideas. He found antique chairs and tables and lamps and filled the Ballroom with little vignettes and built a small stage at one end. The little alcove seated four, with a love seat and two needlepointed Queen Annes with padded, needlepointed arms.

The San Francisco Bay was the special guest at every event; people came for the music and the poetry and the puppets and were mesmerized by the ocean, the majestic view, the rarefied air.

HAYNE AND DIESEL DISCOVER SONOMA

On a rare quiet weekend, Hayne and Diesel drove to St Helena to visits Diesel's friends. The Silverado Trail twinkled in its springtime glory, when the leaves on the vines were young and green, the mustard deepened its yellow flowers and the trees dressed up in bud and leaf. The grasses and wildflowers waved from the side of the road.

Marion and Frank met them with open arms and wove Hayne into their lives as easily as they had Diesel years ago. Over cocktails, they got to know each other. During dinner, they discussed the Napa and Sonoma valleys and what drew Frank and Marion to St. Helena to grow grapes and make wine.

Hayne rarely told much about himself earlier than 14 years old, but, while they slurped the custard for dessert, he mentioned his summer at a CYO Camp in Sonoma.

Frank said, "It's for sale."

"What's for sale?" asked Diesel.

"The old CYO Camp; they call it Sulfur Steam, for some ridiculous reason. It's been on the market for a few years. No one knows what to do with it."

HAYNE AND DIESEL GO TO "SULFUR STEAM"

Hayne was nervous. This visit to St. Helena, meeting more new people and now that CYO Camp in Sonoma, made him jumpy. Too many memories were up close to the surface, like the boys who made fun of him on the bus ride to the camp, calling him the "cheeseburger puppet boy" and other, more unpleasant epithets. He hated the strict rules, when he had grown up with none; and he resented the corporal punishment, inflicted by the counselors themselves. He still felt the sting of the horse whip on his precious hands. The semi-adult counselors never knew what the boys were up to, and the boys were usually up to no good.

No, Hayne's memories of the CYO Camp were not his favorites. But, Diesel had other ideas. There was something up Diesel's sleeve. As the companion to this far-thinking, rich, gregarious Robert DeWayne Edwards, Hayne would just have to be patient and see what happened. There was a surprise every day in Hayne's new world. He thought he had come to San Francisco to finish up a theater arts degree, but he found something quite different.

Up to this point, Hayne's life had been a scramble for everything from how to get food (besides burgers) to digging through the resale shops for a decent pair of pants. His socks had holes in them. Heck, his two pairs of shoes had holes in them. His mother, Fatty, provided all the milkshakes and popcorn he could want. She didn't understand when he turned it down. "It's free food," she'd say. Hayne would roll his eyes and look away. *It's not food*, he'd whisper to himself.

Hayne put one foot in front of the other, with great and deliberate care. His mind focused on minute details: how much everything cost, how slim his chances, how big the box. Diesel was used to big plans and lots of money. He could see great vistas of opportunity before them.

Until Gilmor Brown came along and pulled him off the sand and into an education, Hayne's world was the trailer, the Ice Queen, the vast Santa Monica beach and all it held to entertain him; the Hippodrome was a shadow of its former self, but it still had activities and the carousel, and there was the Ferris wheel, and the concessions stands. His young life consisted of puppets made of used white socks, two size six knitting needles and loose leftover yarn from Glenda. It included collecting tips and sliding the pennies, nickels, dimes and quarters into little paper sleeves to take to the bank. When he left the beach with Gilmor, Hayne's bank account held $400, pretty good for a teenaged puppeteer stuck in a hut full of hot dogs and burgers.

In Sonoma, as they approached the driveway of the CYO Camp/Sulfur Steam Conference Center in Diesel's 1955 Baby Blue Chevrolet Bel Air, Hayne thought, *Here comes the next idea...hope I can deal with it.*

Diesel drove one mile an hour up the paved driveway circling through some stately madrones. As they approached the main area, they first set eyes on a small, octagonal chapel on the right. "The cross is gone," observed Hayne.

"Stop the car right here," he said. "Let's begin at the beginning."

Diesel pulled over, happy to see Hayne opening to this visit. Diesel's mind had room for many possibilities.

They got out of the car and wended their way up the little path to the chapel. "Let's call it a temple, right off the bat," said Hayne. "The word 'chapel' gives me the willies. At camp, the bigger boys tied up us smaller kids and lashed us to the pews with rope. They poured stolen wine down our throats and stuffed our mouths with loaves of dry Wonder Bread, telling us we were sinners and had to eat Jesus in order to be redeemed."

But the interior was not like Hayne remembered. The pews were gone. The dusty floor was a mosaic pattern of a giant blue star. The twelve tall stained glass windows depicting the twelve stations of the cross were replaced with glass art deco designs of pale colors like beige and pearlescent white. Lots of sun shone through and left patterns all over the star on the floor.

The hush in the big open room was other-worldly, bringing into it a God-like presence without even trying. Hayne's heart immediately stilled. Diesel said, "I think they're gone." "Who?" asked Hayne. "Those boys," said his pal.

They could hardly bring themselves to leave, but, excitement drew them out the door. They left the car where it was and wandered through the madrones toward the main area.

The old Tudor mansion nested in a grove of very tall pines and cedar and bougainvillea. The additions on each side and the brick patio gave an oddly modern look, but the Tudor facade made one think of King Henry VIII himself. It was a confusing but enticing mix.

"8,000 square feet? Who lives in 8,000 square feet?" Hayne asked.

Diesel said, "Frank told me a wonderful old story about a madam and her band of merry maids, that's who. It was called Villa Zanetta, after the madam. I don't know why the last owners changed the name to Sulfur Steam Conference Center. No wonder it failed. Let's go see it."

They walked up the brick steps to the patio. This welcoming grandmother of a mansion invited them to explore her. Not that either of them had even known or had a grandmother. But the villa hugged the patio with its extended wings, and, in the process, hugged Diesel and Hayne. The atrium just further enticed them in.

"Why do you suppose it's been on the market for years? It has such potential!" Diesel said. "Can we get in?"

They peered in the atrium windows and saw that the last owners had gutted the first floor to create a cavernous open space. Hayne imagined the atrium filled with palm trees and ferns, and an entry path made of colored rocks, weaving in patterns toward the Lobby.

"Let's walk around to the back," said Hayne. "I remember a back door."

Their path took them through some uncut grasses and broken cement walkways to a side patio and a door into a kitchen. Through a window they saw a high-ceilinged ballroom or dining room, with a stage. "Yes, that's about the same," said Hayne. "The Great Hall, I think they called it. Look, the walls are all polished or varnished maple! That's been updated."

They walked further around the building to a low back door at the bottom of four steps overgrown with Kenilworth Ivy. The door opened into a dark basement or store room or maybe a hallway. Diesel stepped down and jiggled the loose knob. He said, "With one effort, I could get this door open."

ENTERING

Hayne looked at Diesel aghast. "That's breaking and entering! Or at least entering. What if we get caught?"

"What if?" said Diesel, with a bit of a laugh. "We can say we are prospective buyers."

"Are we?" asked Hayne.

"Well, if anyone asks us, we are. Let's just go look."

With no trouble at all, Diesel put his weight against the old door and it opened to him like the arms of a lover. Zanetta practically cooed to Diesel Edwards, who followed, like the enchanted princeling in a storybook.

It's hard not to compare this to falling in love, because it's the same dynamic. All the juices get flowing and the butterflies flutter around, which cranks up the adrenaline and allows a feeling of excitement and creative joy. At least this is what Hayne observed in his companion.

He remembered that look on Diesel's face the day they met. When they stood by the fountain in the lobby of the Art Institute and Diesel had looked at Hayne like, "You. Me. It. Now." He was looking at Villa Zanetta in the same way.

Diesel smiled, stepped into the hallway and headed in, like he was coming home. Hayne followed. What else could he do? Something glittered in the air. Something mysterious and large and bigger than anything he ever knew was showing up before his eyes.

The dark little hallway led to a storage room and a few steps up into the kitchen. They explored its cupboards, the counters, the unplugged refrigerators. A walk-in! It was more like a canteen or a club than a mere kitchen. A big pass through window to the Hall, stations for beverages, for chopping, and cleaning up. Four sinks! Gas stove with eight burners and two ovens.

They passed through the green baize doors into the Great Hall. At one end, a raised stage waited for a troupe of performers to get some ideas flowing and get on with it. The room overflowed with tables and chairs. Diesel could hardly keep his feet on the ground. Hayne could barely keep his lunch in his stomach. Diesel walked into the Hall and, true to his roots, sang the first lines of *Some Enchanted Evening*. Hayne was on the other side of the Hall. They turned and looked at each other. "… and somehow you'll know… you'll know even then…" He couldn't tell if he was excited or scared right out of his undies. Both, he decided. "Who can explain it, who can tell you why? Fools give you reasons, wise men never try."

The walls were smooth and shiny, showing off the highly polished wood grain. Glass sconces were placed every four feet (they imagined moody, flickering lighting) with no overhead lights.

They moved into the big open space that would ultimately become the Lobby of The Well Lit Theater at Villa Zanetta, but that was a few years away. Now, it was a large hall with a circular stairway to a mezzanine. A vintage chandelier, one of the first of its kind, floated over the big room. They climbed the stairs and checked out the offices, at the back of which was a full apartment with its own Great Room and a big kitchen, two bedrooms and two baths. They inspected the winch and the chandelier in the cupola. They walked to the dorm and counted 60 windows for 60 rooms! The unlocked barn had been badly remodeled into little conference rooms.

Hayne and Diesel walked up a path and discovered the murky lily pond and dubbed it Lake Zanetta. They laughed when they thought this was where they might find the sulfur steam, but nary a mist or bubble appeared. A light breeze waved through the grasses. Thousands of birds chirped; the welcome committee. Hayne expected a chorus to serenade them, a rainbow to bloom or a meteor to slash across the sky.

He heard an audience standing up in ovation, clapping and clapping and clapping again. It wasn't just Diesel's homecoming. Hayne knew it. He, too, felt the magic and wanted more.

Diesel looked at Hayne and said, "I think we *are* interested buyers, don't you?"

AN IDEA FORMS

Hayne and Diesel took their thermos of coffee to the patio. They sat on the little brick wall and poured one cup to share.

"You know, Haynie, if the world were a better world, I would ask you to marry me and come away with me to this new palace. As it stands, Just come…come with me and make a life with me, right here. We can do what we're doing in the Ballroom, but bigger, better."

"And move up here? Leave one palace for another?" Hayne wondered.

"Well, we could keep the Little Gem going for a while. We could do both."

"I love my rooftop studio."

"Of course you do! But, we have to remember it's a rental, and we should have a home."

"Where would we live? This place is a conference center, not a home."

"I know. My mind is spinning. I see it in my head like a movie. We keep the Ballroom in the City for a little while and move some stuff into the upstairs apartment here in the Villa. We can build this place into a theater company. There are rooms to stay in. We have several venues. We're in the country but close to the City so people will come. There are 60 acres. We could lease some of the lower flat area out to a vineyard. Maybe we could build a house here sometime."

"You've already moved here in your mind."

"I have, Haynie. I see it."

"This is one crazy marriage proposal," said Hayne.

Hayne wanted another look at the barn. He handed the thermos cup to Diesel and said, "Stay here, OK? I'll be back in a few minutes."

Diesel nodded.

Hayne walked back down the path. He stood outside the front sliding door of the barn. He looked at the lines of the building and how it faced east to the rising sun. He slid open the big wooden door and entered the cool building.

The three horse stalls on each side had been turned into little rooms with wooden floors. He went from room to room, six little spaces. He sat on a chair in the last room and closed his eyes. He wanted to just sit there, alone, and feel the room. The space.

Hayne thought about his Dutch door puppet theater at the Ice Queen facing the Pier, and the little area in Pasadena where the people sat outside on the patio to enjoy his puppet performances, and the three foot wide portable mini-stage he made in scenery class that had served him for six years now as his take-along puppet stage.

Could he do it? Could he design a Tiny Little Puppet Theater in this building? A real theater? Would he, Hayne Williams, be able to create something beautiful? Extraordinary? Worthy?

He didn't know. He smelled horse.

Big deal, Hayne, he thought. He'd just gotten used to the Brisk Mansion Ballroom. *Even bigger deal, boy.* He loved his little glass studio on top of the world. *Fine. Good. That's nice.*

He had organized and performed 20 puppet shows in the last 18 months for The Little Gem, wasn't that enough? *Nope.* And all those other things: readings and one act plays and managing all those people? *Oh dear.*

But, look how happy it makes D. He's in his element. He's twinkling over there right now, thinking about all the pieces it will take to put this puzzle together; designers and builders and architects and people! Lots of people! Just his cup of tea.

But this, we agreed, would be mine. This will be The Tiny Little Theater in the Barn, Puppets only. Yes, of course I can do this. Isn't this why Gilmor Brown lifted me off the beach?

Frank and a local realtor contacted the bank that sat on this albatross known as Villa Zanetta and then the CYO Camp and then Sulfur Steam. Per Diesel's instructions, the realtor did not disclose Diesel's financial condition and, further instructed, made an offer in a very casual way. Diesel was in no hurry, and he knew the bank wanted to offload the place lickety-split.

Diesel and Hayne were back in the City, sitting in their chairs in their ballroom apartment, gazing out the picture window at the vista of blue ocean, when they received a call from the realtor. Diesel picked up the phone. The realtor was so loud (forgive him, his wife was 90% deaf) that Hayne could hear the man say, "Well, you won't believe this, but they accepted. I think the cash offer helped. They do want out."

And so the new Villa Zanetta began.

SURPRISE!

Several months later, Hayne and Diesel settled into the Villa apartment, prepared to break ground for their adventure called The Theaters at Villa Zanetta. The apartment received a thorough cleaning and the happy duo brought in a few pieces of furniture and some beds and cooking utensils until they had a chance to decide about the San Francisco Ballroom.

Delivered this morning, the puppets awaited Hayne in the Barn, ready to be unpacked and settled, too, in their new home. Hayne was anxious to free them from the confines of their trunks.

They walked down to the Barn. Once there, Diesel busied himself with a walk around the outside of the building, checking out doors and windows and drain pipes.

Hayne planned to gut the rooms for a big open space, placing a stage at one end and seating for about 75. A real backstage. Bathrooms!

Hayne dragged his big trunk from the hallway into a room. He heard scratching sounds and figured they were Diesel, making his rounds. Drag, drag, he got the trunk in without calling for help.

Next, in the stack of boxes marked BARN, he found the smaller trunk that carried the Bleeps themselves. He picked it up and began walking toward the end room and heard the sound again. It came from the little store room across the hall. Through the window, he saw Diesel outside viewing the landscape.

What are those sounds? A mouse? Seems bigger. A rat? Oh dear. I might have to call for help after all.

Hayne set the trunk down and moved cautiously toward the door, hoping to not cross paths with a bear or a mountain lion. Hayne's imagination knew no bounds. They were near the forest, after all. He slowly opened the door all the way. Nothing there but dust, and lots of it. Some old boxes in the corner. An old lamp.

He noticed a closet door cracked open. The noise came from there. Diesel arrived from the outside. Hayne put his finger to his lips for a "Shhhhh." They listened. A slight rustling noise came from inside the closet.

Hayne reached into his jacket pocket for the flashlight. He turned it on and went to the door, holding the knob to keep the door from opening any further. He peeked in and shined the flashlight.

Oh! Hayne stepped back and looked at Diesel in shock. His eyes were wide open. He turned off the flashlight.

"What is it, Haynie? Should we run?"

Hayne shook his head. "No, not that. Just a minute." He gathered his wits, turned the flashlight back on and peered again into the darkened closet.

There! In the far corner in a pile of clothes or maybe sleeping bags, sat a small boy, shivering in a tee shirt with short sleeves and overalls that had seen better days. His unwashed dark hair shot out from his head like camel hair brush bristles. His dirty feet were bare. He blinked in the light, trying to focus his eyes. Hayne looked at Diesel and held his gaze for a moment. "You won't believe this." He turned off the flashlight and opened the door.

The child recoiled into the corner. All Hayne could see were the child's eyes, round and kind of wild.

"I won't hurt you, child," Hayne said kindly. "May I come into your closet?" Diesel observed in wonder.

The child didn't move at first. He grabbed his teddy bear from the pile and put it in between him and the man at the door. Daddy had said not to talk to anyone.

But hunger speaks louder than absent fathers, and the boy nodded to the man at the door.

"Diesel, get that small trunk." Diesel, wise man, did as he was told. Hayne opened the door another crack. The boy stared at him, still not moving. Diesel brought the small trunk, out of which Hayne took Bongo Bleep and slipped him onto his left hand.

He stuck Bongo into the closet and said in Bongo's monotonic drawl, "Hi, I'm Bongo Bleep. May I come, too?"

The child almost laughed. "I'll tell you stories if you let me in? May I?" asked Bongo Bleep. "I'll show you my spaceship."

The boy was silent for a few minutes. Hayne peeked around the door. He smiled.

The boy looked up and said, "OK," in a very small voice.

Hayne opened the door and sat down by the door frame, just inside the closet. The boy did not move. Hayne put Bongo up again and said, in his Bongo voice, "Hello, friend. What's your name?"

Hayne could tell the boy was a little mentally disabled, maybe Down Syndrome. His eyes had a very slight lack of focus. He remembered from the beach days a group of "Downies," the beach rats called them, came regularly to his puppet shows. They loved the puppets.

Hayne was patient. *More patient than I could be here*, thought Diesel. "What's going on?" he asked.

'Wait," said Hayne. "Give me a minute. Can you tell me your name?" he asked as Bongo.

The response came out kind of gravelly, and soft, like the boy didn't use his voice much. "Hecto,'" he said, pointing to his chest. "Me, Hecto.'"

HECTOR

"Are you alone, Hector?" asked Hayne, now concerned.

"Daddy gone," said the boy, comfortable now. "Find food for Hecto.'"

"Can you tell me how long your daddy's been gone?"

Hector's eyebrows furrowed. He counted on his fingers. He looked at his pile of coats. He held up two fingers and said, "Thith long. Thith many thleepth. Gone, long time. Thaid one hour a biwwion hourth ago. Hecto' hungry."

Bongo forgotten for the moment, Hayne said, "What have you eaten lately, Hector?" The boy held up a can of red kidney beans and an opener. "Hate beanth," he said and made a face.

"Well, I am Haynie, and this is D. We live here. Come over to our apartment and we'll make you breakfast and you can tell us all about it."

Hector thought about this. He thought about his daddy, who said don't talk to anyone. He thought about the time just before this time, when they walked maybe two thousand miles to get here from the train station. He thought about breakfast. "Eggth?" he said, "and toatht?"

"If that's what you'd like, Hector. Will you come with us?"

"Yeth, Haynie. If you thay tho." Hayne got up from the doorway and stepped back into the room. Hector crawled out of his bed of coats, picked up Teddy, straightened his little shoulders and went into his new life.

Although he didn't know it at the time. Currently, he was thinking about eggth and toatht. Hayne reached out with his free hand, Hector took hold and the four of them (Hayne, Hector, Diesel and Bongo Bleep) walked up the dirt path to the Villa.

Hector had arrived at the Villa at night and hadn't been out of the closet since going in. He was awed by the sights; the big oak tree with a swing, the statue of St. Francis in the garden, the field of mustard, waving in the breeze. He was not so afraid anymore. He wondered where his daddy was, but he liked Haynie and that other man, De… Di… DD. And hunger made him brave. "Will you find my daddy?" Hector asked his companions.

Diesel spoke for the first time. "We'll certainly try, Hector. We will try."

After eggs and toast with lots of jam and a glass of orange juice and then another, Hector felt much better. "Good," he said to Diesel, who was sitting beside him at the table.

"How old are you, Hector?" Diesel asked the boy.

Oh, Hector knew the answer to that! He had it remembered on his fingers. He put up one handful of fingers and one finger of the other and proudly said, "Thix! I am thix yearth old."

Diesel asked, "Can you tell us your daddy's name, Hector?"

Hector looked at Diesel, perplexed by this question. He said, "My daddy's name is…Daddy."

"Do you have a mommy, Hector?" asked Hayne, coming back to the table with a sliced apple. Munching, Hector considered this new question. So many questions. His head was beginning to hurt. "No mommy," he said. "Daddy thay...uhm... Mommy go bye bye."

With that, Hector slipped off the chair, walked around the corner into the living room, wrapped himself in a soft-looking wool blanket, and curled up in the corner of the couch. He was conked out in thirty seconds.

"What do you suppose?" asked Hayne of his friend. "Where is Daddy? What shall we do with Hector? He's like a puppy."

"Well, I think there is nothing to do at the moment. We don't even know Daddy's name, and I'm not too sure we're going to get it. I think his little six year old mind has some limitations."

"Yes, really. Imagine leaving him alone! In a closet! Daddy must be beset with troubles."

"Nothing to do yet but wait til Hector wakes up and ask a few more questions. Poor little tyke. Well, he's lucky we found him."

Hayne wondered who were the lucky ones. "We'd better leave a note in the closet for Daddy."

And that was the beginning of Hector.

HAYNE GOES BACK

While Hector slept on the couch like a little Labrador pup, and Diesel unpacked silverware, Hayne took a little trip back down to the storage room to that closet. He needed to know more.

At the closet, Hayne got the flashlight out of his pocket. Hm. A light socket in the ceiling but no bulb. But he could see why they chose this little closet. Right next to the bathroom.

He shined the light on the pile of coats. Looked safe enough, so he rummaged. Ah. Two army surplus sleeping bags, several men's jackets, not in good shape. Three empty cans of beans, attracting ants. Two empty bottles of whiskey and a plastic cup. A plastic bag with soiled underpants and socks. Ew. A small rucksack.

Hey. What's this? In the rucksack was a wallet. In the wallet, a driver's license— wow! A jackpot! Paul Farmdale. Age 45 Parkerville,

North Dakota. Folded up inside the wallet, a birth certificate. Hector MacArthur Farmdale, October 1, 1951...father unknown...mother, Maria Farmdale.

Well, and where are you without your driver's license, Paul Farmdale? And if the father is unknown, who are you? And where is Mommy Go Bye-Bye? Hayne wanted answers. He left his note and returned to the apartment.

Hayne had found nothing else, but this was enough. In conversation with Diesel, he said, "...and if we turn him in, Hector will end up in an institution. We'll have to wait for Paul Farmdale to return."

"Haynie, you're not saying we're going to keep the boy?"

"Well, what else can we do? His mother has gone bye bye. His father is...who knows where? Who is Paul Farmdale, anyway? Do we hand him Hector and they'll be on their way? On their way to what? He's a bum. They're bums. Hector has nothing but a bag of underwear and that bear. We can't just take him to the police and say, 'Here ya go, one little kid, and oh, by the way, he has some special needs.'"

"Hayne, keeping him is a crime."

"And who would know?"

"If Paul Farmdale turns up here, you cannot keep his child from him."

"I know that, D, but this child... he... he can't help himself. And we don't know if Mr. Farmdale is his father. And, no matter what, I am not turning that boy over to a drunk supposed father or to any heartless authorities. I don't care what you say."

"I know, Haynie."

HECTOR'S "DADDY"

Several nights later, Diesel read through the *Sonoma Times*; the Police Log read like a novel. It could be so funny.

"Mrs. P. on South Fork Lane complained someone stole a cherry pie off her windowsill. Pie remnants discovered near the neighbor's dog house."

"Mr J. needed help with his admittedly noisy weed whacker. It wouldn't start. He thinks his neighbor sabotaged the fuel. A local fight ensued."

"Man wandered into the road, appeared to faint, hit by car. Story on page 12."

Diesel put down the paper. Hayne was watching their new house-keeper, Rosalie Rosario, make Hector some French Toast. "Lotth of thywup, Wothie."

"Lots of syrup, please, Rosie," said Hayne.

"Pleathe, Wothie," repeated Hector, anxious to eat. Hector's tummy always grumbled.

Diesel went back to his paper and found page 12:

An unidentified man, 40-50 years old, with no wallet and no identification, was hit by a car in downtown Sonoma on Friday evening about dusk. He wandered into traffic and Mrs. Margaret Goodbody said, "He looked directly at me but kind of bleary-eyed and walked straight in front of my car. I guess he fainted. I'm so glad I didn't hurt him."

"Mr. X" was admitted to Sonoma Valley Hospital for observation and testing for possible Tuberculosis. He is in isolation.

The article went on to describe the man, who said the name "Paul" before he fainted again. They requested that anyone with information about Mr. Paul X please come to the Sonoma Sheriff's Department.

"Hayne," said Diesel. Hayne looked up. The way Diesel said his name, something was afoot. He saw the paper in Diesel's hands.

"Oh, ho! Information," Hayne said to his companion.

"Yes," Diesel said. "You might as well read it yourself and tell me what we'll do now," he said with a wry smile.

Diesel watched Hayne read. He knew what Hayne was going to say, but he waited to hear it from Hayne's own lips.

"Paul Farmdale."

"Most likely."

"Let's go."

"Right," said Diesel.

The weak and wan Paul Farmdale did not have TB. The pneumonia was more about exposure and neglect, the doctor said. "He's none too well fed, and he's anemic. Looks like he's been a long time on the street. But he finally woke up about an hour ago. You can go in."

Hayne tried not to imagine Hector and his father wandering around on the street, living on beans. This twisted his tender heart around like a pretzel.

After checking in with the nurse on duty, Hayne and Diesel entered the sick man's room. Paul Farmdale was hooked up to the drip, drip, drip of sustenance. He looked worried. And small. And forlorn.

He focused on Hayne and Diesel. "More doctors?" he croaked. "Why now?"

"Not doctors," Hayne said. "We're here to help. Mostly we're here to talk about Hector."

"Oh!...Hector!...Thank God...Where is my boy?...I have been so worried..."

Paul's breath came in and out with short puffs and long pauses between words.

"Your boy is fine, Paul. He is with us. At the old Sulfur Steam Conference Center. We just moved in and found him."

"I was so...afraid...to say...anything...afraid they'd...take Hector... away. I wasn't...sure I left...enough food. Some bread...and beans. I wasn't...sure of...anything. I thought...I'd be...right back." He gurgled and coughed. Then he focused on what Hayne had just said.

"You...bought it?...Sulfur Steam?...Oh my...is Hector...is Hector really ok?"

"Hector is fine. Let's talk about you."

Paul was really Hector's grandfather. The mother (Paul's daughter) died shortly after Hector was born. The father absconded with Maria's car and a jar of her stashed cash before Maria even knew she was pregnant; he doesn't even know he has a son. Paul is all Hector has. Hector is all Paul has.

"What are you planning to do when you are released from the hospital, Mr. Farmdale?"

"I don't know...find another...place to crash. We won't...be in... your way. If you could...keep him...until I get out of here..." He was breathing hard, trying to talk, trying to keep from crying, longing to make sense of any of this.

Hayne probed, still. "Mr Farmdale, why are you on the street with that boy? You seem capable enough to work, except for the pneumonia. Pardon me for asking, but, do you drink?"

"I...drink only...enough to deal...with life. Savings...used up...care of my daughter and then...for Hector. Sold everything...got on the train…walked and hitchhiked…to Napa then…Sonoma, looking for a…warmer climate…than North Dakota. Found Sulfur Steam, empty. And now it's not."

Hayne's mind was working overtime. Diesel could see it happening—the back of his neck was glowing with perspiration, his eyes wandered from sick man to window to Diesel to sick man to Diesel.

Diesel nodded and whispered, "Go easy on the man, hon." Hayne understood.

"Do you have any skills, Mr. Farmdale?"

"Skills?"

"Yes. What have you done for work in your life?"

"Drove a bus…got fired…too much time away…now broke…sick and…a six year old…with needs. I'm handy with a hammer…can drive a nail…you know."

HAYNE AND DIESEL CHAT

"What is it, Haynie? Is it about the boy?"

Hayne looked over at his handsome, brilliant companion, whose biggest hardship in life was most likely spending a week at military camp with a hulking roommate named Victor Magenta who thought of Diesel as the wimp of the decade. Poor Robert.

Poor Robert, my behind. Robert DeWayne Edwards had a father, and a mother, even an aunt who cared about him. He had a brain, and talent and could sing, dance and play the piano. He was well educated and extremely rich.

"D, I know we haven't talked much about my mother, and my life in LA. You know I just can't bear it, it's so not worth sharing, and I'm sorry about that, and you probably won't ever get much out of me on the subject. But there's this:

"When *I* was a scrawny six year old, I slept on a cot on the floor in a falling apart trailer. I had nothing. But, I had me. Which is the point. I was creating stuff and making things up even then, I had a brain and possibilities. I had a mother, but she…Well, I did have her. But I was so lonely. That's why the Bleep were 'born' in the first place. Out of deep boredom and loneliness and general poverty of circumstances.

"And then I met you. And now, this. We have this big place and your big ideas. We have something. A lot of somethings. We have each other. Sometimes I am completely overwhelmed by it.

"This boy, Hector, he has nothing. No mother, no father, no money, no real prospects for a life. All he has is a wobbly grandfather and an innocent sweetness that will last until he dies. Unless he's put in a home or, worse, an institution. What happens to that sweetness then? Who will care? And, who will care for Hector after his father dies?"

"I think I already know the answer to this conundrum, but why don't you tell me?" said Diesel.

"Well, we need a person to do things around here. We're not carpenters, not gardeners, but we can pay to have these things done. I propose we bring Paul home and put the two of them in the caretaker's cottage so they can…care take. And take care of each other."

"But we'd actually be taking care of them."

"Well. Yes, technically. But, Paul can get better, and Hector can go to the school in Petaluma—there is another Down Syndrome boy in the school, in the third grade class. His name is Ralphie."

"You called them?"

"I did. The sheriff, Randy, told me about the school, and the boy. They make special arrangements for him, and he is in a normal situation."

"And when Paul dies? He is a sick man, Haynie. Even if he recovers from the pneumonia, he is weak and anemic and older than his years."

"I know. And we are young and strong and have money and this big place. When and if he dies, we'll deal with it then. Right now, they have nothing. I'd like them to have us."

Diesel pondered this. He got up and strolled around the balcony. His companion sat in the wicker chair, following Diesel with his eyes.

Diesel said, "And what if we die before Hector?"

"Oh, honey, we'll work those things out. No one knows anything for sure. All I know is that I cared about Hector from the first moment we found him in the closet. I relate to him, somehow. And, I just…have a feeling."

Funny, Hayne was usually the more practical worry-wart.

Diesel looked down the road ahead and saw a twist in his plan.

Was he up to it? Could he be unselfish enough to take on a special needs kid for life? He wasn't too sure. But, Hayne was, and, well, he knew Hayne's softness and big heart balanced out his own self-centeredness. Maybe they could do it. Maybe they *should* do it. Something for someone else. Now there's a novel idea.

Chapter Five
Sunday, June 8, 2008

Hayne and Hector Unpack the Puppets

Hayne was not sorry Diesel suggested the Old Play. He missed his little empire in The Tiny Little Theater in the Barn; dusting the velvet curtains and setting up the proscenium, mending the puppet bodies, designing new hairdos and eyebrows and noses. Hayne loved noses best; sculpted, or papier mâché or even some of carved wood. In hand puppet terms, noses made all the difference.

On March 23, 2007, Hayne's 79th birthday, fifty years after conceiving The Tiny Little Theater in the Barn, Hayne and Hector put away the puppets for good.

Hector had said, "It'th not fo' good, Haynie. It'th fo' bad. I mith the puppetth alweady."

This day in 2008, Hayne said, "Here we are, unpacking the puppets, again."

"Again, Haynie? Did we pack up the puppetth befo'?"

"Ah, no, Hector. The very first time was before your time with us. It was long, long ago…"

"Tell me the thtory, Haynie."

Hayne, holding Bongo Bleep, put his hands on his lap and looked off into the distance, as if he could see the year 1942 and everything in it spread out before him. He looked at Hector.

"When I was fourteen years old, Hector, I met a man who changed my life."

"What wath your life like, Haynie? You never told me befo'."

Hayne and Hector sat on stools in front of the open trunk full of puppets. Hector held Grandfather Boodie Bleep. Hayne held Bongo and Bingo in his lap. Hayne sighed.

"Well, it was not like our life here at the Villa. Maybe you don't want to know."

"Oh, Haynie, I do. Pleathe tell me."

"Well, I lived in a little trailer with my mother. They called her Fatty Wills…"

And so, for the first time in many years, Hayne talked about his mother. Hayne was not a big talker, but that doesn't mean he didn't think about things. Hayne was more of an *in the moment* guy—entertain and enlighten, do not look back.

But, Hector had looked at him in that way that tugged at Hayne's heart. And their policy was, if Hector could ask the question, he was entitled to the answer.

Hayne described his life in the trailer, the Ice Queen, the Santa Monica Pier. He skirted around the squalor, the deep-fried "food," and the sloth, no need for that, and focused on the sand, the Pier, the puppets, and Jerry the Juggler and the day Glenda taught him to knit.

Hayne admitted to being a "kind of sickly kid" and described to Hector the very day the puppets were "born."

It had taken Hector fifty years to ask where, and how and why the puppets were born. Hector took it for granted that the Bleeps and all their friends had existed "forevo."

Hayne first unpacked the puppets upon his arrival in Pasadena. A whole new world opened up to Hayne, heady and strange and miraculous.

Fourteen years old and he had never been to Pasadena, eleven miles away from the Santa Monica Beach. When he thought about it, he realized he had never been anywhere but the beach, and St. Michael's School, the occasional dip in the YWCA pool, and that time at the CYO camp right here at Villa Zanetta, that time when the Dominican nuns put ten boys on the bus and shipped them off to Sonoma for two weeks, to get them away from LA, to give them a taste of the outdoors other than the Santa Monica Pier and other LA 'hoods, and to instill in them a little religion.

So, when Gilmor Brown (no relation to Marcus) rescued Hayne from his probable life of roaming the streets of LA, the boy packed up his trunk of puppets and left the every day world of the Santa Monica Pier.

Oh, he returned every weekend for a few years; he couldn't let down his Tiny Little Theater fans and he didn't want to abandon Fatty Wills. He left one of his more elaborate cardboard puppet theaters in the back room of the Ice Queen and, with the puppets of the day in his rucksack, took the bus to the Pier on most Saturday and Sunday mornings.

"And what did you do in Patha…Pathadeena?" asked Hector.

"I moved in with a kind of foster family and went to high school and then to art school and all the rest of the time I was involved in productions and classes at the College of Theatre Arts at the Playhouse. I had jobs at the Playhouse, to pay my way, and I worked in a diner sometimes, making milkshakes because I knew how.

"I learned almost everything I needed to know at the Playhouse, Hector. Not that I didn't learn in school; once I was in the right schools, I started to like it. But, at the Pasadena Playhouse, I learned about art, and writing, and acting, just like we do here at the Villa. I built scenery and learned about lighting and made props. They even let me do my puppet shows. All that opened my eyes to great vistas of art projects and new puppets and shows and all kinds of ways to make people laugh, or smile, or think, or even cry, if it's beautiful.

"And then another miracle happened, Hector. Gilmor Brown sent me to San Francisco to a workshop."

"And that'th where you met DD."

Yes, Hector, that's where I met DD."

AT THE PASADENA PLAYHOUSE

Hayne's memory was still pretty good, for an old man. He never forgot what Gilmor Brown did for him. Gilmor was like…a grandfather or an uncle, a mentor to quite a few aspiring actors and performers in the 40s and 50s. Hayne felt privileged to be among them, and thought wistfully now of those eye-opening days, after Gilmor Brown first saw him at the Ice Queen with the Bleeps on their tiny stage on the Dutch door.

When Hayne was 18, immersed in Junior college (for the "nuts and bolts," as Gilmor said), and the Pasadena College of Theatre Arts at the Playhouse (for everything else important), he was put in charge of organizing the Playhouse library and archive.

The loner, Hayne, slipped right into this role with great attention and intention. In his element, he read everything as he properly filed and cataloged each piece of paper, each little booklet, each script or score.

One day, Hayne came across a tattered 17th-century English transla-tion of an older Italian script called *Le donne ingannate* or *The Deceived Women*.

When Hayne shared this with his mentor, Gilmor told him how a typical Commedia dell'Arte performance explored the same stock char-acters, "like foolish old men, conniving servants, or full-of-themselves military officers who perpetrate nothing but trouble and, in an almost carnival atmosphere, create havoc among the women. It's always the same story, over and over again."

"This play in my hands," Gilmor said, "is, as far as we know, the ear-liest printed version of the story that became the libretto that Mozart set to music in 1790 and called *Cosi fan tutte* (*Women Are Like That*)."

He saw Hayne's eye light up like fireflies. "It would be terrific for The Bleeps. You may have it. Do something with it. Make it your senior project."

Well, what big possibilities for the Bleep entourage! Hayne set out to produce his first Baroque play. New puppets to add to his trunk!

Let's see, he thought, *two silly sisters, two young and shallow but con-ceited officers, a meddling valet, a betraying maid. But! At one point the officers dress up as fake foreigners (in the* Cosi fan tutte *version, the fakes are Albanians – I'll have to come up with something unique) and the maid disguises herself as a doctor, so a total of nine new puppets! Oh boy!* Hayne got to work.

Hayne placed *his* story in a circus. Fiora and Drusina are tight rope walkers and Tristano and Francesco have recently joined the circus as clowns.

Their friends, the Golden Snub-Nosed Monkey named Colombina (who called herself Roxie) and the Zebra who went by the name of Arlecchino, cause all the trouble.

As part of his senior project, Hayne wrote a synopsis of the original script:

Le donne ingannate *"The Deceived Women"*
A one-act Commedia dell' Arte script written in 1591
by Alberto di Nuccio (b. 1555 Napoli, d. 1617 Milan)

Di Nuccio's play greatly influenced Lorenzo da Ponte's libretto
for Mozart's *Cosi fan tutte* in 1780

Cast:

I Innamorati (The Lovers)

Fiora and Drusina, two upper-class sisters

Tristano and Francesco, two aristocratic young men

I Zanni (The Servants)

Colombina, the ladies' maid

Arlecchino, the servant to the men

Synopsis:

Scene One: Tristano and Francesco are in love with Fiora and
Drusina. Arlecchino suggests to the two men that their true
loves might prove untrue if given an opportunity. "All women
are like that," he says. The two men are deeply offended, and
they accept Arlecchino's proposal of a wager: if the women
are untrue, the men will lose the bet. The men exit and
Arlecchino is joined by the ladies' maid, Colombina. Together
they plot to fool the women and win the wager.

Scene Two: The women profess their love for Tristano and
Francesco. The men suddenly announce they must go off on a
long journey, and the two sisters weep and are lonely.

Scene Three: The two men return in disguise and each man
romances the other's girlfriend. They almost succeed, but at
the last moment they are unmasked and their true identities
revealed. The four lovers are embarrassed but reconciled, and
the clever servants, Colombina and Arlecchino, have the last
laugh as they split the winnings.

Marcus took weekly piano lessons for ten years as a boy and dutifully practiced, but, he admitted, he didn't have the chops to "be a contender." He played, but not beautifully. He sang, but not nobly.

What Marcus did have was the smell of the greasepaint and the roar of the crowd in his veins. His parents and aunts and uncles and most of their friends and associates were actors and opera singers; he grew up around show business and show business was his aim. If he couldn't perform, there were other ways to satisfy his longing for the theater and its magic.

In 1997, Marcus escorted a woman he longed to impress to Sonoma to see a performance of *The Magic Flute* at Villa Zanetta. He heard about the place from a colleague and thought Becca Lindstrom might swoon over the Villa and this performance of Mozart's final opera. But it was Marcus himself who swooned and fell in love. Zanetta beckoned, and he followed.

Marcus lay on his bed in the dorm thinking about his first visit to the Villa. After an early dinner in Sonoma, he and Becca arrived at dusk, greeted by a flock of large colorful birds, all of whom seemed to be able to play the flute. They were birds the size of ostriches, with very ungainly, un-birdly feet. But they laughed and played and opened the car doors for the arriving guests and several birds even hopped into the drivers' seats to park the cars in the lot. Marcus noted that these particular birds had the least interesting tail feathers.

The show was marvelous, the music, of course, sublime, but on the way home to the City, Becca declared she was utterly bored by opera and didn't understand one word of it (even with a printed translation in her lap) and didn't care to try.

Well. That did it for Marcus and upon arriving at Becca's apartment in the Sunset District, he walked her to the door and said goodnight. He didn't even try for a peck on the cheek. It disturbed him greatly that someone he considered courting could diss such heart-lifting, wonderful music and amusement. He wrote her off as a lost cause. When he got home, he picked up the phone and called Kendra, starting the late night conversation, which she always seemed to be up for, with, "Can you believe...?"

He went back to Villa Zanetta for the next three performances of *The Magic Flute*. On the final night of that run, Marcus lingered at the bar after the performance. There was a mystical, invisible tug on his sleeve. A muse whispered sweet nothings in his ear. He imagined Thalia and Melopomene swishing their diaphanous gowns and tickling the hairs on his arms, touching his fingers with theirs, whispering, "Mar-r-r-cus, her-r-re we ar-r-re!"

Hayne and Diesel happened to come to the bar for a sherry before walking up the hill to their home. They noticed that man who had been to every performance and wanted to meet him. Anyone that dedicated to the theater was a friend of theirs!

"Hello," said Diesel, sitting down to the left of Marcus. "Hello, from me, too," said Hayne, who stood by Diesel's elbow.

"Well, hello. Oh! You are the founders of Villa Zanetta! How nice to meet you. I'm Marcus Brown, your big fan."

"I'm Hayne Williams," said Hayne, "and this is my partner, Robert, aka Diesel Edwards. You've been to four performances of *The Magic Flute*."

"Ah. You noticed. Yes. I can't seem to tear myself away tonight."

This innocuous little chat at the bar with Marcus Brown began an ongoing conversation between the three men. Within a few weeks, Marcus quit his job as the Manager of SF Opera Light in anticipation of being hired as General Manager of Villa Zanetta. Everything evolved so smoothly that, when they prepared to take their final bows on The Well Lit Theater stage in 2007, ten years later, they dubbed Marcus Executive Director (which title Hayne and Diesel had shared for nearly fifty years).

Marcus sighed. *And the rest is history.* Something about this place pulled him in and pushed him away at the same time. He squirmed around in the bed, feeling a disturbance in his equilibrium. He blamed it on the chandelier, but it was more than that.

FOR IMMEDIATE RELEASE   Sunday, June 8, 2008
The Theaters at Villa Zanetta mourn the death
of beloved stage director Falcon Jennings

Tragedy struck at the renowned Sonoma Valley arts facility Villa Zanetta on Friday evening, June 6, when well-known stage director Falcon Jennings was fatally injured by a falling chandelier in the theater lobby.

Mr. Jennings, 40, was a respected and popular stage director on the West Coast, and his sudden death comes as a shock to the theater and opera communities. At the time of his death Mr. Jennings was serving as stage director for The Well Lit Theater's production of Mozart's *Cosi fan tutte*. His previous productions at Villa Zanetta included *The Magic Flute* and *Don Giovanni*.

In addition to his work on the Villa Zanetta artistic staff, Mr. Jennings has directed productions at Berkeley Repertory Theater, Long Beach Opera, Sacramento Opera, Los Angeles Cabaret Theater, West Bay Opera, and California Shakespeare Theater, among many other West Coast companies.

He was also a frequent director at the Cinnabar Theater in Petaluma, California, where he lived with his wife, Martha Watts-Jennings. (Ms. Watts-Jennings was to be Wardrobe Mistress for the production of *Cosi fan tutte* at Villa Zanetta but has withdrawn from the production.)

Mr. Jennings earned a Master of Fine Arts Degree from the Drama Division of the Juilliard School in New York. He was hailed by all for the performance of his one act play, *Here Come the Lions*, on the Juilliard stage.

Circumstances surrounding Mr. Jennings's death are under investigation.

A private memorial is planned at Villa Zanetta, and a Falcon Jennings Memorial Fund is being established.

Contact:
John Eagle, Villa Zanetta Director of Development and Public Relations. *Email* jeagle@villazanetta.org.

All that glitters is not gold.
The Merchant of Venice
~ Wm. Shakespeare

AND WHAT OF THE CHANDELIER?

Consider the classic 1910 100-light French chandelier with bronze and brass frame. Its arms were adorned with scrolling acanthus leaves and hand-cut crystals; it was easily lowered for cleaning and bulb replacement.

To anthropomorphize the chandelier for a moment, this one did not want to go down in history as an instrument of death, a killer, a snuffer of life. It had survived since Zanetta's time, since her lovely ladies strolled the promenade showing off their attributes under the new electric light fixture. This chandelier had seen some sights, lit some parties, illuminated and sparkled over some pretty illustrious festivities. It had been updated, refurbished, polished and tended for almost 100 years. It was first hung with rope, then chain, finally a thin but much sturdier cable.

During the post-kaboom clean up party, hosted by the sheriff's department, the chandelier let the cleaner-uppers know in no uncertain terms that it did not want to be destroyed or tossed in the refuse heap. If it had feelings, they would be hurt. It wasn't the chandelier's fault that some lunatic cut the "much sturdier" cable and sent it hurtling to the floor to permanently knock the stuffing out of a stage director. This chandelier had purpose, and its purpose was not finished.

And so, a debate ensued: What of the chandelier? Do we dare put it back? Use it for parts? Hang it somewhere else? Put it on trial?

The chandelier now had a past and a reputation. It could not go back up via the cupola's little winch. Something new would have to be done.

The chandelier was fingerprinted and photographed 50 ways from Sunday and then set aside. Priscilla researched more modern lighting.

Meanwhile, Hector, that gardener and lover of "found objectth" for his garden and other endeavors, was invited to look at the chandelier, which Marcus had directed the cleaners to put on the brick patio, sans the bulbs. The brass arms were a bit bent, but most of the hand-cut crystals were still attached, and the rest in a little plastic bag.

Imagine Hector's delight at the gift—all "shiny and thparkley in the thun like that."

Marcus said, "Well, we thought you might make something beautiful out of it for your garden."

"Oh, yeth, Mawcus Bwown. I promithe I will," said Hector Farmdale.

THE COMPANY ARRIVES

Marcus tried to glue himself back together. He had no choice, really—either that or retire on the spot. Priscilla would take over in a flash (he knew that) and he could walk away from this madhouse.

Of course, he would never leave Villa Zanetta that way. But it was tempting, not having to face all these musicians and crew and staff and audience and patrons and whomever else and tell them over and over again about the incident.

He finally resorted to *Memento mori* (Latin for 'remember that you [have to] die,' a little reminder of the inevitability of death), and, "We'll explain at the Welcome Party."

Marcus instructed his staff and volunteers to not discuss the incident, please stay on the topic of Festival logistics and answer any of *those* questions with, "We'll explain at the Welcome Party."

Overnighters were shown their quarters, day players (who lived close enough to go home each night) were taken to the Old Hall, now serving as the incoming participants' lounge, where one could find refreshment, snacks, and a little conversation.

Naturally, the whispered buzz in the Old Hall concerned the incident.

"Where did it happen?"

"The chandelier!?"

"Was it Willard?"

"Falcon Jennings? Who would want to kill Falcon Jennings?"

"How's Martha?"

"Falcon Jennings? Geez. Bet Willard Franklin is happy."

On and on it went.

Marcus was tired already.

Perhaps, he hoped, *we can get through the next rehearsal with a modicum of dignity.*

President of the Villa Zanetta Board, Barton Wyndermere III, arrived in his Bentley from San Francisco to do his part. Marcus usually enjoyed Barton Wyndermere's presence on the compound. Barton had a way of sucking up all the air in any room he entered, in an entertaining way. He was tall and very good looking—Cary Grant good looking. And rich. So rich, he had never done a lick of work in his life, unless you could call being a "professional client" a job. He referred to it as "moving money around." Marcus could not imagine it.

Barton came prepared to officially speak to the company. For once, Marcus could step aside and let the Board President handle it.

"Welcome to all participants in the 2008 Villa Zanetta Opera Festival. By now you have all heard some sort of scuttlebutt about the incident at Villa Zanetta on Friday evening. Here are the facts: Falcon Jennings was killed instantly when struck by the 100 year old chandelier. Mr. Brown was the only witness and barely escaped injury and perhaps even death.

"Please do not give any interviews or speak to the press. Any questions from the outside, either press, police, legal or personal, should be directed to Mr. Brown.

'There is a suggestion of foul play, the sheriff's department has representatives here, combing through the theater and various other sections of the Villa for clues. They will do their best to not interfere with our production.

"We have, unfortunately, also lost our conductor due to conflicts and differences. Mr. Franklin has resigned his position as Music Director for *Cosi fan tutte* effective immediately. We are especially proud of our Assistant Conductor and Choral Director, Sampson Powers, for making a seamless transition."

Well, that was perfunctory, Marcus thought, as Barton Wyndermere III roared off in his Bentley for dinner at the home of Bill and Odella Palmer. *I'll bet Bill Palmer told him to stick to the facts.*

He sighed again and wondered how he would solve the next problem.

> And I here make a rule-
> a great and lasting story is about everyone or it will not last.
> The strange and foreign is not interesting-
> only the deeply personal and familiar.
> *East of Eden*
> ~ John Steinbeck

THE OLD HALL

After that brief and, to Marcus Brown, unsatisfying update from Barton Wyndermere III, the Villa Zanetta Opera Festival 2008 ensemble gathered in the Old Hall; the familiar place, that comforting old room full of friendly and sometimes mysterious ghosts of other festivals, other performances. On the polished wood walls were posters and gowns and doublets and swords and all kinds of theatrical memorabilia: here, some feathery plumage from *The Magic Flute*; there, a hand painted mask from Britten's *Curlew River*; around the frame of the door hung a watery-green satin curtain salvaged from the set of *Cleopatra*, right off her barge.

Marcus's favorite item was the handwritten list on a scroll of white butcher paper hanging on the wall. The list? Every performance at the Villa since 1958, mostly in Hayne Williams's small, neat handwriting, including puppet shows, all operas and musicals, dance and art shows.

The familiar was necessary at times like these, when emotions are high, thoughts are dark and feelings fraught. Chef Henry prepared a luscious and welcoming buffet, with all of the choices for the grieving and the sad, comforting foods like sausages and rolls, steamed green beans in garlic butter sauce, pans full of warm mashed potatoes and pots of soup. Henry's famous mac and cheese. Three kinds of salad. Fresh fruit compote. Pie.

Although the rest of Sonoma boasted a perfect 80° day, the weather in Villa Zanetta's Old Hall was chilly; the combined nervous energies of the 60 or so musicians and crew and staff and volunteers coming together to share a meal and hear the rest of the story. There has to be more to the story. This is a theater company!

Marcus sat with his friend, Kendra, at his personal table in the far back corner. It was dark there, sheltered by the sound equipment and a stack of chairs. Marcus needed a few minutes to gather his wits before stepping up to the podium another time to address the tribe.

"No more wine for me, Kendra, I am not going to embarrass myself in front of the entire company. Perhaps *after* I tell the story one more time, but not before. But don't let me get drunk. I would prefer to keep my sloppy moments on the QT." Marcus straightened his red bow tie, touching it like a talisman. He thought he might never take it off. It, and his torn sleeve, had become symbols of survival.

Kendra smiled at her friend. "No problem, Marc, hon. Your secrets are safe with me."

"Do I have 'wants to go home' written on my face? Because that is how I feel. I'm not sure how much more of this I can manage."

"No, actually, you just look like the rest of us, tired and a bit frazzled. I am sure you can fool them. You've done it before. You'll be fine."

Marcus stepped up to the front of the stage. He waited quietly for a few minutes until the din died down. The wine was poured, the buffet on the counters, and the people spread out among the tables and chairs and little couches around the Old Hall. The company had buzzed all afternoon and would keep buzzing until late at night, but right now their attention was all on Marcus Brown.

Marcus was about 5'6" tall. In his younger years he played a lot of tennis, but after he set that aside, he thickened slightly around the middle. He was cute, not handsome, self-effacing, and prone to worry. His one vanity was his hair; thick and salt and peppery with gentle curls. When not worried, he had a lovely smile, and when perplexed, mystified, tense or angry, the deep lines between his brows just closed in on each other and created the most glorious frown. After Kendra once pointed out his frown lines, Marcus began to practice *not frowning* in the mirror, by raising his eyebrows and forcing a squinty-eyed fake smile.

On this evening in June in Sonoma, Marcus's sport coat (the one with the telltale rip in the sleeve) and red plaid shirt and red bow tie blended in with the artistic crowd. After years of herding actors and artists and musicians, the color red rubbed off on him and he could never get it off. He surrendered in 1992 when his confirmed bachelor's wardrobe began to fill up with reds from crimson to maroon. If you could see his socks under his khakis and inside his saddle shoes, they would be red.

Marcus usually took his glasses off while giving a speech, but he was afraid he might cry again so he left them on as protection.

He looked at his audience. (That was another thing that rubbed off on Marcus Brown in the theater world—the dramatic pause.)

"Greetings, all. We are very glad you're here with us at Villa Zanetta. It is a special 50ᵗʰ anniversary festival, and we have chosen story, ensemble, and music carefully to show us off at our best. So, thank you for being part of that.

"I will go over the changes in the ensemble and schedule with you again in a moment, but first, let's address what is on all your minds tonight.

"We have lost a dear friend and colleague this weekend and, to keep rumor and gossip from ruling the day, I will tell you exactly what happened, in my own words. After I tell you, I ask that we keep gossip to a minimum and honor Falcon Jennings by going on with the show.

"Further, I tell you this now so I don't have to repeat it 60+ times.

"I happened to be the only witness to this tragedy and, the more I look at it, the more I feel it is a miracle I survived. Falcon was hit by the chandelier as he walked across the Lobby. I had just come down the stairs from the office. We were three feet apart and about to greet each other when Falcon looked down and, in an instant, the chandelier was crashed to the floor and he was under it. It missed me but tore a hole through my jacket sleeve." He held up his arm to share the visual evidence.

Marcus had his audience now. He heard satisfying gasps from several people and went on with his story.

"It appears that the cable was cut." Another gasp.

"The sheriff's department has spent several days collecting evidence and fingerprints. Until tomorrow evening, the theater is off limits. The updated rehearsal schedule is on the table by the door. Please see Priscilla if you have any questions.

"The sheriffs are still around so please be cooperative. However, remember, no interviews, and direct all questions to me or Priscilla.

"I'm very grateful and happy that Diesel Edwards is stepping in to replace Falcon Jennings as Stage Director for the production of *Cosi fan tutte*. Mr. Williams and Mr. Edwards have both emerged from their brief retirement to contribute their efforts to going on with the show. We have added Mr. Williams (Hayne), performing *The Deceived Women*, with his baroque puppets in The Tiny Little Theater in the Barn on the two Wednesday afternoons and on the second Sunday." (Applause erupts, Marcus notes this to tell Hayne.)

"Martha Jennings has, of course, withdrawn from her post as wardrobe mistress, but as you can see, Smooch McGuinn has risen to the occasion and will be with us. Soloists, if you need adjustments to your costumes, she will be in the hall after supper for about an hour to discuss.

"Sampson Powers is well prepared to assume the conductor's position on the platform and we are grateful to have him.

"We ask that you help us carry on in the creation of beauty, to fill the holes in our hearts. In memory of Falcon Jennings, let's take this moment to weave ourselves together into a powerful tapestry of thespians, musicians, artists, crew and staff, to become more than the sum of our parts to inspire and uplift us all. I'm glad you're here."

SMOOCH'S DAY

Smooch McGuinn had arrived at the Old Hall after a brief and very disturbing visit with Martha Jennings in Petaluma and an even more distressing phone call.

Marcus could tell there was something going on in Smooch's mind. She was one of those transparent people whose face told the story. Smooch's hair was pulled back tighter than usual, and she kept her paisley pashmina wrapped tightly around her, like she was cold. She opened her eyes wide at Marcus, like, "We'd better talk." He invited her to step outside.

They sat down at the big table with a green umbrella. Marcus chose to remain quiet until she was ready to talk. Smooch looked at her hands for a few minutes, touching the tips of her painted nails against the pads of her thumbs.

Finally, she said, "I have two things, and one alone is hard, but this is a sack full of cats."

"OK," said Marcus. "Where do you want to start?"

"Well, first I'll tell you about Martha. I went to her house in Petaluma, you know. Have you seen her since Friday?"

116

"No, I haven't even talked to Martha since she left with her mother. I've been pretty busy here. Diesel talked to Mrs. Watts about a memorial on Wednesday. How is Martha?"

"She's awful, Marcus. She's practically catatonic. I think her mother has her pretty doped up, I hear she can get quite histrionic when she's upset. But, this is different. It's like she's lost her mind. Her eyes are focused on something invisible and she can hardly speak. I tried to ask her about costumes, but she was unwilling or unable to talk. It was like her mouth had been glued shut. She looked right through me, like I was invisible."

"Well, it's only been two days, hon. She's upset."

"I know, Marcus, but I'm worried about her, that's all."

"OK. I'll check on her. And number 2?"

"Willard called me," said Smooch. Her eyes filled with tears.

"Oh no," said Marcus. *What next?*

"Do you want to tell me about it?" he asked.

"No! Yes! Of course. I don't know why I got the crazies today," she said, "but that man called to try to talk me into getting him out of the country."

Marcus swallowed his sip of Sonoma Cutrer. "What?"

"He's hiding out somewhere nearby, he didn't say where. I heard birds, so he might have been outside. He knows I'm here at the Villa. He's drunk and frantic. He wants to disappear."

"And he called *you*?" Marcus asked.

Smooch shook her head no meaning yes and then no, like, *the gall!*

"You know the sheriffs want to talk to you," said Marcus. "They'll be here shortly."

"I know. That's why I'm here right now. What should I tell them?"

"Well, Smooch, you have to tell them everything."

"I don't know where he is."

"I know, but still…you kind of have no choice."

Smooch sighed deeply. "OK. I guess I signed on for this."

GRADY, PATRICK AND SMOOCH

Grady Mulligan and Patrick Delaney arrived in their respective vehicles at 6pm. (Grady wouldn't get into Patrick's old Ford pickup, full of hay remnants and the redolent odor of manure as it was).

They met, as usual, in the lower parking lot and walked up to the Villa together. Grady said, "I heard from Marcus Brown. He says our conversation with Samantha Margaret McGuinn is going to be very interesting."

"Smooch."

"Yeah. I know. It's hard to be serious about that. Do we call her Smooch or Samantha?"

"Smooch, from what I hear. Kendra Masters says everyone calls her that."

"Yeah."

"Did Marcus say why we'd be so interested?"

"Nope. Just a text."

"OK."

Their Villa "office" in the Not-so was still a good place for a conversation. When Grady and Patrick invited Smooch in, she looked so stricken and shaky, they allowed Marcus to be with her.

Grady said, "We hear there's news."

Smooch tore her tissue into little pieces. She sighed deeply and said, "Willard called me."

"Ah," said Patrick and Grady in unison.

"Where is he?" asked Patrick.

"I don't know. This was about two hours ago. He was outside somewhere, I think, on his cell phone. I don't know how close. He hung up, saying he had to charge his phone."

"And what did he want?"

Smooch looked at Marcus and rolled her eyes. "Go on," said Marcus Brown.

"He wanted me to pick him up, make him a plane reservation, and take him to the airport."

"Where is he going?" asked Grady.

"First he said 'Mexico.' Then he said, 'Argentina.' Then after a few seconds, it was, 'Spain.' I think because he speaks Spanish."

"And what did you say?"

"I laughed like a maniac. I told him he was either drunk or crazy. He started yelling at me like he did when I found out about his affairs.

He yelled like it was all my fault. Then he started blabbering about Falcon Jennings."

She pulled some more flakes off her tissue and they fluttered to the floor.

"Yes?" said Patrick.

"Well, he kept saying he didn't do it but that he wasn't sorry. And then he said something really strange about a secret staircase. He said only two people knew about it. He didn't say who. He said it would explain everything. Then he hung up. Does this make sense to you?"

"A secret staircase? Marcus?" asked Grady.

"No." Marcus shook his head.

"Can you ask someone who might know?"

Marcus looked at Smooch. She said, "It's OK. I'm OK. Go ahead."

Marcus left the room. First he went outside for some fresh air and to think. Obviously, he had to call or visit Hayne and Diesel. They would be the two who would know about it, if there was such a thing as a secret staircase.

And so he called, but Hayne and Diesel knew nothing. Marcus went back to the Not-so with no news.

ANOTHER MARCUS LIST

Marcus sat in his bed in the dorm and listed the pros and cons of his predicament.

First item on the lit, of course, was his commitment to Hayne and Diesel.

What would the old gents do if I left? They'd have to come back. Although Marcus had every confidence in Priscilla Pendleton, she was unprepared for a full directorship. She was strong, and smart, and masterfully organized. She could handle eight things at once and plan for another ten while juggling the rest. But her skills were best used in handling all the people under her, as it were, and not with the people beyond the Villa, like the press, and the board, and the conductors and directors.

Plus, his gave his word. His word! Does that mean that no matter what, no matter his own feelings, or health, or well-being, or judgments, he would have to stay at Villa Zanetta forever?

Well, what would Hayne and Diesel be doing right this minute if it had been Marcus under the chandelier? If *he* were dead?

They'd be back in the saddle in a minute. You can see it in their faces; that love, that desire, that drive to keep going. But, they were 80 and 81 years old! Still sharp, but, was it fair to ask them to find someone else to train and take his place? Would it take another ten years?

That's ridiculous. And, looking back, it didn't really take ten years train him. They just got comfortable in the situation and went on with the work.

HAYNE AND DIESEL CHAT

In their fireside chairs, Hayne and Diesel knitted together the stories of the day. Diesel's first tech rehearsal went well, and he was comforted by the extra efficient Kendra Masters.

"She was terrific. One of the best. She had most wonderful notes. I sat in a chair and let her handle it. I hardly had to move. It was perfect. Once she gets her feet wet, she'll be great. She understands the job. How about your unpacking? Did it go well?"

"My assistant isn't as efficient as yours, D. Hector and I got to talking about the past. We took an hour for the Gilmor Brown story, and I even found myself telling him about Fatty Wills.

"You know, Hector's got the most interesting memory. Sometimes he can't remember what he ate for breakfast, but he can tell me exactly which puppet is what character and what body goes with which head." Hayne smiled at the thought of his puppet buddy. "I couldn't do this show without him. He makes me...able."

Diesel smiled. Just then, Hector came up the stairs from his old room, which had become storage for his "art partth," and "found objectth," he'd scavenged for his faerie garden forts.

He was carrying art parts for his next building project, a gnome house in a gourd. He carried a big homegrown pear-shaped gourd by the stem between his forefinger and his thumb and in the other hand, a small red-hatted gnome he'd found in the thrift shop in downtown Sonoma.

"The focus is back on Willard, I take it?" said Hayne to Diesel. "Seems worse and worse for him. He shouldn't have run off. Everything that happens seems to put him more and more in the soup. What did he say about this secret staircase?"

"He said only two people know about it. I have no idea."

Hector, who had just seated himself on the chair at the table to begin his tiny construction, looked up. His eyes moved back and forth like they did when he was thinking things over or confused.

"I know 'bout it," he said.

Chapter Six
Monday, June 9, 2008

No legacy is so rich as honesty.
All's Well That Ends Well
~ Wm. Shakespeare

Marcus and Hector Chat

Marcus knew the best way to talk to Hector was to just let him tell the story, and the best place would be in the morning and in the garden.

Hector's garden was something of a phenomenon. Or perhaps the phenomenon was Hector himself, he being the entire and full creator of the Villa Zanetta gardenscape.

Long ago, it was supposed to be Hector's daddy's garden, but Paul Farmdale wasn't very good at it. Paul's health never did bounce back, and Hector, well, somehow he just knew what to do. What started as a plot behind the cabin soon wrapped itself *around* the cabin and meandered over by the barn and followed walkways and filled up areas that used to be grass, until the 14 year old Hector looked at the lawn one day and said, "What a waithte." Soon, there were flowers here and trailing beans there and then, Hector's garden was big enough to feed the Villa.

They sat on a bench by a deer-fenced area, watching the bees buzz Hector's flowerbed. Over by the little gate to the fenced-in garden, one of Hector's "Faerie Fortth" nestled under a bush; a tiny hut with tiny wheel barrow and a little pitch fork. Several deer, no doubt pondering those fenced flowers, flicked flies in the wild mustard field to the left.

"I have to gwab it," said Hector.

"What's that?" asked Marcus.

"The memory. I have to wait till it…floatth by and then…I will gwab it like a fly…and then I try to keep it. In my head."

"Do you write it down?"

"Thometimeth. Not awwayth. No. Ha ha. I made a joke. Memorieth… they move too fatht. And, I don't thpell too good…too well."

"So how do you remember all the things to do in the garden?"

"Mmm. That'th not memowieth, Mawcus Bwown. That jutht came with me, in my body."

Just then a hummingbird buzzed Hector's red hat. "Oh!" he said. "Willard told me the thecret thtairs were a thecret. He found a...a doo-er."

"Can you show me?"

"He thaid it was a thecret."

"OK, but he must want us to know, because he told Smooch that only two people knew about it. Maybe it will help us find out what happened with the chandelier."

"And who made Falcon Jenningth D.E.A.D.?"

"Yes."

"OK."

THE DOOR

Hector and Marcus walked to The Well Lit Theater. Hector started at the spot on the east side of the mansion where the 1970 construction of the theater joined seamlessly with the back. Hector walked very close in, scanning the fake Tudor wall with his hand. He took off his thick glasses and let his nearsighted eyes focus in on the building.

Hector whispered to Marcus, "I think I will know it when I feel it. I jutht have to 'member how it feelth."

Marcus gestured like, "Lead the way." Slowly they walked along the south side of the theater building, Hector's hand moving along the surface, like he read the wall through his fingers, like braille; but nothing, so far. They passed around the darkened stage door at the end and, where they turned the corner to the north side of the building, the bushes were thick.

"Oh! Yeth! Willard thaid, 'Leave thith bush alone.' It'th over here... the door. Not on the new part. On the old houthe part." Hector led the way to where the theater joined the mansion. The bushes had to be held back to get through. "I will fix thith," he said about the overgrown bushes. "Thnip, thnip!"

Hector ran his hand along the mansion wall close to the join. He felt a tiny, perfect seam. He jumped up and down. "Here," said Hector.

"Here ith a door." He pushed in and the secret door gave a little *POP!* like a kitchen cabinet on a spring. It opened into an ancient, rickety, 18 inch wide stairway, two steps up and a sharp turn to the right, sidling up between two dark and dusty walls. It looked to Marcus like the theater builders had just ignored the secret stairway and built around it.

Hector was smiling. Marcus said, "Where does it go?"

Hector shrugged his shoulders and said, "Up! To Heaven, maybe."

"Oh my," said Marcus Brown.

"Is Willard in twouble. Trouble?" Hector asked.

"I don't know, Hector. But someone is."

THE SECRET STAIRWAY

"You didn't go up the stairs?" Patrick asked. They met in the parking lot and waited for Grady.

"No," said Marcus. "I saved you that privilege. Seems like the fewer people in there the better."

"You're beginning to sound like a detective! Had Hector been in there?"

"No. He said it was too dark. And, he said Willard told him to keep it a secret."

"When did this occur? This secret?" asked Patrick.

"Well, I haven't asked him that yet. It's not good to bombard Hector with questions. What he did so far this morning was a big deal. I'm sure he's digging in the dirt somewhere right now, cooling off. "

"Yes, but he's become a key source of information, Marcus."

"I know. I've talked it over with Hayne. We agree that I should continue to talk to Hector. It's really more about sitting with Hector and letting him talk. He's slow, but he remembers everything, sooner or later. One just has to be patient."

Patrick sighed. "Make it soon, if you can. Sooner or later we'll have to talk with Hector again, you know."

"Yes. I know. We'll prepare him for that."

When Grady arrived with Joe Budd, the four of them walked back to the secret door. Although Hector had wanted to go get his clippers immediately, Marcus said to wait—that the bushes should stay like they were so the sheriffs could understand the secret, secluded spot.

So, Marcus pushed aside the bushes by the corner where the mansion met the theater, a dark and secretive spot, all right, surrounded by an untended thicket. When the sheriffs' deputies snooped around the other day, no one had thought to look for a secret door.

Marcus felt along the wall for the seam and pushed. *POP!*

Patrick stuck his head in and said, "Why would there be a stairway like this at the back of the house?"

Marcus said, "I've been thinking about that. I imagine there is a tiny landing up there and another hidden door like this at the top. It *was* a 'pleasure house,' Sheriff."

"Yeah? And...? Ah! A get-away!"

"Yes. The story goes that Madam Zanetta catered to a high brow clientele. I suppose there were certain citizens one wouldn't want to run into. Or a police raid. She *was* in business during the thirteen years of the Prohibition. At first, I thought the builders in 1970 ignored it. But, I don't think they even knew it was there. This wall was never in their purview."

WILLARD'S RUIN?

Grady, Patrick and Joe Budd flicked on their flashlights and looked inside but did not go in. Patrick said, "We'd better let forensics in first. There's not much room in there and there are a lot of opportunities for prints or threads or other clues to this ever-growing mystery. So much ancient dust, and like it's been swept by a big broom. Close it up, and Joe, go call in the troops."

While they waited, Marcus offered coffee in the Old Hall. Marcus went into the kitchen and came out with a French Press, three cups and a pot of foam. Grady and Patrick smiled like, "Who are these people?"

"Hayne and Diesel like to do things right," said Marcus.

"I guess," said Patrick. "I'm not complaining."

Grady interrupted, "Can you think of any reason why a man would incriminate himself this way?"

"What do you mean?" asked Marcus.

"Well, if only two people knew about this stairway, Willard must be one of them. If the other is Hector, I'd say Willard Franklin is your man. Why point it out?"

"He's not exactly operating with a clear head, Sheriff," Marcus said. "What I'd like to know is, how did Willard find this secret door? No one else, including Hayne and Diesel, ever knew it existed. Hector, who knows everything, didn't know about it until Willard told him, or showed him. When we parted this morning, Hector was trying to remember. He kept saying, 'Latht time. Latht time.' And then he'd shake his head, like clearing fog. I think it helps his eyes. I'm sure he'll get there. He always does."

THE SHERIFFS AND HECTOR

Hayne sat on his favorite stool in The Tiny Little Theater in the Barn, repairing the mustaches of the puppet Francesco, preparing him for the performance of *The Deceived Women*. He clipped bristles from an old brush and, with his medium tweezers, glued them one by one to the upper lip of the long-suffering Francesco. He held the puppet away from him and admired his work. *Very good*, he thought. *We'll have to freshen up the black in his irises, and then I think he's good to go.*

Hector burst through the door, panting. Hayne put Francesco aside and stood up. "What is it, Hector? What's happened?" Hayne asked.

Hector shook his head. "No, no," he said, breathing hard. "Nothing happened. I 'member a thing. I r-ran like the wind to get here to you befo' I fo'get."

Hayne asked Hector where he'd be most comfortable talking to Sheriff Grady. Hector said, "Big table' on bwickth, you n' me."

Allowing Hector to find his own words, Hayne watched out for the signs of confusion; Hector's eyes would flick from side to side, like his vision went internal, to escape the feeling he described as "a headache with pinth inthide my bwain."

Hayne said to Grady, "Hector has something to share with you, Sheriff, and he asked me to write down a few words to help him remember." Looking at Hector, Hayne said, "OK, Hec, here are the three phrases: 'Last year' and 'I heard a noise' and 'Willard in Love.'"

Hector nodded. "L...latht thummer, I...I trimmed the busheth in front of the houthe. That thide, over there," he said, pointing around to the north side of the mansion.

"I heard a noithe. Like birdth in the busheth. But then I heard a *POP!* And a thcweam. Like a…laughing thcweam. Tho, I ran into the busheth by the houthe…Willard wath in there, fwooting."

Grady, taking notes, looked up.

Hayne said, "Hector means 'flirting.' It's a way of talking about what Hector calls "lovey stuff" [wovey thtuff]. He doesn't really approve of flirting."

"That'th it," said Hector. "Willard wath fwooting thomeone by the houthe and she flew' backwardth into the houthe—through the door that opened with a *POP!* They laughed and laughed. She had her feet in the air." Hector frowned. "He had hith pantth down."

"Who was it, Hector? Who was Willard with?" asked Grady.

"No. I don't know. Willard thaid, 'Keep uth and thith door a thecret, Hecto', there'th a good boy.' I…I hate it when people thay that. Like I'm a dog. But I kept Willard'th thecret tho he can fwoot more with a blonde perthon."

"She was blonde?" asked Grady.

"Oh! Yeth! I thaw blonde hair. That'th all. It was dark in there, and I thaw thtairth, to the thky, maybe."

"Did you ever go back there, Hector?" asked Grady.

"No," he said. "It'th eathy to keep a thecret, 'cauth I fo'get."

MARCUS

Marcus, who had been at the meeting with Hector and the sheriffs, took a few minutes for a sit-down at Gabe's Bench. He tried to remember who Willard toyed with last summer during *The Marriage of Figaro* events.

He remembered Willard at a party up on the hill. He played duets with the local pianist—what was her name? She only lasted one season and left for Hawaii in the fall. Margaret something. A brunette. Hmmm.

There was the blonde soloist, Sandra McDougal, but she wasn't his type. Too old. Too sure of herself. Like Kendra.

There were a couple of blondes in the orchestra: the flautist, Penelope Saunders, and the viola player, Ingrid Tomas. No, not either of them. Not sexy enough, too studious and geeky.

Marcus's mind flew around through the company assembled last season and could think of no one who might have "fwooted" with Willard Franklin in that secret place.

FOUR FOR DINNER

Marcus, Sampson, Smooch and Kendra brought their trays of dinner to the popular big table on the brick patio. They settled their plates and cutlery, glasses of wine and iced tea, and passed the salt and pepper.

Marcus said, "Is it just me, or is there a cloud over the Villa tonight?"

"Honestly, Marcus, I think it is you," said Kendra. "I'm not kidding. You have the worst job of all."

"Oh, well, that's helpful."

"No, I mean it. Look at it. Take this table full of people as an example. The rest of us, Sampson, Smooch, Kendra, we all have something creative to do. We are engaged and focused. We're picking up creative pieces all over the place. Carrying on. It helps us deal with the reality of the grief. It helps *us* get on.

"You, on the other hand, are mired in a murder. You have to deal with all the suspects, all the things that point to some dire end while we're all here going 'la la la, let's make a play.' Plus, you were hairs away from dying yourself."

"Well, when you put it that way."

Smooch said, "She's right, Marc. What would you be doing right now if Falcon Jennings had not been killed? I mean, on Monday evening at 6pm during the week of final rehearsals?"

"Well, first of all, you are making an assumption that Falcon was murdered. And…don't interrupt me…and, you're also probably assuming that if Falcon *was* murdered, it was Willard. And I'm not so sure that's right, either."

"You're not answering my question," Smooch said.

"I am answering your question. I just don't want people to conjecture. I would be home with my feet up on the coffee table, drinking a glass of Sonoma Cutrer, nibbling Cowgirl Creamery Mt. Tam cheese on a cracker and watching the sun set over the hills. Well, that's where I might have been Friday evening by this time. By Monday, I'd being doing just what we're doing now. But, with a better frame of mind."

"You are right, of course, Kendra, but I really have no choice. I am in a movie of my own making. I should have had the gumption to retire last spring. But, I made a promise to the old gents and I have to see this through. And, I *am* mired in the case. The M.U.R.D.E.R., if there was one. But in reality, it's just one more thing.

"Like Roseanne Roseannadanna said, 'Life is just one damn thing after another.' I'm in *that* place."

MARCUS IN THE TINY TEMPLE

Marcus's moments alone in the Tiny Temple had been soothing his flustered nerves for ten years. He checked the temple schedule every week to discover which times would be best; this week, for instance, the temple was free after the Sunday chanting circle and Angel Romero's yoga classes on Monday and Wednesday.

Tonight he desperately needed a good talking to by his better self. All he could think about these days were these five things:

1. The kaboom

2. The moment the chandelier hit Falcon's head (the sound!)

3. The metallic smell

4. The slammed door/like Falcon leaving

5. His own near death

And there were so many other issues to deal with; not only the Villa and its schedule but the thoughts and feelings of everyone else on the Villa Zanetta compound. He had put his own angst aside to...be there...for the rest of the company.

Maybe he should see a therapist. Too bad the men's group isn't meeting for the summer; that would be a safe environment to talk about his state of mind.

He could talk to Kendra, of course, but she has her own set of puzzle pieces to sort out. *Besides, how much does anyone want to hear about my close encounter with a chandelier?*

Combine all this with the growing feeling of burnout, mix it with a few sleepless nights and a diet of pretzels, pizza and Chinese takeout, throw in a little loneliness, and you have the plight of Marcus Brown.

After dinner, Marcus said to Kendra, "I'm going to the Temple for a sit-down. I'll check in with you later."

A "sit-down:" everyone's clue that Marcus needed to be alone. He took a regular sit-down every day, either in his office or in the Tiny Temple, or sometimes on Gabe's Bench. And who can blame him? He has been "on" since Friday at 5pm with very little sleep.

Sampson whispered to Kendra, "OK, so we're all set. Now that we know he's at the Temple, I'll go get the chorale and we'll just slither in the door and sing. This is great. Much better than his office. You're sure he won't be mad? Like we're intruding?"

"No. He'll be delighted. You'll see. I'll go in before you and put my finger to my lips, if he sees me. He'll know what I mean. You just slide in around the back wall. Tell the chorale to not speak—to be like temple mice until they sing."

Sampson smiled and went to gather his people. When the 16 singers plus Sampson returned, Kendra silently led them down the path to the Temple. She knew Marcus would be on a chair right in the middle of the small room. It was a holy and ecumenically balanced place to Marcus— it held the remnants of prayer and meditation and yoga classes, gospel singing and rabbinical meetings and every spiritual get-together there ever was in the Tiny Temple for the last fifty years.

He soaked it all up, especially right after a yoga class or meditation; he loved the lingering aroma of the temple incense. Here, he gathered his wits, pondered, breathed and, as Priscilla might say, calmed the EFF down.

His friend Kendra understood he needed cheering up, and she thought she knew what might help. One night a few years ago, they had been together at a gig. She was all strung out and nervous (she couldn't even remember why, now) and Marcus took her into a room, sat her in a chair, put his earbuds into her ears, and pushed a button on his iPod. He played her a recording of Mozart's *Ave verum corpus*, one of the most beautiful pieces of music she'd ever heard and perfect for that moment, such peace in the midst of a crisis. The vocal vibrations settled her nerves, like a hymn, or a prayer whispered in her ear by sixteen angels. The absolute beauty. The peace. The love. It whooshed into her consciousness, wholly permeating Kendra Masters 5'2", 100-pound body.

This afternoon, she'd heard the Bella Voce Chorale rehearsing that very *Ave verum corpus* in the Old Hall and she knew what to do for Marcus.

Kendra led the chorale to the door of the Tiny Temple and put her finger to her lips. She could see Marcus sitting in utter stillness on a folding chair in the middle of the room, facing a sleek art deco stained glass window shedding golden evening light. She directed the chorale around Marcus to the back and moved to where he would see her if he opened his eyes.

Settled into quiet space, his eyes stayed closed. The chorale crept around him like a band of angels. All one could hear was the lightest murmuring of wings. A few minutes of focused silence, then Sampson lifted his baton and their voices whispered into the rarefied air. Their harmonies rose and lowered, reaching up to the ceiling and into Marcus's heart and down into the very bones and nerves and cells of his body. The music reached into his spirit. He opened his eyes for just a moment and saw Kendra, who smiled at him. He closed his eyes again to stay in that special place and time with this soothing, warm hug of a prayer, the blended, beautiful voices lifting the ceiling right off the temple and carrying Marcus away with its penetrating peace. A sense of harmony and some kind of unknown-before joy overcame him, he wasn't sure why, and the chorale repeated the prayer of his heart three times before they, and Kendra, left as quietly as they came in.

HAYNE AND DIESEL CHAT

Diesel brought two glasses of sherry and handed one to Hayne sitting in his green wingback chair by the fire. Diesel sat down beside him in the other wingback and took a sip. Hector curled up in his beanbag chair with the cat, Furry Bells, nestled in beside him.

Hector had experienced a very big day. Furry Bells knew it, of course, like cats do. She cozied up against Hector's chest and let him scratch her behind the ears.

"You should be very proud of yourself, Hector. You did well today. I know it wasn't easy," Hayne said to his protégé.

Hector, back to his normal quiet self, had settled down after the agitation of the discovery this afternoon. Hector spoke more complete sentences today than he had in all his 56 years.

"It'th OK, Haynie. Poor Willard. He did thomething bad, I think."

"Well, we don't know that, Hector. But the sheriffs need all the help they can get to find out what happened to Falcon Jennings. You may have helped them get closer to the truth of this story."

"It'th not a good thtory, Haynie. Thomebody died."

'I know." Hayne looked at Diesel and said, "Don't you kind of miss the days with Gabriel? Everything was so much simpler then."

Chapter Seven
1957–1958

A Sunday Morning at the Brisk Mansion

Diesel and friend, Gabriel Michaels, sat at the little ice cream parlor table and chairs outside the rooftop conservatory, surrounded by Hayne's plants. Diesel poured coffee out of a silver pitcher and Gabriel stirred sugar into his cup. Hayne set down the plate of pastries and sausages and sat in his favorite place—the one chair left at the table, slightly overrun by a massive and fragrant Cecile Brunner rose bush.

"What an amazing event last night," Gabriel said. "Didn't you love the mime troupe? Such excellent moves. Incredible timing. I'm glad I walked through Union Square that day and saw them cavorting in the gardens. I think you should have them back at The Little Gem soon. Before they get famous and expensive."

Gabriel could tell that Diesel and Hayne were both preoccupied. He babbled on for a few minutes and then abruptly stopped. "OK. What gives, you two? There's something up, but I don't know what. You've been quiet since I got here this morning."

Diesel looked over at Hayne, who nodded and meant, "Let's get to it." Diesel said, "We want you to join us."

"I have joined you. I'm sitting here dunking my donut into this fantastic coffee."

"He means he wants you to join us at The Theaters at Villa Zanetta," said Hayne.

"Ooh, I'd love to come see it. Thanks for inviting me. I thought you'd never ask. Is it ready to be seen?"

"No, Gabe." Diesel put his hand on Gabriel's arm. "You're missing the point. We want you to go into business with us. We need a music director. We want you."

Gabriel Michaels was, for once, stunned into silence. Oh, he knew he was good, and he wanted nothing more than to soar with eagles like these. These two men were true entrepreneurial spirits in the world of theater. They were almost as good and definitely as charismatic as Herb Blau and Jules Irving over at The Actors Workshop. And into opera! Alas, they were untried except for these one-off extravaganzas they've created here at the Brisk Mansion. And, this new place of theirs was in the boonies of Sonoma! Gabe wanted city life! Sonoma was for couples and old people and families. What would he do there?

But what he said was, "Tell me more about it."

So Hayne and Diesel took Gabriel Michaels for a drive. They tried to not talk up the idea too much. They wanted Gabe to fall in love, like they did, with this piece of the earth the gods had just asked them to take care of for the rest of their lives. Part of taking care of it was to produce something beautiful, extraordinary, and grand. And for that, they needed a music director.

Gabriel Michaels held his own with any accompanist or pianist or conductor Diesel and Hayne knew or knew of. His brain stored volumes of creative information, from musical scores and operas and plays to bebop and boogie woogie. He was charming, accomplished, and well educated. His future was wide open and they knew it and wanted him to be with them.

They let the drive, the sunshine, and the madrone trees do the talking. When they arrived at the Villa, they took Gabriel on a tour. They showed him the refurbished Great Hall with its walls of polished maple, the little stage, the new carpet. They climbed the stairs to their apartment and proudly showed him their remodeled kitchen, where Rosalie Rosario rolled out pie dough and little Hector sat at the table with a grilled cheese sandwich and milk froth on his lips. Hector kicked his heels under the table and grinned at Hayne and Diesel.

"You back! You back!" And they all smiled and hugged.

They took Gabe to the barn and watched a few minutes while the carpenters put finishing touches on the puppets' proscenium in The Tiny Little Theater. The thick velvet curtains, created in miniature for The Tiny Little Theater's miniature actors, lay spread out on a table, ready for hanging.

From there, they visited the dorm, still in disarray but ripe with possibilities, Gabriel could see; nice little bedrooms for actors, staff, musicians.

"What a novel idea. Like a music and art camp for grown ups," he said.

They saw the Tiny Temple and wandered around the grounds and Hayne and Diesel spoke as subtly as they could about the future of Villa Zanetta; the plays they'd like to produce, workshops to teach and support, art shows and other events, classes and parties and performances of all kinds. Even weddings and other ceremonies.

Gabriel had never seen Hayne and Diesel so animated, and they were an upbeat pair! He listened and weighed in and pondered and fantasized.

Of course, by the time they were done, Zanetta had cast her spell and Gabriel Michaels said, "What's your plan?" He could still live in the City and be a part of this.

Hayne Williams and Diesel Edwards and Gabriel Michaels thus began the conversation and the creative partnership that would last for thirty years.

On this very day in October, 1957, the Villa Zanetta Triumvirate was born.

Robert "Diesel" Edwards: Stage Director

Hayne Williams: Art Director

Gabriel Michaels: Music Director

They celebrated.

ON THE STAGE IN THE GREAT HALL

"The big question is, can we do an opera on this stage?" Diesel stood on the stage in the Great Hall. Hayne and Gabriel sat on two chairs on the newly carpeted floor. Diesel opened up his baritone voice and sang a few lines of "Some Enchanted Evening," which he would ever remember as the song that spilled out of him on the day they found Villa Zanetta.

Many times over the years Diesel would walk into the Old Hall and, if it was dark or empty, sing a few lines and remember that vivid moment.

Gabriel said, "I didn't know you had that voice!"

"I don't really. I'm out of practice."

"Well, you should get in practice, because that's beautiful."

"Gabriel, you'll probably only hear him sing at garden parties and that is if he's very drunk, which has only happened once since I've known him," said Hayne. "Diesel gave up singing, *and* dancing, actually—he's a beautiful dancer—for the other side of the curtain. He won't listen."

"Hmph. That's too bad. Maybe someday we can change his mind. Well, we can certainly do an opera, as long as there aren't too many characters. The stage isn't big enough for a huge production. And your orchestra has no pit, so they'd have to take up seating space on the floor. You have to work within your confines, here. What did you have in mind?"

Diesel said, "A shortened version of *Cosi fan tutte*."

"Ha. Perfect. I can see it already. Do I get the honor of conducting *Cosi*?" asked Gabriel.

"We're hoping you will," Diesel said.

Hayne said, "Tell me the story."

Gabriel got up and went onto the stage with Diesel, where they acted out the entire first act: the two silly sisters and then their boyfriends, those two arrogant soldiers, and the meddling friend who said women couldn't be trusted and the conniving maid who helped cook up a plan to prove it. They stuck their fingers across their upper lips, like pretend mustaches, to transform the arrogant soldiers into the fake Albanians who then wooed the sisters. They did every part and sang little bits of arias and rolled around pretending to be dying, like the pretend Albanians in the story pretended to be dying.

Later, they all sat down at the table in Diesel and Hayne's Villa apartment to eat the apple pie Rosalie Rosario had made for them that morning. Hayne sipped tea. Diesel toyed with a glass of sherry. Gabriel told a story about a time he directed a short version of *Cosi*, with no orchestra, just two pianos, which sounded quite doable to Diesel as their first performance at Villa Zanetta. He thought about where they would get another piano and who would be the other pianist besides Gabriel.

And then Hayne's mind grasped what he'd been trying to remember all day. "Oh, my glorious God in the sky!" he blurted. He jumped up from the table and said, "I'll be right back." He skipped out the door and headed for the Barn. Hector, playing in the dirt where his father was planting Azaleas, said, "Woosh! A birdie flew by." And in just a few minutes, Hayne flew by again, back in the door with some old papers in his hand. He handed the translation of *The Deceived Women* to Diesel. "This is the same story," he said to Diesel.

And it surely was. Diesel, amazed by this, said, "How in the world did you ever come across this? It's a gem." As he handed it to Gabriel, he said, "An English translation of the 16th century storyline that became *Cosi fan tutte!*"

And that's when Hayne knew what *he* and his puppets would perform at the opening event of The Tiny Little Theater in the Barn. He's been waiting for this for ten years.

OCTOBER

LA

To further Hayne's knowledge of *Cosi fan tutte* and opera in general, Diesel bought three tickets and took Gabe and Hayne to see *Cosi* at the San Francisco Opera.

Well! The stage itself took Hayne to the moon. The proscenium, entirely in gold, knocked his socks right off his feet; gold curtains, gold walls, gold-leafed trim. That alone glowed in Hayne's creative mind for weeks. He learned to love opera right then, before the music started, before the soloists appeared, before anything happened at all. He settled into his seat and prepared to be amazed. And he was not disappointed. He read every word of the translation, watched the musicians in the pit, drank up the colors and the costumes and the glam. Hayne wallowed in opera after that, and took every chance to see and hear a performance. His sketchbook filed up with proscenium ideas and set designs.

HAYNE GOES HOME

While in Los Angeles for the *Cosi* auditions, Hayne visited Fatty Wills. He arrived unannounced, early enough to catch her before she opened the Ice Queen at 11 (Fatty had no phone, of course). Hayne had not been to the Ice Queen or the trailer in over a year.

Looking at the state of his mother's trailer and the general dishabille of her person, Hayne could see she'd not spent the money he sent on her own behalf.

When questioned, Fatty said, "Oh, my boy. I gave some to Stanley, he needed a new tooth. And, Jerry the Juggler, you remember Jerry,

well, he got the cancer, and, well, you know, I had to help him, and…
well, I don't really need anything…"

"That's utterly crazy. This trailer is ancient, you are still slinging burgers, you do nothing to improve your life. Fatty, please, what can I do to make it better? You don't do anything. Why don't you spend any money on yourself? I mean, lovely for Jerry and all, but you could have lived on that money for months."

"And, what? Quit the Queen? What would I do?"

"I don't know, Fatty. Anything. You could do anything."

"No. I couldn't do *anything*, Hayne, and you know it. I'm already doing what I know how to do. You don't need to do things for me, Hayne, really."

"Oh, but I do. I can't stand that you won't even fix up the trailer. You could have new sheets, or new curtains, at least."

"But, I don't care about those things. You do."

"Well, what do you care about?"

"Oh, I don't know. Maybe I'd like to have a cat. It's been lonely here since you've been gone."

"You won't let me fix up the trailer?"

"No. Buy me a big ol' TV in a console." Pointing to the space next to the sink, she said, "Look, we could put it right there. I'd like to watch *Gunsmoke*."

Things were quiet in the trailer for a moment. Fatty laid back in her recliner, exhausted by this conversation. Hayne sat on the edge of his old and still rumpled bed and noticed that Fatty's ankles were swollen and puffier than ever. And she walked with more difficulty; over-worked knees, he supposed.

"Hayne," his mother said. "I know yer happy up north and that's good. I'm glad. But ya can't change me to fit you. I am who I am. What's that saying, 'Ya can't make a silk purse out of a sow's ear'? I'm the sow, and there ain't no silk in sight. I know you won't bring yer friend here. That's as may be. But, you gotta go on and do yer life. You gotta stop worrying about me. You know, I've been right here all my little fat life. I'll die here. Probably right here in this chair. So, go on, make some-thing' of yerself and send me pictures. I love yer pictures."

While Diesel and Gabriel were ordering the Blue Plate Lunch Special at the new and trendy Pann's Coffee Shop in LA, Hayne was getting his heart broken at the Ice Queen Concession on the Santa Monica Pier. He knew his mother was dying, and he knew she knew it, too. Her face had lost its steaming, red-glowing luster, her eyes were tinged in green. Her hair hung in thin wisps. Fatty's poor knees and ankles were just not up to the job anymore.

Hayne took a cab to the Melrose Theater, where the auditions for *Cosi fan tutte* were underway. He sat down next to Diesel, currently wincing at a voice ever so slightly off key.

What was Hayne going to do about Fatty Wills? He couldn't just walk off and leave her there, by herself in the trailer. Jerry the Juggler was in a home for recovery of "the cancer," and Glenda had left him for a traveling salesman. Pete the Pilgrim died in a halfway house about three years ago and Sandbox Sam was in worse shape than Fatty.

Hayne got a glimpse of Sam as he left the Ice Queen. He sat in his old chair in front of his tent/store with a ratty blanket around his shoulders. He was coughing. Also unshaven, shoeless and badly in need of a bath. His table of surf-side baubles looked sparse and pitiful; no Glenda-knitted scarves or garments to soften the harsh and dreary scene. The neighborhood itself slowly upgraded and changed around these two relics of the past.

Hayne hardly noticed the auditioning singers, barely tracked the audition at all. Fatty Wills occupied his mind. There were so many conflicting thoughts, Hayne hardly kept up with his own head. Fatty loved him in her own way, he knew, and he supposed he loved her, at least he appreciated what she tried to do for him, which was generally in the form of a milkshake or burger. And she did bring home that trunk. But, he had no idea where she came from, how old she was, who her people were, if she had any siblings, and if she even knew who had fathered him, a longtime frustration for Hayne, who asked repeatedly. He thought it might be Jerry. Fatty never, ever changed her position. "That's not for you to worry about," she'd say. "It don't make no nevermind."

That just made him more curious. She never did produce a birth certificate for him, although he knew she had one, somewhere. He didn't know where she was born, much less where *he* was born.

The next morning, Hayne went to the school, wondering why he'd never thought to ask the nuns a few questions. They seemed to have known his mother for years. Maybe she went to St. Michael's, too. Maybe they could help her.

At the front desk, Hayne told a young novice he needed a St. Michael's history lesson; there was a person he needed to investigate. *That's good,* he thought. *I sound official, like a detective.* He was directed to the convent next door and told to see Sister Agnes, keeper of the St. Michael's history and alumni stories. Hayne waited about fifteen minutes; Sister Agnes was at prayers.

When she emerged, he thought she was an ancient elf hiding out in nun's garb. She was tiny, very wrinkled and hunched over. When she walked, her head bounced a little, like a goat leading a herd behind her. Her small face and body were draped in the full habit of the Dominicans: long white tunic, black leather belt, black stockings and brogans, voluminous black veil flowing behind her little bobbing head. Her shiny black rosary clacked at her waist, the silver cross dangled and bounced against her knee as she moved.

Although Hayne was not tall, when she looked up at him she had to lean back and hold onto a chair. She asked him to sit back down on the bench in the hall.

When they were at more or less eye level, she said to Hayne, "How can I help you, young man?"

He said, "I'd like to know about my mother, Charlotte Williams, otherwise known as Fatty Wills."

Sister Agnes looked at him, eye to eye. "So. You've finally come."

"I beg your pardon?" said Hayne.

"You're Hayne Williams. I've been waiting for you."

HAYNE AND SISTER AGNES

Hayne just stared at the old nun. In this moment, Hayne dropped all expectations about his life forever and decided to just follow the clues. He was, indeed, gobsmacked. Sister Agnes had a lot of explaining to do.

Sister Agnes took Hayne by the hand. She led him into a little sitting room. She bid him sit on the sofa and went into a tiny kitchenette to make tea.

Funny. In all the years Hayne had attended St. Michael's, he never once went into the convent. He considered it a "house full of penguins," and he had enough of nuns in the school.

He envisioned taciturn women living in "cells" along dark gray corridors, with low light and a mournful hum in the background. This was a marble mansion full of fine furniture and Asian rugs, even nic-nacs. Hayne never expected nuns to have rooms full of nic-nacs. And the light was bright via the big open windows. The curtains fluttered gently.

Sister Agnes came over to the sofa with two cups of tea and set them on the table.

She said, "I hoped you'd get here before I die. I'm not getting any younger, you know."

"Sister, who are you?" Hayne finally blurted out. "You've got to tell me what I've stumbled upon here."

"You haven't 'stumbled' upon anything. These things just have their own time. I lost track of you when you left St. Michael's and went to Pasadena. Glenda kept me informed, until she left town with that new man. But, I knew you were in school. That made me glad. And, I just knew you'd be here, eventually."

"Why?"

"Because you'd want to know things."

"Why didn't you come find me?"

"Because I promised Charlotte I wouldn't go looking for you. So, I figured, if you ever showed up here on your own, I could tell you everything. That wouldn't be lying. I knew you'd come. Everyone has a story, Hayne. I've waited a long time to tell you yours. How old are you now?"

"I'm 26, Sister."

"Well then. I've waited 26 years. First, tell me about yourself. I want to know what you've done, how you've prospered. You're better dressed than you used to be. And you look, well, healthy. And happy. Glenda used to tell me about how sick you were all the time."

"Glenda taught me to knit," Hayne said.

"Yes. I know that, too. I know about your puppets. And I know that great man, that saint, Gilmor Brown, took you under his wing. What happened next?"

Hayne was glad he had an hour before meeting Diesel and Gabe.

After Hayne had exhausted himself with details of his life, he hoped she'd get on with his past, but she hopped up and told him to wait there, she'd be right back.

She returned, wrapping a leather apron around her crooked middle. The silver cross wiggled at the bottom of the apron. She said, "I forgot, I've got nuns in the workshop. I've got to go before they hurt themselves." Hayne looked at her quizzically. "Ah. You see, I'm kind of in charge of the studio/workshop, where the nuns get to make candles and bang nails into things. Right now they are building little boxes."

Sister Agnes handed Hayne an envelope. "Better than my taking up another hour telling this story, here is a letter I wrote to you a few years ago and never sent. You'll find it all in here. You can write to me if you have any questions."

Hayne just nodded.

Sister Agnes agreed to keep an eye on his mother. They contrived to help Fatty via the convent—Hayne would send money to Sister Agnes, Sr. Agnes had a novice she could send on a mission to befriend "Charlotte" (he'd have to get used to that!) and bring her things: a bag of size 10X clothes, or maybe dinner some night. "Maybe a new towel or a curtain," said Hayne. "Not too soon. So she doesn't think it's from me. And if she needs meds? Or help? You'll call me.

"And, do you think you could find her a cat?"

COSI AUDITIONS
MELROSE THEATRE, LA

Hayne was just in time for the last *Cosi* audition of the day at the Melrose. He stopped in the back and saw his partner in the thick of the things he loved best. Diesel sat in the 20th row, Gabriel behind him, leaning over the seat in front, whispering in D's ear. They watched the soprano warble her way through two of her best arias. Hayne's admittedly uneducated ear thought she might make the cut.

Diesel turned around to say something to Gabe and noticed Hayne. He waved and touched his heart. Hayne waved back and touched his heart. D turned around to face the singer.

Hayne was thrown into the past, spending this time in LA. He saw himself in the back room of the Ice Queen, or in the trailer. A small, sad boy. A small, sad, sick, raggedy boy. He leaned against the back wall of the Melrose, on this fine day in December, 1957, and skimmed back through his life on the road to here.

Being an artist, and a visual person, he clearly saw significant moments in his life like a mural, from the trailer and Ice Queen, the only home he'd ever known, to a foster "home" in Pasadena, not a home at all—more of a flimsy tent over his head while he discovered the world through Gilmor Brown and the Pasadena Playhouse. Then, the College and the summer workshop at the San Francisco Institute of Art that turned Hayne around a corner smack into the world of Robert DeWayne Edwards. And let's not forget that moment with Queen Elizabeth and Aunt Hazel at the wedding of the third cousin once removed. Then, the profoundly disturbing visit with Fatty/Charlotte, yesterday. And Sister Agnes! Sister Agnes!

He could paint a 12 foot wall depicting his defining moments. This was a big one. He didn't know why. He *did* know why. It wasn't just Robert and the Ballroom and the Villa, although all that was pretty heady and exciting. But, here was Sister Agnes. He had a feeling he might be close to solving the mystery of Hayne Endicott Williams! Fatty used to tell him she chose his middle name out of a book, but Hayne was sure it had some kind of meaning. He wanted it to have meaning.

When he was a little kid, he imagined the Endicotts were a family from Connecticut. He liked the sound of Connecticut. He imagined that the Endicotts were his real family and that one day they would swoop in and pick him up and return him to his people in Connecticut. Then he'd feel badly, because he didn't want to hurt Fatty's feelings, even in his mind.

While he was thus ruminating, D and Gabe finished up and said their thank yous and good byes. They walked up the aisle to meet Hayne, and they all went out on the town to have a good dinner and talk about art and music, but not mothers.

Hayne understood he could never take his mother out of himself, and he had to let her be whoever she really was inside all that protective fat. He did get it, kind of. But, he still wasn't planning to take Robert DeWayne Edwards to the Santa Monica Pier.

Sister Agnes looked after his mother until Fatty died of liver failure just a few months later. Hayne was deeply saddened, but not surprised. The good Sister Agnes sent him her effects; a key to a safe deposit box in Los Angeles and an unopened package of sheets. Hayne donated the console TV to the convent. He gave the sheets away to a sad looking bum on the street. He sent the safe deposit box key back to Sister Agnes with the request that she retrieve whatever was in the box and send it to him in Sonoma. He thought he might never go back to LA or the Santa Monica Pier.

Hayne tried not to imagine Fatty sitting in that recliner, dying alone in her Covered Wagon trailer. It was the saddest thing he ever thought of and he couldn't help but feel guilty that he didn't *make* her do something, knowing he could never *make* her do anything.

Hayne didn't open the letter. It all had to wait until he had the courage…and the time…and the focus to take it all in.

JUNE 1958
THE LAUNCH

Diesel and Gabriel prepared their streamlined version of *Cosi fan tutte*. At lunch in the apartment one day, Gabriel presented Hayne and Diesel with arias and duets to be cut from the performance, which Diesel carefully looked at while Gabe explained his reasoning.

Gabe, who could never sit still for more than ten minutes unless he was at the keyboard, paced around the room while he spoke, his expressive hands waving, fingers constantly moving, like air piano. He said, "We're doing it in English, which is very upcoming, and I like that. And it's a sweet and very charming English translation, you know, by Ruth and Thomas Martin, who are very romantically inclined in their speech. It's quite beautiful. But, our band is two pianos, not an orchestra. And there's not much room. And it's a long opera, almost three hours!

"So. Here's what I think. I believe Act One is OK as is—the characters all get to sing about their personalities and struggles, so we'll just cut the two men's duet. Then, a few internal cuts within the recitatives. Nothing more. In Act Two, we can eliminate the opening recitatives with the women and Despina's aria. Sorry to our Despina, but I think we will be happier without it.

144

"Then we'll cut what I call the Big Five: it's a series of arias for tenor, soprano, baritone, tenor, alto, numbers 24 through 28. We'll cut all of them and their connecting recitatives.

"So now Act Two looks like this:

Despina's aria is cut,

we keep the duet where the women decide to go for it,

the men serenade the women (with chorus),

they have a little party,

then the alto-baritone duet,

the five solo arias sequence is cut,

keep the soprano-tenor duet,

wedding (with chorus),

and the complete finale."

Hayne smiled and set the cut list aside, remembering D's explanation of a recitative: the "talky, narrative bits, the *then they did this and then they did that* parts."

Hayne went to the Barn to meet with his people. In the Barn, It was *all* emoting. Hayne performed all dialogue and every voice. No narrator, no such thing as a recitative. There was no time for an explanation. In puppet theater, it is all action all the time.

A CROWN FOR THE QUEEN

Hayne's fantasy circus setting of *The Deceived Women* turned Fiora and Drusina into Harlequin tight tope walkers. Tristano and Francesco have recently joined the circus as clowns. Their friends, the Golden Snub-Nosed Monkey named Colombina (who called herself Roxie) and the Zebra who went by the name of Arlecchino, cause all the trouble.

Hayne sat on the front brick patio, painting the face of the Golden Snub-Nosed Monkey named Colombina (who called herself Roxie). He worked out the timing of his script in his mind. He pondered his setting in a circus and added some new dialogue. Lost in creative thoughts, he didn't notice the messenger in uniform shirt, shorts and knee socks until he was up on the patio five feet away.

"Oh!" Hayne said.

"Telegram, sir," said the messenger. "For Mr. Robert Edwards or Mr. Hayne Williams. Is that you, sir?" The messenger came towards Hayne, who took off his painting gloves, signed the receipt on the deliverer's clipboard and opened the envelope. "Thank you!" he called, as the messenger skipped down the steps.

TO: ROBERT EDWARDS/HAYNE WILLIAMS
ABOARD USS MATSONIA JUNE 4.
ARRIVING SF FROM HONOLULU ON USS MATSONIA JUNE 8.
COMING TO SEE YOU AND OPERA OPENING.
AT SONOMA MISSION INN JUNE 9-14. WILL CALL.
KISSES AND HUGS. ELIZABETH AND HAZEL

Holy Mary, Hayne said to himself. *They'll be here tomorrow.*

Later, Hayne said to Diesel, "OK. Now I'm nervous. I wasn't really nervous before, just excited. But your mother and Aunt Hazel. I mean, could they have planned a more inopportune moment to drop in? Shall we have to entertain them while we piece together the first big event of Villa Zanetta? Will they be disappointed? Will…"

"Haynie, stop this. Mother and Aunt Hazel are fine, you know that. They won't interfere. What's wrong? Really?"

"Nothing is wrong. It's just that I wanted everything to be perfect before Elizabeth and Hazel came to visit. Our apartment is a mess, the dorm isn't anywhere near ready, the grounds need a lot of work…" Diesel just looked at Hayne in that way; his brow furrowed and you could see a question mark appear in the thought bubble over his head.

Hayne stopped himself. *What are you doing, Hayne? D's Right. Stop.*

He stopped imagining the worst, but Hayne didn't stop thinking about the differences in their mothers. Fatty was dead and he hadn't opened the letter from Sister Agnes and now here were these two magnificent, strong, and powerful women coming to see what he and Diesel were up to. Of course, he was nervous. He had a lot to work out in his mind.

But, Elizabeth and Hazel never seemed to be anything like what Hayne imagined. Oh, he remembered them, all right, and held them close to his heart these days. They had opened up to him in the most trusting and beautiful way, he couldn't deny it. But, he had the idea they'd be high maintenance—women with servants and Jungle Red polish on pointy nails usually were.

Surprise, surprise, Haynie. After Aunt Hazel helped Hayne sand the old paint off some boards and a gloved Elizabeth finished digging out the front garden beds and planting 25 Gerbera Daisies and four containers of bougainvillea, they all met in the apartment for tea and sherry. The next day Elizabeth helped Paul Farmdale plant some fruit trees. "No, no," he heard Elizabeth scold Paul. "Not like that. Be gentle with the roots. Like this."

On the third day of their visit (and Opening Night, to boot!) Elizabeth took Diesel away to lunch and to a notary to sign some papers. Hayne was mildly miffed, and thought it odd and distracting that she chose this day to do business.

Hazel brought a cup of tea to Hayne where he was painting and said, "I thought you'd like to talk. I'll fill you in on the business that had to be accomplished while we are here."

Hayne accepted the tea. "Business?" he asked.

"Yes, it really is business, and a boon for you and Robert, but Elizabeth asked me tell you the details. We are here on somewhat of a mission."

"OK," said Hayne, putting his brush down.

"Elizabeth is selling EDEC."

"Oh my! What prompted that?" asked Hayne.

"Well, here's the truth, friend. It's good news and bad news. It's good news because it will make your partner a very rich man. The bad news is that Elizabeth has decided to sell because she has been diagnosed with a slow growing cancer. She does not want to have the new chemical treatments, they are risky, and without them, she might live up to ten years. She wants to be free to travel and, well, just do whatever we want. She is talking to your Robert to make sure just one more time that he wants nothing to do with EDEC."

"I'm so sorry to hear this about Elizabeth, Aunt Hazel. Sorry for us all, but especially sorry for you. Your best friend of all time."

"Yes. Well. Yes, it is true. And I need not explain to you that I will be with her all the way.

"I know that, Hazel," replied Hayne.

"We've been together since the eighth grade, Hayne. I can't imagine my life without her."

"I understand," said Hayne.

"Yes, I rather think you do. And, I want to tell you something else. I want to tell you about my history, because I think it will make you feel better about yours in relation to the Edwards family."

"Mine?" said he.

"Yes, dear Hayne. I know you don't talk about your mother or your past, and you've only offered little hints that you might have had an unusual childhood and upbringing. No, Diesel has never told us anything, but I have eyes, and I have a heart, and I come from a very, very different world myself, so I think I understand."

Hayne was thoughtful. "I'm not sure any of you would understand."

"You'd be surprised," said Hazel.

"You are constantly surprising me, Aunt Hazel."

THE STORY OF AUNT HAZEL AND HER BROTHER, MONTY

"Our mother's name was Giselle Dubois. We believe she arrived in New York on a ship from Paris in about 1898, following a promise of work as a bookkeeper in the garment business. She spoke no English, and was sequestered with other young Parisian girls who also understood they were going to the United States to work 'in offices.' Well, those offices turned out to be bedrooms, where they were stripped of their clothes, given flimsy nighties, and were locked in their rooms, forced to pleasure many men in one day. My mother lived like this for three years, until she became pregnant with my brother, Monty. She was immediately thrown out on the street with a bag of clothes. It was her fault, of course, that she was pregnant.

"She still had little English, as there had not been much need to speak in the bedroom, and her meals were delivered, and she bathed under the supervision of a matron. White slavery proliferated in Chicago in the early 1900s, and poor Giselle fell into the trap.

"A pregnant French girl on the street? Well, you can imagine her vulnerability. On the street she met Harry Balding, who promised her shelter and took her home. He cared for her and helped her have the baby and gave little Raul to the Chicago Orphan Asylum before Giselle could even hold him in her arms. Raul was adopted by the Edwards family and named Robert DeMontfort Edwards. I'll tell you how I know this in a moment.

"Balding, promising marriage, groomed Giselle back to health and then sold her to a 'resort,' where she was again pressed into service and could not get free. When she became pregnant again, she was of no use, but the kindly madam sent her to Ada and Minnie Everleigh at the Everleigh Club in downtown Chicago. Ada Everleigh took pity on pregnant girls, especially the ones with possibilities. They took Giselle in, she had her baby, and Ada, too, sent the baby to the Chicago Orphan Asylum. Call it a coincidence, or call it kismet, but I, too, was adopted by the DeMontfort Edwards family, and given every chance of a life.

"We know all this because my mother, Giselle, reluctantly agreed to let me go, and wrote a long letter in French containing the above facts, which my adoptive mother set aside and gave to me upon my 13th birthday. Giselle had no idea that both of her children were adopted by the same family, but we were able to find this out with some sleuthing.

"We do not know what happened to Giselle. By the time I was old enough to read the letter, the houses of prostitution like the Everleigh Club were dismantled and the women dispersed or deported. The heyday of tolerated prostitution in Chicago was coming to a close.

"I never liked my brother, Monty. He grew up spoiled and secretive and ashamed of our mother and our origins. He was haughty and kind of a bully. When he married Robert's mother, well, it was just perfect for Elizabeth and me and we put up with Monty, for Robert's sake and ours. Elizabeth will never tell young Robert these details, but it is good for you to know them to put your own origins in perspective.

"My adopted father, DeMontfort Edwards, was a kind but weak man. Mabel Edwards ruled the roost and treated Monty like a little prince. I didn't mind her neglect. I didn't mind at all being left alone. The only thing I didn't like was when Monty pulled my hair, or pinched my arm or once locked me in a closet with a live squirrel. No, I never liked Monty much.

"So, now you know. I have told you this so you feel more at ease and maybe won't worry so much about whatever it is you hide about your upbringing. If you want to tell me anything, I am all ears, with no judgment whatever."

And so it was that Hayne found himself spilling his entire story to Aunt Hazel. It took an hour, and when they heard Diesel's car coming up the driveway, Hazel said, "And you haven't read the letter?"

"No."

"Funny that we both received letters. Women are more prone to the truth and the longing to tell it. The truth is the greatest equalizer, you know. Pretty much everyone I know has a story in their background swept well under the rug."

"I'll let you know what Sister Agnes's letter says when I have the guts to open and read it. Thank you, Hazel. You are right. Thank you for telling me your story."

"And thank you for trusting me with yours, Hayne. And for loving my nephew. He's lucky to have you."

Diesel and Elizabeth arrived with little Hector, who had been waiting for them in the driveway, clutching a box. They all sat down on the patio and the seven year old Hector gave the box he had been carrying to Auntie Queen. It was wrapped in newsprint and tied with garden twine. "Thith ith fo' you, Auntie Queen, 'cauth I never knew a queen befo.'"

Elizabeth carefully opened the box and brought out a paper crown covered with gold foil stickers. She placed it carefully on her head and proudly wore it for the rest of the day.

JUNE 11-14, 1958
THE FIRST OFFICIAL EVENT AT VILLA ZANETTA

Thursday
Launch Party for 50
Puppet Entertainment in the
The Tiny Little Theater in the Barn
Directed by Hayne Williams
Dinner by Chef Butch Barclay

Friday Evening
Hayne Williams's Puppet Version of
The Deceived Women
The Tiny Little Theater in the Barn

Saturday Evening & Sunday Afternoon
Cosi fan tutte - W.A. Mozart
The Great Hall
Stage Director: Robert Diesel Edwards
Music Direction and Piano: Gabriel Michaels
Second Piano: Bethany Davis

Thursday evening, the seats in The Tiny Little Theater in the Barn were replaced with tables and chairs and set for a five course dinner for 75. The rental piano (smaller and easier to move than Diesel's grand) sat in a corner by the tiny little stage.

Hayne and company prepared their little Baroque thespian puppets for their first appearance on any stage, and the two *Cosi fan tutte* sopranos warmed up to present a little taste of what was to come on Saturday.

Butch's five course dinner was presented:

Passed hors d'oeuvre and champagne
The "new" Limestone "Butter" Lettuce Salad
with French Vinaigrette
Butternut Bisque
Boeuf Bourguingnon, Parsley Potatoes,
Fresh English Peas
Creme Brûlée

Wine was served, and coffee. Hector sat with Diesel, Auntie Queen and Aunt Hazel at the table closest to the stage. Hector held his special puppet Guiliano in one hand and Teddy the Bear in the other. His eyes were wide with joy. He squirmed in his chair, waiting impatiently. Hector could hardly wait until he was tall enough and old enough to be the hands of the "puppetth."

When the guests picked up their spoons for the Creme Brûlée, Hayne squeezed Hector's hand and snuck backstage. The baroque puppets came to life in Hayne's Tiny Little Theater. Each voice was Hayne's, each movement through his movements and, although Hayne longed for a few more hands, the little synopsis of the play that would be performed in full the next night went off without a hitch.

Cosi fan tutte (All Women are Like That)
Synopsis by Robert DeWayne (Diesel) Edwards
Villa Zanetta Program Book 1958
(Accompanied by the R. & T. Martin English translation)

Scene 1: In a coffeehouse
Two soldiers, Ferrando and Guglielmo, express their certainty of the faithfulness of their beloved fiancees, Dorabella and Fiordiligi, respectively. But, their friend, Don Alfonso, declares that there is no such thing as a faithful woman. He claims that All Women are Like That and cannot be trusted and he can prove it. He wagers with the two soldiers that their girlfriends can be easily seduced.
They make a plan. Ferrando and Guglielmo will pretend to be called off to war but will return in disguise and try to woo the other's lover.
They go to tell the sisters and the sisters wish them safe travels. They are bid farewell and the men sail off to sea. The sister are sorry to see them go. Alfonso predicts the sisters will soon be unfaithful.

Scene 2: In the sisters' home
The sisters lament that their lovers have been called away. The maid, Despina, advises them to take new lovers. Do the sisters really think that their soldiers will be faithful to them? Ha! Soon, the soldiers appear disguised (with mustaches) as foreign Cowboys, in our production. They toy with the women, express their love, the women resist. Despina, that traitor, working in league with the plan, gets the fake mysterious cowboys to go to the sisters and pretend to take poison in despair over the sisters lack of love. Despina comes in disguised as a doctor with a magic remedy—a magnet to relive the fake

cowboys of the fake poison. They pretend to hallucinate, demand kisses to revive them. They revive enough to continue their fake pursuit of the two sisters.

Act 2

Scene 1: In the sisters' bedroom
Despina urges them to relax and enjoy the cowboys and they all agree that a flirtation would do no harm while their lovers are away. It will help them pass the time. One said to the other, "I'll take the brunette."

Scene 2: In the Garden
Much wooing and flirting ensues.

Scene 3: In the sisters' bedroom
Much more flirting. The sisters finally surrender. A wedding is planned and Alfonso gloats over his prediction. *Cosi fan tutte.* All women are like that.

Scene 4:
A fake double wedding between the sisters and the fake cowboys is in process. Despina, oh the despicable Despina, pretends to be a notary and is creating the fake marriage contract. The fake cowboys leave for a moment and the soldier lovers return from the war and pretend to get furious when the fake notary shows them the fake marriage contract.
The women begin right here to lament their ways. The soldier lovers leave in a huff. Then the soldier lovers return with their cowboy disguises. Despina is revealed, and, although the sisters have been duped, they actually apologize to the men for being unfaithful and they all get married and live happily ever after.

On Saturday night, Hayne took an actual seat in the back of the Great Hall with Elizabeth and Aunt Hazel to watch *Cosi fan tutte.* But, on Sunday afternoon, he watched from backstage right, out of the way of the soloists and performers, but with a view of their comings and goings, their set up, their backstage selves, costume changes, different ways of handling nerves and distractions. From this day forward, Hayne had a regular backstage seat with his name on it: up close to the action, to absorb the sounds, the smells and the colors, to be permeated with the music and enveloped by the beauty.

The performing arts center which would become known as The Theaters at Villa Zanetta had begun. They were on their way.

THE MORNING AFTER CLOSING NIGHT

On the Monday morning after the Sunday night wrap party, Diesel slept in. Aunt Hazel and Elizabeth were on their way back to Chicago to map the rest of their lives. Hayne sat in his window seat with a cup of steaming coffee, looking at Sister Agnes's handwriting on the plain white envelope.

OK. Here I am. The moment has come. I can wait no longer. I am afraid and elated at the same time. What will I find? What truth to be uncovered? What road did Charlotte Penelope Williams take to get to the Ice Queen? To me? To becoming Fatty Wills? Am I crazy to hope for any real explanation, or will I still know nothing and keep my past forever buried in the Santa Monica sand?

To Be Delivered to
Hayne Williams
From Sr. Mary Agnes, OP

He was downright afraid to open this Pandora's Box of a letter. He had carried it in his shirt pockets for months, never knowing quite when the moment would come to dive into this world Sister Agnes was about spill out to him on paper.

Short and to the point communications came to Hayne from Sister Agnes over the few months after they met. The 80 year old nun's notes told him Charlotte was "well-enough," or "slowing down," and that she had been "delivered a kitten she named Barney." Sister Agnes said Charlotte hired a girl to do most of the Ice Queen work, which dwindled anyway, now that Currie's Ice Cream Store and a few other more trendy burger places thrived in the neighborhood.

On the QT, Sister Agnes discovered that Charlotte's boss, Andy, the same guy who hired her and kept her on all these years, even as the place deteriorated, was heard to say, "When Fatty dies, I'm tearing that place down. It's over."

A young novice enlisted to visit Charlotte regularly and provide a few things "from the holy spirit." Odd, to Sister Agnes; Charlotte seemed to accept the gifts from God, but not her son.

And then, Fatty/Charlotte died quietly in her sleep in the recliner, just as she predicted. Sandbox Sam found her after waiting an hour for Fatty to show up in the lean-to for their nightly party of two. All their friends were gone. Just the two of them drank beer and played some cards, every night. But it wasn't the same. And now, Sam was alone.

Perhaps it was better that Hayne waited to read the letter about his mother until after her death.

St. Michael's Convent, Los Angeles California
September 23, 1950
Dear Hayne,

If you are reading this, it means you have come to see me or I am dead. I hope it's the former. I still have the Lord's work to do in this world. As of this day of September 23, 1950, I am in good health and expect to keep on for a few years, bringing solace to a few and hope to a few more.

This letter is a chronology of events in the life of Charlotte Penelope Williams because she is unwilling or unable to share this information herself. Charlotte knows her own mind but does not read or write well. And so, I will put down these details on paper so you will have them, eventually. Mind you, it is not a window into the inside of Charlotte's head, or her heart, or her soul. That is another matter.

Charlotte came to the convent as an orphan postulate in 1920 at the age of ten. Her parents, Mathilda and Roger Williams, had recently died in a fire and no relatives were found to take Charlotte, who was a difficult child and seemed to leave a trail of stories strewn like dirty clothes behind her.

Charlotte's grandmother had been my best childhood friend, and I was godmother to her only child, Mathilda. When Mathilda died in the fire, the Dominicans were asked to take Charlotte in. At the time, we took a few girls each year to groom for the novitiate, to train them to be good nuns. We took in my friend's granddaughter, Charlotte.

We tried to fit Charlotte into the mold that forms a nun, but she rebelled at every corner. She was pretty then, and saucy, and attracted much attention. I must say, she made the Dominican postulate habit look sexy, and that is spoken by a nun of sixty five years.

What to do with Charlotte? She had an apathy about things we couldn't figure out. We had to coax her to change her bedding and coerce her into bathing. She didn't care about school, didn't care to read or sew or make anything. She liked to lie on the floor and count shadows. She counted blocks and stacked them up and knocked them down and stacked them up again.

When Charlotte was 17, a priest visited from Ireland. He was an unscrupulous young man and wooed the unsuspecting and innocent Charlotte into a closet and lifted the skirts of her habit. What a discovery for Charlotte! Sex became the one thing for which she perked up. She even took a bath or two.

But they were soon discovered. The young priest was disgraced and sent home. Charlotte was essentially de-robed and relieved of her commitment to be a bride of Christ. When she turned eighteen a few weeks later, she was asked to leave the convent. As a parting offer, Charlotte received $200 and a letter to the Young Woman's Club in Culver City as reference for a room.

She never made it to the YWCCC. Instead, she went downtown; she heard that's where you could disappear. She stayed with some bums until she started feeling queasy every morning and one of her bums suggested she might be pregnant.

She came back to the convent to ask my help. I almost said no, as a nun. But as her grandmother's best friend, I said yes. She was 18, true, but she made decisions as if her brain had atrophied at ten. She also said, "So that's where babies come from. I'm never having sex again. One baby is enough for me. Why didn't anyone ever tell me about babies?" She said "babies" like one might describe a pestilence.

When I asked her where she was staying, she said, "With a friend at the beach," and of course, I believed her and assumed she meant in a house at the beach. In fact, she was with a forty year old man in a tent behind a dumpster in downtown Los Angeles, but I did not know that fact until later.

When it came time for Charlotte to have her baby, I made arrangements for her to go to a home for unwed mothers in downtown LA, hoping she would give the child up to a family with the means and ability to care for him or her. She stayed long enough to have her baby and then disappeared, with you in her arms.

It took some time to find Charlotte, although we knew she wouldn't go far. She had a baby on her back and no money. Someone sighted her at the Santa Monica beach. Nuns are quite noticeable at the beach, so I asked a friend to poke around. That was back when the Santa Monica Pier was becoming quite the thing—the Hippodrome, etc.

We found your mother and baby you in the Ice Queen. She had convinced the owner of the new burger concession that she (and you) were the ones to live in the backroom and she would run the place. And she did.

Then, in 1935, the Fearless Flyers trapeze artists performed at the Hippodrome. The five of them became friends with Charlotte and played pinochle with her and Sam and the others on their nights off. When they left town, Charlotte inherited their broken down, unfixable Covered Wagon trailer. Her boss at the Ice Queen gave her ten dollars to have it towed to the back parking lot of the Ice Queen. I suppose you'll remember that. You were about seven years old. I suppose you remember living in the back room of the Ice Queen.

I've got to hand it to her, she may have grown fat and fatter and no wiser, but she kept that job and kept you in school on her own money. I'll bet you didn't know that, either. I can imagine you never even gave a thought to the money needed for your education at St. Michael's.

She visited the convent a few times, and made me promise not to take you away or come looking for you. I kept my eye on you as long as you were in school.

There is nothing wrong with Charlotte's brain. The problem is, she just doesn't care. I hope you can forgive her. I believe it is either how she was born, her wiring, so to speak, or the trauma of losing her parents was more dramatic than we thought.

There is just a piece missing in her puzzle. An empty space.

The funny thing is, though, that she cares about you. She fought to keep you, and, as she agreed, she kept a roof over your head and fed you and loves you in her way.

When you left with Gilmor Brown, it wrenched her heart. It was not easy for Charlotte to let you go. But, she has seen you grow to be a "pretty good artist" she said, and she knew you'd go nowhere living with her.

Also funny that she didn't care to educate herself, but she wants you to have opportunities, and you certainly have. She said Gilmor Brown's arrival in your life was a miracle, and that you deserve to "be somebody."

As to the man who fathered you, his name was Michael Gilley. He died in 1937 in Ireland. He never knew about you.

May the Lord Bless you and Keep you,

Sister Mary Agnes, OP

HAYNE CONSIDERS HIS LIFE

Hayne curled up alone in the corner of his window seat, like a cat gravitates to a soft blanket or a bird tucks itself up under the eaves. He wiped his eyes and considered the letter from Sister Agnes.

Imagine his mother, putting him through school! Agnes was right – he had no idea. *What kid ever thought about where the money came from for school? Wasn't school free to everyone? And my father's name was Michael and he died in 1937—the year the Bleeps were born, so, I was nine. My father's name was Michael. Presumably, I was conceived in a closet by a priest and a nun. He never knew I existed.*

Hayne was used to being alone. At the trailer, he was always alone. Even though the Ice Queen Concession sat in the middle of the middle of everything in and around the Pier, when Hayne lay in his usual rumpled sheets in the trailer, "ad nauseam," as he later learned to say, he could have been anywhere: in Alaska on a fishing boat; on a fantasy island, drinking rum in coconuts; at Carnegie Hall, puppeteering.

The dark red and chrome trailer, only seventeen feet long and nine feet wide, soon booted Hayne out of itself entirely, and he did not mind one little bit. By the time Gilmor Brown came along, Hayne was living by himself full time in the back room of the Ice Queen again. Fine with him; it had the tiny "real" bathroom.

Hayne happily left his past full of mean and ugly and yet sometimes utterly beautiful memories to go to Villa Zanetta in Sonoma. He knew and felt the deepest truth: that at the Villa, they had landed, they had come home; a most novel feeling. He'd become more accepting of Diesel's zillions; he'd be stupid to complain about that. And, besides, sitting on a couch with Diesel's arm around him, looking at photos or planning some big event, was the most secure and tender feeling Hayne had ever experienced in his life. He never thought he would ever amount anything, much less this. This was magic.

Hayne wondered if he would ever stop comparing his surroundings to the trailer. Could he ever feel completely at ease in these opulent (to him) environments? Would he stop thinking about Fatty Wills dying in her recliner all alone in a twenty two year old, seventeen foot trailer? Stop thinking about the Santa Monica Pier? And the lonely life he lived there?

And yet, *there* is where Gilmor found him. And now, because of Gilmor's astonishing scholarship, and Gilmor's belief in him, Hayne went to San Francisco and there met Robert Edwards, and now he was embarking on something new. With a partner. Two partners, artistically speaking. But, he had D. At his side.

And there was Hector.

A whole new life.

Andy did tear down the Ice Queen and had the trailer hauled to the dump. No, Hayne couldn't go back there again. He wrote a note to Sister Agnes, asking her to find some kind of home situation for Sam. Hayne would pay the rent.

Now Hayne prepared himself for the contents of the safe deposit box. What could be in it? What on earth was important enough to Charlotte Penelope Williams, aka Fatty Wills, who lived on next to nothing in a glorified metal box, to keep in a bank vault?

This is what he found:

159

January 1957

Deer Hayne,

I borrowd a portable typwritter from Madeline over at the Hippadrome to write you this letter cause of my bad handwritting. I'm not good at writting, and a bad speller, to, but I will try. I'll make it short, but I'll make it as true as I can.

I never had much and I don't deserv much, cause heres why. I made a mess at home and I think I started the fire on accident that killed my parents. I never told ~~no one~~ anyone because I wasnt sure. But I left the ~~keroseen~~ kerosene heater on near the curtains that caught on fire and burned it all down to the ground and I wasn't even good before that - my father called me a "royal pain," so I guess I'm to blame for everything.

Im to blame for you, to, and all you didn't get to have. But, yer better off now without me, even tho I tried.

Im sorry I got fat. It happened overnight and I could not fight it. It was like 400 pounds of fat attached to me and came to stay. Im sorry. Im sorry for any shame.

Im glad you have a friend. Im sorry not to meet him. Im just plain sorry for everything I ever wasn't.

Im dyin soon, Hayne. No one told me so. I just know. I can feel it, even threw all this fat. It's like, death has visitid me. He stands outside the door of the trailer, waiting. I think he is impatient.

But, here. This is for you. Here is the little book to the bank. Its not much, but I saved it for you. I never needed it. And here is your birth certifikit and a lock of your baby hair.

Hayne, you ~~were~~ are the only thing that ever mattered to me.

From

Charlotte Penelope Williams

Fatty Wills, yer mother

Hayne wiped his tears and opened the bank book. With interest compounded yearly, the final entry, in December, 1957 was $53,567.43.

160

Chapter Eight
Tuesday, June 10, 2008

Wake Up! Wake Up!

It was still dark on Tuesday morning when Marcus shot out of his bed as if it were on fire. He ran to the door, flew it open and stepped out into the mist. The blast of cool air quite suddenly woke him from the dream, like a slap from the hand of a friend. *Wake up! Wake up!*

His heart pounded and he put his hands on the wrought iron rail to steady himself. He stared into the bushes to get his bearings and realized he was on the front steps of the Villa Zanetta dorm, buck naked. He looked around. Not a soul in sight.

Marcus thanked the muses that the door didn't slam shut and lock him out. He went back to his room, got into bed, pulled the covers up to his chin and thought, *Marcus Brown. What was that about?*

The shock of waking from the dream snapped details out of his head, but he reconstructed the pieces to get to this: in the dream, he was naked and alone in a woods, sitting on a log inside a big circle scored by red paint which sloshed over the pine needles and twigs and grasses. The log he sat upon came instantly alive with giant mosquitoes and other big flying creatures—lady bugs and dragonflies, and some faeries and other elementals—which started poking at and buzzing him like hungry bombers seeking a destination. They were big and all had needle noses and those noses were focused on him. This sent Marcus flying but when he got to the edge of the circle, a force prevented his going further. Then, the force became a family of fierce bears with claws the size of his hand. He turned to run. Just before he popped awake in the night air, he sensed the bears patting his head with those great paws.

Sitting in his bed, and much calmed down, Marcus laughed. He was reminded of the Vision Quest with John Eagle two years ago on Mount Shasta.

Alone in the woods in the evening, but not naked, he had marked a six foot circle around himself with a stick in the dirt. He nestled into his sleeping bag, leaned against his chosen tree trunk, and settled in for the 48 hours of contemplation, with no food or water, hoping for a vision.

In the night, when hoot owls began to speak and the woods were alive with a chorus of rustlings, a scourge of a million mosquitoes emerged from Marcus's chosen tree trunk and swarmed around him for hours. He buried himself deep into his sleeping bag, determined to not leave the circle, thereby breaking the power of the quest. This, he decided, was his experience to endure.

And so, he rolled into a ball like a caterpillar in a cocoon and studied the insides of his eyelids. He could faintly hear the steady beat of the drum, thumped throughout the night by those friends down by the campfire "holding the space" for the Questers. *Ha*, he thought in 2008. *A group of All-Nighters.*

While he lay throughout that night in a fetal circle, something large sniffed around Marcus's bedroll. Two somethings! He felt a nudge, and then another, which woke him out of a fitful sleep. He lay still, like a part of the log itself, like a mummy, waiting and waiting, barely breathing until the nudging stopped and the very large somethings wandered away.

In the morning, he slowly emerged from his cocoon to see two brown bears about twenty yards from his spot, just waking up, yawning, and sniffing at bushes. They paid no attention to Marcus, but Marcus paid very close attention to their every move, and yet, he never felt afraid.

Forty hours later, Marcus, refreshed in spirit, unharmed in body, and hungry, returned to the camp and, while wolfing down a bagel and cream cheese, told his fellow questers and guides of his encounter with the bears and mosquitoes. It was unanimously agreed by the guides (this illustrious group included John Eagle) that Marcus had good solid Bear Medicine. These are Marcus's notes, scribbled with a ballpoint pen on the back of a paper napkin:

> Bear Medicine = strength and confidence
> bear spirit in dreams means take action,
> provide leadership in your tribe
> Bear says, time to heal
> Bear Medicine needs solitude, quiet time, rest
> Pay attention

He remembered hoping they wouldn't tell him he had Mosquito Medicine.

In the Old Hall, Marcus sat at his table with Kendra. A pot of coffee, a small pitcher of foamy milk, and basket of little rolls sat on the table and each had a piece of broccoli quiche on a plate.

"I eat better here than at home," Marcus said for no reason. Kendra, pouring coffee, said, also for no reason, "What would you be eating at home?"

Marcus laughed. "Nothing." Kendra laughed, too.

Marcus retrieved his wallet from his back pocket. He took out a folded paper napkin that looked like it had been in the wallet for quite some time.

"Can I tell you about a dream?" he asked his friend.

"Of course," she said. "You can tell me anything."

"So, I woke up this morning in a very compromising position," said Marcus.

Kendra raised her eyebrows.

"Not that kind of compromise. I woke up naked at the front door of the dorm. I leapt out of bed and, I guess, ran straight to the door and dashed outside. Kind of sleep walking. Or, sleep running. I remember I was afraid, at first. Then, when I really woke up and looked down at my naked body, I started to laugh. Not for long though. I ran back inside like a rabbit and crawled back into bed."

"And what was this dream that made you run outside in your altogether?" asked Kendra.

"Well, remember my Vision Quest at Mt. Shasta with John Eagle?"

"Oh, yes," she said. "I remember it well. It had a lot to do with bears!"

"Yes," he said. "And here is the dream – kind of and exaggerated form of the Vision Quest." Marcus described the red paint circle, the giant bugs and faeries, the big bears in the circle in his dream. He told Kendra that he felt vulnerable and yet protected. It felt like a message. He said, "And this is what I scribbled at the end of the Vision Quest, listening to John and the Elders discuss my time on the mountain. It's basically John Eagle's interpretation of my so-called Bear Medicine." He showed her the piece of paper. "It's telling me to pay attention, I think."

While she read the notes, Marcus studied Kendra's face. He liked her nose. He said to her focused profile, "I haven't thanked you for last night." Kendra looked up. He said, "That was a wonderful thing you did for me. I assume it was you. No one else would think to do that for me. You know, it is such a prayer, the *Ave verum corpus*. And you know how I feel about it. And, as I remember, you were there. In fact, I think you kissed me on the nose and left before I could thank you or say anything at all."

"I know," she said.

"Why?"

"Because...I wanted you to bask in that beauty for a bit. We didn't need to talk."

"Well. I am talking to you now. It took me right down to my knees. I think I sobbed all night. Until I dreamed of bears."

"Oh, Seriously? It made you cry all night? I'm sorry."

"Don't be sorry. It was perfect. I might even be on the road to recovery. Maybe you started it. And then, the bear family."

Kendra smiled.

Marcus said, "Kendra, why are you so incredibly nice to me? I can be such a pain in the patooty."

Kendra, about to take a bite of her quiche, put her fork down. She looked at Marcus and scrunched through a few funny faces, like she was going through a whole list of possible answers. She sighed and said, "I don't know, Marc. Because I'm your really good friend, I guess." She smiled in a mysterious way Marcus didn't understand.

Marcus and Kendra drank coffee and ate quiche and nibbled rolls, both lost in thought. Marcus glanced through the Chronicle, finding nothing to grab his attention. Kendra pretended to look through her *Cosi* notes. When it was time for Kendra to meet Diesel in the Well Lit, she gathered a few belongings together, stood up, put the long straps of her satchel over her shoulder and prepared to go. She stopped and looked at Marcus.

She said, "I'm only going to say this once and then I will never refer to it again. I love you, Marcus. I have loved you since the beginning and I will love you til the end. You may need another vision quest to wake up to this fact."

Kendra turned and left the Old Hall with as much dignity as her tight jeans could manage.

HAYNE AND HECTOR HAVE A CHAT

Hayne set the six papier mâché-headed Baroque puppets on their stands and examined their fabric bodies. "These Baroque people look good, Hector. They are ready to go again after a twenty five year hiatus."

"Hi...ay...tith?"

"Vacation. They've been relaxing in the trunk for a long, long time."

"It'th nithe, Haynie, to be with the puppetth again," said Hector, fondling the paper mâché head of Ferrando... "And thethe old guyth, I like their headth."

Hayne pick up the hot glue gun to make a head-to-body correction.

Hector said, "Haynie?"

"Yes, Hec?" Hayne put down the glue gun.

"Haynie, did your mommy go bye bye?"

"What do you mean, Hector?"

"My mommy, she went bye bye, when I wath thmall."

"Yes. That's right."

"It meanth she died."

"Sometimes it means that, Hector, but sometimes it means they just go away."

"And, my daddy went bye-bye, too."

"Yes. He died."

And Gabwiel Michaelth. He died, too."

"Yes."

"Tho, I never thee your mommy. Did your mommy go bye bye?"

"Oh, I see. Yes, Hector. My mommy died a long time ago."

"And Auntie Queen. And Aunt Hathel. I 'member when they died. I 'member it 'cauth they both died in the thame year—1975. I 'member it cauth it made me thad they didn't want to live without each other."

"Oh, yes, Hector. You are very right there."

A minute passed.

"Doeth everybody die, Haynie?"

Hayne's eyebrows raised about an inch and stayed there until he exhaled.

He looked at Hector, whose eyes were beginning to show the signs of angst.

"Yes, honey. We all die, sometime."

"I will die, too?"

"Yes, Hector. But not right now."

"Will it hurt when I die?"

"Oh, probably not, Hector. When it's your time to go, you'll be just fine."

"Doeth that mean you're D.E.A.D.?

"Yes, D.E.A.D."

"And you will die and DD will die, too. And will we aw' be jutht fine?"

"I expect so, Hector. Dying is just part of living. Everything passes. Give me those brushes, OK?"

"OK, Haynie. If you thay tho." Hector grinned at his friend.

Hayne took the brushes. Hector was quiet for a few minutes. Then, he said, "It'th like plantth. They live…and they die…and you put them in the dirt and they make more plantth."

BETTE WANTS A NAP

Bette Belle was tired after the 2:30 Act 2 rehearsal and longed for a nap before dinner. She skipped tea time with the other singers and went back to her room in the dorm; a nice room, at ground level, with a view of the woods and a sliding glass door to a little enclosed patio.

She moved to the side of her bed and began to pull her dress over her head, to get half-naked and under the covers for a snooze. She heard a voice behind her.

"Please don't scream."

She flipped her dress down and spun around and said, "Holy Mother of America! What in blazes are you doing here? How did you get in my room? Are you now a Peeping Tom?"

"Im sorry to sneak up on you but I had to."

"No, you didn't have to. You're on the lamb and I hear potentially dangerous. That little scene in the conductor's room proved that. Get out. Get out now."

"Well, I can't. I'm not dangerous. Really. But you have to help me. I have no one else to turn to."

"You still have no one to turn to, because I am not it. Get out."

"But-"

"Get out now or I will start screaming and the cops will be after you in a heartbeat. They're here. I mean it, Willard."

He leaned toward her in a gesture of pleading. She picked up the first thing she could reach on her bedside table, a little lamp with a glass shade. "I'm small, but I have a mean right arm. Go out the way you came in. You have three seconds."

Willard, defeat in his eyes, slipped out the sliding glass door, scaled the fence and was gone. He wasn't going to force her to do anything. By now, he knew he was being a jerk, but not *that* kind of jerk.

Bette Belle took her cell phone out of her purse and called Marcus Brown, who called Patrick, who called Grady Mulligan.

No Time for a Nap Today!

Bette Belle did not get her nap. Instead, she found herself explaining to the sheriffs why Willard Franklin chose to visit her by scaling the wall and entering her room through the sliding glass door.

"Well, until Saturday at about 3:47pm, I had a crush on Willard Franklin, and thought we were nearing a date situation. Boy, was I wrong."

Patrick asked, "How does one 'near a date situation,' in your mind?"

Bette Belle had calmed down her fierce stance with a cup of tea. "I have to laugh, really, considering. He has the worst reputation, but can be so persuasive in the short term. It's all in the eyes, when you're in a professional setting, like a rehearsal. A lot can be said via the eyes. His eyes said, 'I'll see you in Sonoma.' He's very dramatic. Marlene Dietrich dramatic. A professional flirt. I am susceptible to professional flirts. Especially tall, handsome, musical ones." She laughed.

"And?" asked Patrick.

"And nothing, I was up close and personal with the real Willard Franklin on Saturday and I uncrushed myself in a New York hurry."

"Bette, did you look through your things? Is anything missing? Moved?"

"I did not stop to think about it. I locked the sliding door and came up here."

Grady said, "Well, I'll escort you to your room so you can check it out. Why didn't you tell us before about you and Willard?"

"Because there *is* no *me and Willard*, Sheriff. You must not date much. Flirting with someone is one thing, but it doesn't mean you're an item."

Sampson was about to begin a rehearsal for the trios and ensembles when Grady and Patrick came into the theater and walked down to the stage. They asked for a few minutes to speak to the group. Sampson, of course, offered the sheriffs the podium.

Patrick stepped to the side of the podium and addressed the soloists on the stage as well as the musicians in the pit. The chorus wasn't involved with this rehearsal, but they would get the message.

"Good morning. I'm Sheriff Patrick Delaney, here with my colleague, Sheriff Grady Mulligan." He pointed to Grady standing off to the side in front of the stage.

"This is an unusual case," Patrick said, "and even though none of you were here or directly involved in this incident, many of you have worked with the deceased, Falcon Jennings, and with other colleagues who might be associated." (Patrick didn't want to imply to anyone that they were sure it was Willard Franklin, who had gone off the deep end.)

"We are here to help, and need your assistance. Sheriff Mulligan and I will be on the Villa compound today and tomorrow and we will be at your service. If any of you have information that might contribute to the solving of this puzzle, the untimely death of a man you knew, please come see us. Thank you."

MARCUS'S LIST

Marcus sat in the back of the Old Hall during the chorus rehearsal. He closed his eyes and ran through the day's happenings in his busy mind.

In his usual way, he listed the highlights of the last 12 hours, finding only one crisis, Willard's surprise visit to Bette Belle. Otherwise, a breathable day.

Bear Dream
Breakfast

Meeting/Hayne/Hector/Grady
Chef Henry & Priscilla/Gala
Lunch with Sampson/Diesel
Priscilla/schedule/Wednesday/Falcon Wake
Bette Belle/Willard
Grady & Patrick/Bette Belle
Dinner at my desk
Priscilla

This imaginary list was not new. What *was* new was that he didn't care that it took up his entire day. Every moment was filled, a mountain of unfinished work lay ahead of him, there were little chaotic fires (both logistic and emotional) to put out everywhere: a murder to solve, a trauma from which to recover, an opera festival opening in four days, a puppet show added to the festival line up, an impromptu wake causing his schedule to cascade, a four course dinner for 100 at Friday night's Gala, and at least three primary artistic team changes.

But, it was OK. He didn't want to quit and walk away. He felt able to handle it. Can beautiful music do that? A good cry? A note from a spirit guide? Bear Medicine? A declaration of love?

Marcus had to laugh. He noticed that he didn't put Kendra's name on his list next to "breakfast."

Well, one thing at a time, he thought. *I can't even think about that right now. It's just too big. Can I be like Scarlett O'Hara and think about it tomorrow? Although, it is pretty eye opening, right alongside that message from the bears.*

Is it that I just don't pay attention to the signs? Were there signs? Have there been clues all along? No. We've been buddies for years. I would have known.

But she does make me laugh. And we do talk about everything.

Independence makes me cross my arms in front of me, to ward off the evil eye. Nay, nay, says Bachelor Marc Brown. Sex would ruin a perfectly good friendship. Intimacy would mean I'd have to share my closet. My bed. My life. My nonexistent dog.

Stop now, Marcus. Stop thinking about it. It's too big.

Put it in a safe place until you can think about it.

"So, D, do you think Willard would keep coming back if he's guilty of doing away with Falcon Jennings?"

"I assume that is a rhetorical question, Hanyie, and will not even try to answer it."

"No, I know. It's just so odd, his behavior. Why did he leave his car? Why is he popping up and spooking people? What's he trying to tell us? Or is he just off his personal rocker? So many unanswered questions."

Diesel said, "Fortunately, solving this puzzle is not our job. Personally, I am full up with *Cosi* and I think you ought to focus on your performance tomorrow. Let it go."

"Oh, I try, but you know how these things worry me."

"I know better than anyone, Haynie, but the world needs your art, not your detective skills. We have more than enough sheriffs on the job."

"OK, D. I know you're right. I think I'm a little nervous now because Hector is involved. I so hoped to protect him from all this."

"You can't protect him from everything, and, besides, we agreed a long time ago that one of our gifts to Hector would be to let him live a real life."

"I know. This was not what I had in mind, D."

"I know, Haynie. Just hold his hand. That's all he needs. You're doing a fine job of that."

"OK, D. If you say so."

Chapter Nine
Wednesday, June 11, 2008

> No, I will be the pattern of all patience; I will say nothing.
> *King Lear*
> ~ Wm. Shakespeare

Fingerprints

"The strange thing is," Patrick said, stirring a cup of Henry's powerful coffee, "the entire area is completely free of fingerprints. All up and down the little secret stairs, the steps to the cupola, the winch, even the cable. We found the upper door, under several layers of wallpaper, very cleverly concealed. Everything was stripped clean inside. Whoever did this took their time to dust or sweep their way out the door. These cable cutters were tucked down in between one secret step and the wall. No fingerprints on them."

Patrick put the heavy duty cable cutters on the table and took a sip of coffee. He resisted putting his feet up on the hassock placed near his Queen Anne. Grady would surely disapprove of his boots on that tapestry.

"No footprints, either?" Marcus asked.

"Nope," said Grady. "The killer raked out the whole place. Now it's just all mixed up leaves and mulch. They used a spray cleaner on the stairs. And some kind of duster. Pretty thorough. Gotta be a fairly smart person behind this. And determined. And strong."

A Celebration of Life

Up on the hill, Hayne, Diesel, Hector, Chef Henry, Magnolia Jones, and Jake Ortman prepared for Falcon Jennings's Celebration of Life. Hector and Jake pulled the big white event canopy out of storage and set it up on the flat grassy area beyond the deck of the house. The sides were left off the tent for a full view of Lake Zanetta and its quivering lily pads, and, beyond that, a backdrop of manzanita and madrone, clacking branches and rustling leaves.

Chef Henry provided an elaborate "brunch picnic." All of the attendees were given tea or coffee on their way into the shade of the tent. As people settled into their chairs and tables, MeiMei and Lulu passed around baskets of small breakfast pastries and napkins. Chef Henry and several other minions spread out the fare on the long tables covered in white linen: chafing dishes of sausages and scrambled eggs, and bacon. Pans of huevos rancheros. Bowls of black beans and tortillas and chips and salsas. Asian Slaw, Warm German Potato Salad and a Golden Beet Salad with Goat Cheese and Shredded Romaine. Strawberries and cream.

Over at the side, Henry set up his biggest griddle and prepared to make 600 pancakes. Just before Marcus stepped up to the front of the group to say a few words, he watched the right-handed Chef Henry giving the left-handed Hector a lesson in pancake flipping. Hector focused in close, turning it over in his mind so he could manage the job with his left hand.

Priscilla set up a big display of Falcon's Villa gig photos. Marcus brushed by the display. Then he stopped. He made himself look into the photos as if they were true windows into the past. He missed Falcon. He saw his Gene Kelly face, his wispy, long brown hair. He remembered the conversation they had right there, in that photo of the two of them by the walk-in in the Old Hall kitchen. Their first serious discussion, about the difference between a job and a calling. They agreed, like Giorgio, the old trapeze artist, that almost all parts of show business were a calling. He was close to tears.

Marcus spoke first, of course, as the head of this company of thespians and musicians and artists. He kept his glasses on and fingered the little heart shaped piece of pink quartz he'd found in his coat pocket this morning. He remembered the twelve years he'd known Falcon, and listed his many accomplishments. He admitted to the whole company gathered there in grief and sadness that he could barely say more about his now late friend without crying. To himself he said, *and without seeing the moment of Falcon's death yet another time.*

He most of all wanted this celebration of Falcon's life to help put the man to bed. To let him rest. Once a formal closure took place after a death, and everyone has had their moment to speak of the late loved one, to say goodbye, shouldn't the healing commence? *Can that happen before the slayer of the beloved stage director has been found?* Marcus sighed at the thought.

Priscilla and Marcus had agreed on an open mic "roast and toast" with minimal formality. All of the people gathered in the tent knew Falcon, and some knew him well. No one had yet approached Grady or Patrick with any new information, but all were affected by the death of their colleague. Everyone had a story, or a memory, or a thought about the quality of the man now dead, whose ashes sat on the mantel in Martha's living room amidst a shrine of flowers and memorabilia.

Martha sat like a zombie at the front table; her first appearance in public. She dressed in black taffeta with black petticoats. Her face was hidden by a black hat's veil, but Marcus knew her eyes were vacant. She appeared unmoved by the words of the congregation gathered to honor her late husband. She was somewhere else. Her mother held her hand.

HAYNE REMEMBERS

A few string players brought their instruments and played softly from their seats in the back of the tent. Lulu and MeiMei passed around boxes of tissue.

Hayne's mind drifted into the past while sixty people had their say. Of course, other deaths showed up: Queen Elizabeth, when her illness finally took her away, and Hazel a few months later. Hector was right. Hazel just didn't want to remain on earth without her lifelong companion. And he remembered Gabriel Michaels's death, which made him think of Gabe's last days.

He remembered Gabe propped up in his bed, saying, "I know I'm going to die soon, because I've gone through the entire last thirty years, every event at Villa Zanetta, in order. If I've counted right, we've prepared or performed nearly ninety stage productions in almost 31 years."

In 1989, they moved Gabe full time up to the Villa so they could care for him. His eccentric city life was over anyway, as the ravages of AIDS took their toll on his body.

When they began to reminisce that day, Hayne went to the kitchen and brought back a whole roll of butcher paper. They listed every show and hung the paper like a precious scroll in the Old Hall, which Hayne kept current still.

Hayne and Gabe placed asterisks on favorites, like the ten minute standing ovation they received for the *Cosi* production in 1965, their first show with a full-size orchestra.

They listed and starred the gala opening of The Well Lit Theater in 1970, with a performance of Benjamin Britten's Opera, *The Turn of the Screw*.

Starred in red—the sold-out SRO performances of the famous Bialystok Puppet Theater from Poland. The puppeteers stayed three extra days and taught Hayne all about marionette puppeteering.

And the great Russian director and teacher Boris Goldovky, directing Mozart's *Don Giovanni* and leading a week-long workshop for stage directors. Oh!

"Boy, that was fun," Gabe said. Hayne didn't know if he meant that workshop or the entire run of his Villa Zanetta career.

Gabe's young friend, Robert Mapplethorpe, died of AIDS related infections in March, and Gabe was sure he would be next. They became sick at the same time and kept each other up to date by long letters detailing their afflictions; New York to California, California to New York. After Robert died, Gabe wrote to him anyway and tucked the letter inside his journal.

> Dear Lucky Bob,
>
> Well, you won the bet. You first. Now I am here in California, alone in grief and in my illness. I am lovingly cared for by the two best men on earth, and yet, I am still alone.
>
> Did you feel alone when you died? I'm sure you were surrounded by all those sycophantic friends, but you were alone inside. I know it, if I know you. Knew you.
>
> I am glad we met. It made New York all the better for me, and your friendship carried me through the pain, agony and torture of this worst of all diseases.
>
> I am next, I am sure of it. The aloneness is more complete, and it chokes me. I hope to join you soon and we can play canasta together in Heaven. Save me a seat.
>
> Love, Unlucky Gabe, still here

Gabriel died two weeks later of *Pneumocystis carinii pneumonia* (PCP), one of 100,000 people to die of AIDS in America in 1989. Gabe became a statistic and it was Hayne's and Diesel's, and the Villa Zanetta's, great loss. This made for Hector's second experience with D.E.A.D. (the first being his grandfather/father in 1963). Hector didn't really understand and, like with his grandfather/father, kept looking for Gabe for weeks afterwards, asking, "Where ith Gabwiel Michaelth?"

Diesel nudged Hayne and whispered, "Are you asleep? I'm hungry." Hayne realized that the Falcon Jennings roast and toast (of which he'd heard not one word) had ended and it was time for sausages and Hector's pancakes.

But he thought about Gabriel Michaels for the rest of the day, and missed his brilliance and energy and calm presence, even at the end.

KENDRA LEAVES THE EVENT

Kendra prepared to leave the event for her meeting with Grady and Patrick in the Not-so. Suddenly shy, she hesitated at the sight of Marcus.

Wretchedly sorry she'd exposed her innermost feelings, Kendra wondered if she had time to flee. But, Marcus turned from his conversation with the chef and saw her standing in a shaft of sunlight by the front of the tent.

Kendra wore a dress; shocker enough, but the sun backlit her hair like a halo. She braved a look at Marcus and smiled.

Marcus looked at Kendra as if he'd never seen her before. Perhaps he never had. Her usual tough little New Yorker posture was absent. Her golden hair hung free, she wore very little make up, and her dress floated in the breeze. Marcus remembered only one other time he'd seen Kendra in anything but jeans or tights; at a very formal wedding, in which she was the Best Woman. And for that, she'd worn a tux!

Great Caesar's Ghost, Marcus thought. *She's beautiful.*

GIRLFRIENDS

Kendra left the tent and began to walk down the hill. Since there was no one at the moment to whom she could admit this (Marcus having been successfully avoided and no girlfriends on this particular gig), she admitted to herself that she was a bit worried.

Why would Grady and Patrick want to talk to her again? Did they suspect *her* now? They've had their suspicions about everyone onsite, but now they were singling her out.

"Kendra?" said a voice behind her. "Wait up!"

It was Smooch, who waved and said again, "Wait."

When she caught up, Smooch said, "Do you have time for a chat?"

"Well, no. Not right now. I am on my way to *chat* with the representatives of the law. Don't know why they want to see me again, but I don't expect it's because they like me."

They walked down the hill together. Kendra continued, "But, if they don't keep me too long, I have some time before the 2:30 runthrough. What's up?"

"Uhm. I could use some time with another woman, that's all. This whole thing bothers me and I just need someone to talk to."

"That's so funny, Smooch. Sorry, not funny, ha ha. Just funny because I was just considering that *I* have no one to talk to."

"What about Marcus? You always have Marcus."

"Do I? Then, it's even funnier, because what I need to talk about is Marcus."

Kendra looked at her watch. "Look, I'm a bit late, but I can't imagine they'd need me for more than 30 minutes. Let's meet at 1:30 at Gabe's Bench. If one of us is late, we can at least enjoy Hector's garden. Bring a hat or a visor. That bench is in the sun in the afternoon."

"Good idea," said Smooch. "I'll be there."

They walked in companionable silence, each woman glad for the other's company, if only for a few minutes. Kendra felt completely out of sync in a dress, but she felt she owed Falcon some respect, and all she had was this rag she threw in her suitcase at the last minute.

Smooch, in a black mini skirt, black leggings, sandals and a baggie shirt tied in front over a tank top, looked so completely comfortable, in her own skin. Kendra wondered if she would just end up jealous of this gorgeous creature or if she might really like her. She didn't know her that well, but she was interested.

When they got to the front door of the Villa, Smooch unexpectedly hugged Kendra and said, "I look forward to it. I'm going to practice my millinery skills on cowboy hats. See you later." Kendra turned right into the Not-so and Smooch went on to the Well Lit, to her station in the wardrobe department. Kendra and Smooch had agreed to create elaborate cowboy hats to go with the big, long fake fur coats for the fake Albanian cowboys' costumes.

Grady and Patrick came into the Not-so behind her and they all sat down in an amiable triangle at the smallest table.

SMOOCH AND KENDRA

In the hot afternoon, Kendra put on a wide straw sun hat and left her room in the Villa Zanetta dorm. The walk up to Gabe's Bench gave her time to consider her recent interview with the sheriffs. She meandered slowly through Hector's garden, stepping on the flagstones like a hop-scotch grid. She stopped to smell some jasmine growing by the side of the dorm, picked a few sweet peas to give to Smooch (she knew Hector wouldn't mind), rubbed the dry lavender flowers with her fingers and put the tips of her fingers to her nose.

By the time she reached Gabe's Bench, Kendra had a sheen of sweat on her skin and longed for water. Smooch reached into her big straw bag for the two glass bottles of sparkling water she'd smuggled out of the kitchen (she figured the "no glass water bottles outside" rule didn't apply to her, for some reason). She offered Kendra a bottle and a chocolate chip cookie.

Kendra, grateful, gave Smooch the flowers and sat down. They were quiet for a few minutes, and each waved to Hector, tying up vines in the Concord grape arbor about twenty yards away.

"What did the sheriffs want, if you don't mind my asking?" said Smooch.

"I'm not rightly sure," said Kendra. "They asked a lot of the same questions they'd asked me before, but with more intensity. They dared not imply I was having an affair with Falcon, but they want to think that. You can tell. It would be so convenient. I didn't think about this before, but I actually have no alibi for 5pm on Friday evening of the 6th of June 2008. I was alone in my car, eating a whole bag of Cape Cod Potato Chips, trying to keep from smoking a pack of cigarettes."

"You're not smoking now."

"No. I'm tryin to quit."

"Why now? Seems a stressful time to quit smoking."

"It is."

"But…"

Kendra looked at Smooch, like, *Can you be trusted?*

"Go ahead. Tell me. I think I've figured it out anyway."

"What? What do you think it is?"

Smooch said, "Maybe Marcus would like you to quit?"

Kendra laughed. "Well, you're half right."

"How long have you two been lovers?"

Kendra laughed again. "We're not! That's the point."

"Ah. Well, I do see, now. You've been friends forever, Kendra. What's changed?"

Kendra considered this. She watched Hector for a few minutes before she responded. Watching Hector's sweet monk-like presence while he worked around the grounds was a regular pastime for the company in residence; an accidental calming influence.

"Nothing has changed, Smooch, except I'm tired of waiting for Marcus Brown to notice that I am a woman."

"How long have you felt this way?" Smooch asked.

"Ever since the day we met, eleven years ago on a ski lift ride in June in Telluride. We were both participating in the Bluegrass Festival. We laughed all the way through the ride and have been buddies ever since, and he hasn't had a clue. Until yesterday."

"Oooh. What happened yesterday?"

It seemed so natural to be talking with Smooch that Kendra opened up and told her everything. She told Smooch about all the times she'd seen the confirmed bachelor go after or notice the wrong women. Or he'd call her and talk about his disappointments, or love affairs gone wrong.

"He'd come to the City to meet me for dinner and dump all his life and work issues in my lap and then go home. I guess I'm at the end of my tether. I'm 45 years old, not getting any younger, and he is 55. I might be crazy, but I think we would be amazing together. But, he is blind."

"Not so blind as you think. I saw him watching you up the hill there."

"That's because I blurted out the truth yesterday and I wish deeply that I had not."

"What did you say?"

"I told him that I have loved him from the beginning and I would love him until the end."

"Well, that's pretty hard to turn down. What happened next?"

Kendra said, "Chicken that I am, I left. I couldn't even look at him. I have most likely ruined our perfectly good friendship forever. I can't take back the words. And even if I could, I wouldn't. I'm tired of pretending."

"What do you want him to do?" Smooch asked.

"I want him to love me back."

Smooch took that in and nodded. Kendra said, "What's on *your* mind? You didn't meet me just to get an earful of my little internal dramatics."

"I guess I'm just nervous, with my ex, Lurch, lurking around everywhere. Did you hear about Bette? This is all surreal, made worse by Martha's behavior. She's not the least bit helpful, and I can't help but blame her INCREDIBLY OVERBEARING MOTHER for her catatonic state. I'm beginning to think that Mrs. Watts is a shrew who thinks of her daughter as just a passel of trouble. Other than that, I'm fine."

Kendra laughed again. "Lurch. That's perfect."

"I know. Don't even ask me why I ever married him."

"No, I won't. I have an old friend who often said, 'Love is blind and sex makes you stupid.' Tell me about Martha. I only know a little of their story. Falcon was careful not to discuss her. I wondered if one of them was having an affair. But, if it was Falcon, it was not with me!"

"I don't know. I hardly knew him and only connected with her a few times by email and phone, ages ago. I went to their home thinking Martha might fill me in on a few details, but that was a black hole of disappointment. She's in no shape to share anything coherent with me. Her mother keeps her loaded. It's pretty extreme."

There were just too many missing pieces and the final statement in conversations like these among the company members was always, "And who would want to kill Falcon Jennings?" And always, the same obvious conclusions crept in.

On Sunday, John Eagle had announced to the fans and friends of Villa Zanetta that Hayne Williams was emerging from brief retirement to perform *The Deceived Women*, on Wednesday, the 11th of June at 5pm, Sunday the 15th at 2pm and again on Wednesday the 18th at 5pm. Within 24 hours, the 80 seats available were sold out for each of the first two performances and at present, there were about 20 tickets available for the final Wednesday.

The audience—overjoyed to be there with Hayne, the beloved puppeteer, and his sidekick, Hector Farmdale, once again—clapped and clapped on that first night. Both Hayne and Hector were surprised their performance went on without so much as a hiccup. Hector said, "We 'member it so well, Haynie. We did a good job."

And Hayne fully agreed.

But the sweetest part about the event were the interactions with the audience after the show. Hector was enjoying a particularly good day and besides, everyone loved Hector. As John Eagle one said, "What's not to love? Hector is an enlightened being." (And John Eagle should know. Marcus had once noted to Falcon that for John Eagle, show business was a job. John's true calling was connecting people to spirit and recognizing enlightened beings).

Someone in the audience asked Hayne, "Would you tell us about the first time you performed this play?"

"What we call The Old Play, *The Deceived Women,* was the first performance ever at Villa Zanetta. It was almost exactly 50 years ago right here when our Tiny Little Theater was still brand new." He looked at Hector. "What year was that, Hector?"

"Nineteen…fifty…eight!" Hector smiled.

Hayne looked at the audience. "Hector's memory is much better than mine." Hector smiled again.

"The story of how I came to have the Old Play in the first place, is worth noting…" While Hayne shared the discovery at the Pasadena Playhouse with people in the packed audience, Hector had Tristano and Francesco in his lap. The puppets soon got into a silent kerfuffle, smacking each other on the head. They rolled around on Hector's lap, kerfuffling in disagreement. Hector, unaware of the audience, silently imagined the voices of the two puppets arguing about who would poke the holes in the dirt and who would plant the carrot seeds in the holes. After they planted all the carrots and made up and hugged, they got into a fight again about how to water the carrots and then who would get to pick the carrots. Finally, they agreed to take turns harvesting, cooking and eating the carrots. The audience clapped for Hector's spontaneous encore.

Hector looked up and beamed at his fans.

MARCUS GOES HOME

Marcus wanted a night at home. He was afraid to keep dreaming. Next time he might end up in the driveway in his birthday suit. *I'd better go home and get some PJs.*

After checking in with Grady, Priscilla, John, Hayne and Diesel, he put his things in a bag and drove over the Oakville Grade to Highway 29 and turned left toward St. Helena.

On his mind were many things, the greatest of which was Kendra. How annoying that Willard and his shenanigans took up most of his thoughts and Kendra was pushed to the side.

'Twas ever thus, he thought. Willard was an outright problem. Kendra was...Kendra was a conundrum, a complex puzzle to solve.

Getting away for a few hours will be good, he thought. *Clean out my internal data base. Let me just wallow in thoughts the rest of the way home.*

First, Willard. There is a big piece of information missing here. Someone is lying big time. Why does he keep sneaking around? Who will he freak out next? He is leaving a trail behind him and he will most likely never work again. Who would hire him now? I'm sure Hayne and Diesel are over it.

Would Willard be lurking around if he'd killed Falcon? Well, I suppose if he's this crazy he might be.

And the blonde woman with whom he was "fwooting" last summer? There were several blondes here for The Marriage of Figaro—*there is always a blonde.*

I do wonder if Falcon was having an affair. He seemed so desperate to talk on Friday. Martha is adorable, but I can imagine she is a handful.

Hmmm. What's next on the list? Am I responsible for checking on Martha and her overprotective mother? Could I possibly send Priscilla? Perhaps she'd be a be a better judge than I.

Of course all this thinking led him right back to his crying jag on Monday night and his dream of bears. This led to *Ave verum corpus*, which led him to Kendra, which led to the pink quartz heart in his pocket. Down the path he went, right into her parting words at breakfast yesterday.

"I have loved you from the beginning and I will love you til the end."

Does she have any idea how she has changed things? I can barely look at her now, much less talk to her. And I have so much to talk to her about! Why now? Why in the middle of this crisis of craziness does the woman choose to tell me she loves me? Can't she just like me a lot?

Plus! Grady and Patrick think she might have been involved with Falcon! Now that is a laugh. They obviously don't know my friend, Kendra. That tough little New Yorker would not dare "fwoot" with her boss.

Marcus pulled into the Spring Mountain Condominium driveway, wound through the complex to Number 12 and pulled into his parking spot. *This is where I need a dog to greet me,* he thought. *Someone to come home to.*

As it was, he heard his tropical plants and delicate bonsai calling out to him when he opened the door. Nothing had been watered since Friday morning. He dropped his bag and went to the sink. *First, water the plants. Second, pour a glass of wine and march your silly arse directly to the deck. Do not pass GO.*

And for Pete's sake, stop thinking about Kendra Masters. Think more about the fact that we got through one day without a crisis. That I know of.

HAYNE AND DIESEL CHAT

"I'm so proud of you, Haynie. What a wonderful show today. I'm amazed by how well it went after so many years," Diesel said.

"25!" said Hector from the dining room table. He looked up from his project and smiled. His gourd gnome house was almost finished and he could hardly wait to put it in his garden.

"25 years ago almotht to the day," he said. "I counted."

Hayne smiled and said, "I couldn't do it without you Hector Farmdale." Hayne almost cried, he was moved by, oh, so many things. He didn't have much conversation in him tonight. He was too busy conjuring up the past and wondering where it all went, and so fast. Just yesterday he was young and vibrant and falling in love with that hunky guy standing practically naked in front of his Life Drawing Class.

Thinking about Gabe today brought up many memories and much joy about the simple act of creating beauty. The three of them, the Villa Triumvirate, Hayne, Diesel and Gabriel, spent thirty years together building this company into a thing, a viable, beautiful, heartwarming thing, that will outlast the founders, he hoped, by many years to come.

Sometimes Hayne felt like he was at the end of his life's rope, and that any minute now he would pass on and leave behind all this beauty and go, well, *wherever we go next*, he thought. *Sometimes, I am ready. And then sometimes I look at these two, my family, and want it to last forever.*

CHAPTER TEN

THURSDAY, JUNE 12, 2008

Virtue is bold, and goodness never fearful.
Measure for Measure
~ Wm. Shakespeare

MeiMei and LuLu Talk

MeiMei and LuLu enjoyed many opportunities to observe and swoon over the two sheriffs, Grady Mulligan and Patrick Delaney. But when they finally had an official reason to talk to the sheriffs, they were shy and afraid of the consequences. Afraid of getting up close to the sheriffs.

In all their years at Villa Zanetta, MeiMei and Lulu Chinn had relied mainly on each other's company. They slept in the same room in the dorm, worked the same jobs, ate the same bowls of rice and sometimes spoke the same words at the same time.

Same. Same. They did everything together and had done so from first emerging from their mother's womb on a sampan in Hong Kong in 1978; first MeiMei, then LuLu. Exactly alike. They feared it would be this way all their lives if they didn't do something to change it.

At thirty, they began to want more. Their biological time clocks ticked. Their desire to be loved tocked.

They had grown up at Villa Zanetta after landing in the United States in 1993 at the age of 15, abandoned and alone. Their mother had died, like many others, onboard the ship of smuggled immigrants from Hong Kong, and their father was lost to them years ago in a fishing boat accident in the Hong Kong Harbor.

When MeiMei and LuLu arrived in San Francisco, the smugglers were arrested and the 15 year old twins taken in at Cameron House, a Presbyterian Church community center created to protect young Chinese immigrant girls from being sold to a brothel.

The girls had no papers, no parents, and nowhere go. Gabriel Michaels's brother, Francis, an immigration consultant in San

184

Francisco, thought MeiMei and LuLu might fit in at the Villa. Hayne, remembering Aunt Hazel's story, took MeiMei and LuLu into the Villa Zanetta family like a mother hen.

In Sonoma Adult School, MeiMei and LuLu received high school diplomas, and Hayne and Diesel sponsored them both at Santa Rosa Community College where they would soon receive AA degrees in Office Administration.

But, all that aside, they had information. They didn't like to spill the beans out of other people's jars, but they talked it over (in Chinese, of course—always Chinese when the stakes were high and secrecy in order) and decided it was important for Villa Zanetta that they step forward and dump Willard's beans on the table.

On Thursday morning, MeiMei and Lulu went to Priscilla, finally back in her office. MeiMei asked Priscilla to call Grady or Patrick, or better, both. Her sister elbowed her in the side. MeiMei looked at LuLu like, "What?" LuLu's eyes bugged out, which MeiMei read as an admonition. "It's OK, honey. I'm just making sure."

Priscilla knew her team. If MeiMei and LuLu were ready to talk, who was she to get in the way? She thought maybe she knew the reasons. Priscilla had eyes. She called Grady's cell phone.

When they met the sheriffs downstairs, MeiMei and LuLu were like five year old girls wishing for their mother's skirts to hide behind. Where had all that self-assurance gone? Out the atrium window.

The twins sat down at the table as close to each other as possible. Their first time in actual conversation with the sheriffs since the first day, and they were nervous. Not because they were sheriffs, but because MeiMei was very aware of Patrick Delaney as a man, and LuLu just wanted Grady Mulligan to stroke her hair.

As soon as they sat down, Patrick looked at MeiMei. He remembered the day the twins took him and Joe Budd up to the cupola—remembered how he loved her lilting, singsong Chinese. Patrick had no idea that that was the beginning of MeiMei and LuLu's obsession over the two handsome sheriffs, Grady and Patrick.

Grady was very uncomfortable. These foreign women made him anxious. Maybe it was their Chinese chatter. He did not like *not* knowing everything that was going on around him.

But right now, he said, "What was it you wanted to see us about, ladies?" *Son of a biscuit. Really, Grady? You sound like a dufus.*

MeiMei, the bolder of the two sisters, and older by two minutes, jumped out from behind her invisible late mother's skirts and looked at Grady, so she wouldn't have to make eye contact with Patrick. She said, "We have important news. We must speak about Mr. Willard."

"What about Mr. Willard?" asked Patrick.

MeiMei kept her eyes on Grady. "We know where he is."

Patrick said, "Tell us everything."

GRADY AND PATRICK AND WILLARD

Grady and Patrick thanked MeiMei and LuLu and walked to the parking lot, where a surprise discussion took place.

Patrick, said, "OK. First things first. I know this is unprofessional, but I've gotta say it. Those two Chinese women are adorable."

Grady said, "I don't believe you. You are going to talk to *me* about women? And on the job?"

"Well, who else? You're the only person I ever see anymore, except our mothers. I'm too busy for any *real* friends. I have to rely on *you*. Besides, you're here. And I saw how LuLu looked at you. She's smitten."

"Oh, she is not. You are imagining things." Grady shook his head.

"No. No, I'm not, cousin. I think we've been tagged by these two girls and I have to say, I'm intrigued."

Grady cleared his throat and shook his head again. "Well, put your Irish imagination away right now, Detective Delaney. We have a man to catch." Patrick laughed and rolled his eyes.

Grady and Patrick chose to perform this duty themselves rather than farm it out to the troops. It seemed kind of delicate. They armed themselves and started up the path to the woods behind the Villa. It took them half an hour to find the path leading to the Villa water tank, per MeiMei's instructions. They followed the path and walked about ten yards before they split up and diverted off the regular path. MeiMei said Willard's camp was right under the water tank.

"How do you know?" Patrick had asked her.

MeiMei finally looked at Patrick and whispered, "Because we saw him lurking in the woods and we followed him."

The sheriffs heard him before they saw him. A whiny babble came from a moving sleeping bag. They crept in from different angles, but saw that they didn't need to even be quiet, much less try to sneak up on Willard Franklin. He was half in his sleeping bag, rolling on the ground. He moaned and babbled and groaned.

Grady and Patrick came together and stood over the rolling body of the disgraced conductor.

Willard perspired like he'd run a marathon. Grady saw his trembling hands, in fact his whole body quaked. His head moved from side to side. He rolled one way and then another.

Willard's babble became more distinguishable.

"Mother of Mercy, give me a drink. Take some soap. Put away the dope. Handle the pope. Sink the ship. Call the dog. Kill the mob. Frickin' twerp."

Patrick leaned over the man, tried to look in his eyes.

"Pupils dilated. Doesn't see me." He put his hand on Willard's head. "He's hot. Like, really hot. I'd say he's in the middle of a powerful case of DTs here. Better call for an ambulance."

"Oh, man, do we have to get an ambulance with sirens and all? That'll cause a ruckus for sure. I think you should get your unmarked truck and we can take him down to the parking lot. You can get your truck up to the main path, at least. We can haul his butt down there in his sleeping bag, use it like a stretcher. No sirens."

Patrick looked at Grady. "Since when did *you* become so thoughtful?"

"It's not thoughtful. It's just common decency. Let's just get the guy out of here. I have oxygen in my Jeep. Let's just save his life."

Patrick looked at Grady with new respect.

"Yeah, OK. I'll go get Molly McGuire. You'll have to ride in her, though." Patrick smiled at his cousin. "I'll be right back."

The ride in Patrick's truck lasted long enough to get the still babbling Willard to Grady's Jeep. Grady, trying to hold his breath, sat in the back with Willard's head in his lap. Grady felt something wet on his thigh.

Grateful to expel himself from the stinky back of the farm boy's Molly McGuire, Grady took a breath of fresh air, brushed off his pants, and said, "Let's put him in the wayback. You'd better come with me and hold onto him and get some air up his nose. Let's skip the EMTs all together." He checked his pants and realized that Willard had been crying in his delirium.

Willard was taken straight to the hospital in Santa Rosa, where he was put in isolation, strapped to a bed, hooked up to more oxygen and poked with an IV. Grady placed a guard outside his door.

Willard continued to babble while his mind meandered through a dark forest of his demons, including a big one named Falcon Jennings. Monsters heads loomed in his dreams and pictures of the dead man rattled his brain. His mumblings rose and fell, increasing here, whispering there, babbling constantly of "boost the rooster, dangle the fangle" and such nonsense that so fascinated the nurse in charge of Willard that she kept a notebook of babblings and turned them in at the end of each day.

HAYNE PONDERS

Hayne thought he would be exhausted after the past few days of preparation and then the puppet show at The Tiny Little Theater in the Barn. Rather, he was strangely elated. He didn't know how many more shows he had in him at this point, but he loved every minute of the work; the planning, the primping of the puppets, the rehearsals, voicing his characters. The (probable) murder of Falcon Jennings notwithstanding, these had been some very satisfying days for Hayne Williams.

He felt so alive. Odd to say after a year of retirement, but he looked back on the last twelve months as kind of boring. He loved their trip to Paris, and had wallowed in art galleries and shows in London. But, he had missed Hector. He always did when they traveled. And he missed the act of creation. When they returned, he took up his knitting with a fervor and there were already enough afghans to cover every bed in the Villa Zanetta dorm.

When Falcon died and everything changed, Hayne had been contemplating another hobby. He considered everything from building tall ship models to working on a 5,000 piece jigsaw puzzle. The call to help at the Villa brought him out of a fate worse than death; apathy.

Hayne considered his place in the world. No, he wasn't planning to go back to the Villa. His job there was over. That was clear and that was fine. But, even at 80, he knew he wasn't finished. There were times…when his bones ached or his feet hurt or some old beach injury throbbed with arthritic pain…he felt every bit his age.

However, his mind, still sharp, wanted something to do. Hayne sat down and pondered the future; what was he going to do with the rest of his years? He had to do something. Otherwise, all he would do is remember. His memories were so vibrant, like through a clear picture window into the past. Being an *in the moment* guy, though, he had to deal with *what's happening now.*

Not to diss memories, he thought. *Memories keep the heart pumping and the creative light bulb shining. But, what worth are memories other than pacifying my mind?*

Thalia and Melopomene happened to be sitting on his left shoulder at the time, giggling. They whispered ideas and blew them like gentle zephyrs into the ear of their favorite puppeteer.

Hayne looked at the table spread with 50th anniversary photos for the Gala.

I suppose I could write all these memories down.

MARCUS RETURNS

A full night's dreamless sleep in his own bed gave Marcus another boost. He walked a mile around the Spring Mountain Condo grounds, admiring the little flower gardens and blooming bushes. He took a shower and walked to downtown St. Helena to the Model Bakery and ordered bacon, eggs, a chocolate croissant and a double latte and watched others come in and out of the cafe.

How novel to be away from the Villa and separated from all the drama; a bit of perspective after five full days ensconced on the compound. The Villa Zanetta is not the center of the universe!

Marcus read the paper, ate his substantial breakfast and sipped the latte. He dallied; there was no reason to hurry. Priscilla had his cell number; she'd call him if there were any kind of need.

Priscilla. What would he do without Priscilla? Another big realization. She made the Villa tick like a clock. The woman was a masterful multi-tasker and made his job easier. *I should be more grateful.*

Marcus walked down the street to the St. Helena Florist and bought a red rose and a little bauble.

He drove his silver BMW 328i back down Hwy 29 and turned right onto the Oakville Grade. This drive over the hill turned out quite differently from the drive home yesterday.

It was an odd feeling for Marcus, to be this awake. He noticed the sun on the trees and the shade on the ground, the deep yellows of the mustard in between the grapevines. He rolled down his window to sniff the air, drink in the sky, feel the breeze on his face. He didn't remember what CD was in his player, he hadn't played a CD in ages, but he pushed it in anyway. And there it was again.

Marcus found a turnout and pulled over. He turned up the music and let the *Ave verum corpus* wash over him. He looked out over the canyon and then closed his eyes. With every reach of note, harmonies to the heavens, his breath followed, in and out. He let the *Ave verum corpus* repeat a few times.

And of course, he couldn't help it. Kendra appeared in his mind.

He let her in. He let her in, just to try it. To imagine how it might feel if he had someone to love and who he knew would love him back. With every crescendo, with every note in the prayer he loved (although Marcus knew the Latin, he cared more for the vibration and the sounds that penetrated his bones, whispered to his soul) he breathed in Kendra Masters. He let her be…just who she was, and perhaps not the pal, but the lover.

How does that feel, Marc Brown, so-called confirmed bachelor? Someone loves you.

Can you dig that in real life and let her in?

Can you honestly say you've never thought about Kendra as a woman? As a lover? A wife, even?

Marcus's eyes flew open liked someone poked him in the behind with a stick.

Wife! Whoa, Nellie. One baby step at a time!

First: how does it feel? Like a sweet song on the wind.

What do you want? Perhaps more than a dog.

What do you see ahead, alone? Just a dog and a cabin on the coast.

What are you willing to change? Well. Not too much. But, I might be able to learn.

Do you love her? I don't know. I like her so much.

Do you want to be alone in your old age in cabin on the coast? Maybe.
Really? I don't know.
And he honestly did not know. Two days ago he had a buddy. Now, they were like reverse magnets, forced apart by a declaration of love.

PRISCILLA'S MANY HATS

Meanwhile, at Villa Zanetta, Priscilla commanded the Gala and Opening Night crew in the Old Hall.

MeiMei and LuLu sat at a table, slipping a little "change of participants" note into each of the 2008 Opera Festival program booklets. Next they would go (together) to the table to their right, where two volunteers filled Gala swag bags and little table favor gift baskets.

Even Hector got dragged in from the garden to help out; he sat a table with John Eagle while they slipped white napkins into golden rings. Hector had said, "Yeth, I will help. I am good at thethe napkin thingieth."

Priscilla stood in the doorway of the kitchen in conversation with Chef Henry. The Chef had prepared a tray of Opening Night hors d'oeuvre samples for her and the crew and they munched and laughed and talked.

When Marcus arrived at the door, all hands were busy. He scanned the big room with, not just his eyes, but his whole being. He took in, right down to his toes, the acts of creation before him. He saw Priscilla, and Henry, LuLu and MeiMei, the two most dedicated of their volunteers, Susan and Sandie, and of course, the amazing little force of nature in every way, Hector Farmdale, who conversed with John Eagle.

Marcus just stayed unseen by the door.

He thought about Hayne and Diesel and what they had entrusted to him ten years ago. In his mind, he scanned the whole property: the three venues, each with its own unique purpose, this beautiful old room, Hector's thrilling garden. The shows. These people. The lovely art.

You know you can't leave this, Marc Brown. Not now. You're just getting good at it.

Marcus walked through the wave of energy created by all the worker bees at Priscilla's fine command.

He went to Priscilla's side, gave her a hug, handed her a little package and said, "Meet me in my office in half an hour."

MARCUS RETURNS TO HIS OFFICE

Marcus faced the Lobby. He had avoided the spot easily while the crime tape encircled it, putting the space and the scene out of his mind whenever he came through the side door to the Old Hall. The Villa had been opened up for over 48 hours, but Marcus had not ventured through the Lobby or up the stairs.

The cleaners had done a pretty good job, but Marcus thought some new carpet was in order. And he'd have to replace that vase with something before tomorrow night. He'd talk to Hayne about that.

He took a big breath and strode right over the spot; just over it, straight through the Lobby, a walk of fire. He felt a slight tug at his heart, a flash of memory, a noise, a death. He moved through it to the other side. He moved through it and over it and under it. He commanded it, "Over. Done with." Falcon was gone. Time to move on to the continuation of living.

Marcus stopped by the Well Lit and left a note backstage. Then, he braved the steps up to his office to see if he could actually get back to work. He had a grant proposal to approve for John Eagle, six individual thank you letters to compose, a conference call with the sheriff's department and the Villa attorneys, and three interviews about Falcon Jennings's "murder" to turn down.

As he walked slowly up the steps, his cell phone rang. He pulled it out of his pocket, hoping to ignore the outside world. But it was Grady Mulligan. He pushed the button and said, "Hey, Grady." And then he heard.

Willard was in custody.

PRISCILLA

At 2, Priscilla arrived in Marcus's office with her gift (a two inch ceramic square with the question, "Pardon me, which hat am I wearing?" inscribed in black) pinned to her lapel.

"It's perfect," she said from the door. Marcus looked up. "Thank you, Marcus." They both laughed.

Marcus said, "Have a seat, Priscilla. We need to talk."

For a split second Priscilla thought he was going to fire her, but common sense told her people don't usually give *You're Fired* presents.

192

Marcus said, "How's it going down there?"

Priscilla said, "OK. It's the first day of actual work with no excitement."

"Well, here's some for you: Willard is in custody at the Santa Rosa Hospital. Grady and Patrick will be here later to fill us in."

"Oh! That's what they were doing here this morning in the red truck! They were certainly subtle."

"Yes. We can thank MeiMei and LuLu, and Grady and Patrick, too, for saving the probably ungrateful Willard's life. I'll tell you more about that later. Right now, I want to talk about you. And us."

"Us?" she asked.

"Yes. Us, as in the Villa. Are you happy here, Priscilla?"

"Yes, of course. You know I am."

"Yes. OK, then. First, I want to apologize for not noticing this before, but you are a powerful ally. I don't want to lose you as an Arts Administrator, but I would like to add General Manager to your title."

Priscilla almost rolled out of her chair in a faint.

"And of course, I'd like to give you a substantial raise." He slid a new contract across the desk. "We can work out the details later, but, I'd really like your help in moving Villa Zanetta forward."

Priscilla said, "You're not going to retire?"

Marcus laughed and said, "You knew about that?"

Priscilla said, "I know everything. Except the door. I didn't know about the secret door."

"Will you join me?"

"Of course, Marcus. I'd like nothing more."

COMPANY BUFFET OLD HALL
FOR COSI SOLOISTS, CHORUS, AND ORCHESTRA

Kendra walked into the Old Hall with a red rose pinned to her denim jacket. Naturally, the first group she encountered included Marcus Brown, who smiled at her in almost the same way he used to, before she blundered into his heart to scramble it up.

Marcus said, "Oh good, you're here. Patrick and Grady were just about to tell me about the, uhm, collection of Willard Franklin."

To the sheriffs, he said, "Go on."

When Patrick got to the part about driving Molly McGuire up through the property to the trail, Marcus asked, "Why didn't you just call for an ambulance?"

Patrick said, "Because my cousin here thought it might cause more scandal. He didn't stop to think that the guy might have died in his Jeep. But, all in all, it worked out and Willard Franklin is now in the hands of the sheriff's department, tied down to his bed."

Grady put in, "And he is still babbling about Falcon Jennings. He's not been charged with anything yet. When he wakes up, it will be soon enough."

THE ROSE

Kendra sat in the middle of The Well Lit Theater, watching the run through of the opera. Diesel sat next to her and Hayne next to Diesel.

Kendra smelled the rose pinned to her jacket. She didn't want it to wilt, but she never wanted to take it off.

It didn't mean anything, it was just a rose. One could put any number of meanings on it, but at least Marcus had told the simple truth.

She fingered the note in her jacket. She didn't need to look at it. She knew it by heart already.

Marcus wrote,

"I went into the florist. This message greeted me by way of a rose poster:

'A single red rose may be the perfect way to express an unspoken love now coming into the light— like when two close friends realize there is more than just friendship between them.'

"Kendra, we should have a good long talk. I miss you. Marcus"

HAYNE MUMBLED TO THE ALMOST ASLEEP DIESEL

"I'm going to write a book, D."

"That's so good, Haynie. G'night."

CHAPTER ELEVEN
FRIDAY, JUNE 13, 2008

What's done can't be undone.
Macbeth
~ Wm. Shakespeare

50ᵀᴴ GALA PREPARATIONS

The entire company got booted from the Old Hall in honor of the Gala. But, no one minded. One day wouldn't kill them.

Besides, in the spiffed up Tiny Little Theater in the Barn, tables and chairs were already assembled. Not quite as comfortable for the ensemble as the Old Hall...but the Old Hall had experienced this switch before.

The Queen Annes' curvy wooden arms were polished, the table and chair arrangements organized, flowers brought in from Hector's garden.

On the tables, glass fish bowls twinkled with tiny white battery-driven lights, bowls and vases of flowers filled the air with the fragrance of jasmine and lilies and spicy elements like mint and parsley.

Jake brought in Hayne's five giant boards filled with decades of captioned photos and spread them around the room; a 5' x 5' board for each decade. Hayne had carefully chosen pictures from favorite shows, old programs and other printed memorabilia.

Hayne particularly enjoyed the 70s board, perhaps because of the colorful shows produced. There was Gabe with the *Godspell* cast. And Diesel directing *Fiddler on the Roof*. Ah, and Diesel's most famous role – as Elwood P. Dowd in *Harvey*.

And the operas! *La Boheme, The Magic Flute, The Barber of Seville!*

Hector leaned over Hayne's shoulder and said, "Haynie, you put *my* picture in there. I thee me there. Ha ha! I wath nineteen yearth old."

"Yes, and here's Diesel directing *Charley's Aunt,* and look, here I am with the Salzburg Marionettes."

"It'th beautiful, Haynie. You did a good job."

MARCUS CHATS WITH PATRICK

"Don't let your guard down," Patrick said to Marcus that morning. "This isn't over yet. We can't charge Willard Franklin without tangible evidence, and he is still out like a light. It will be days before we can really talk to him."

"So, you're not as sure as you were that he did this thing?" said Marcus. "His babble gives you no further clues?"

"Not really. I'm afraid 'frickin' twerp' and 'throttle the bottle' mean pretty much nothing in terms of confessions. We'll just have to wait and see what happens."

"And will you be at the Gala?" Marcus asked with a pang. He sighed at the thought of men in uniforms with badges mingling with their 100 guests.

Patrick smiled. "Yes, but we'll try to be discreet. It'll be just Grady and me."

"OK," Marcus said. "Can I put you at the back table with the staff?"

Patrick tried to stifle another smile. "Yes, sure. That's fine," he said.

GALA INTERRUPTED

Martha came into the Old Hall at 3pm, as if it were any other day on the compound. She blithely said hi to people and looked around the room. She saw Priscilla and, as if they were the surf, waded her way through the five busy waiters setting tables.

She got to Priscilla and, on the loud side, said, "Hi, hon. Where's Smooch McGuinn?"

Priscilla stepped back from Martha as if she were an apparition. Something was very wrong; Martha would never call her "hon," had never called her anything but Priscilla, and they were not friends. "Wow. Martha," she said. "What are you doing here? Uhm, I mean, how are you?"

"Fine. Fine. I'm just fine. I'm looking for Smooch. Do you know where is Smooch? Smoochie smooch?"

"I...do...not know, Martha," said Priscilla, as she gestured to MeiMei to go get some help. "Have a seat over here, Martha, and MeiMei will find Smooch for you."

She whispered to MeiMei, "Anybody. Get anybody."

Priscilla sat Martha down at a table. Martha tapped her fingers on the surface like she was playing the piano. She wore a red skirt with white poodles connected by a wavy rope, dancing around in a circle, with multiple white petticoats, and saddle shoes with ankle socks. That might have been all right if it hadn't been for the white mink jacket, pearl covered handbag and twinkling tiara. It wasn't like Martha to mix her genres.

Priscilla got her talking. "What's up, Martha? Is everything OK? Smooch might be busy. Is there anything I can do for you?"

Martha said, "I'm here to help. Falcon would want me to help. Help. Help. I'm here to help out."

Chef Henry appeared at the kitchen door. "Martha," said Priscilla, "would you like some tea? Henry would like to make you some tea."

"Tea," repeated Martha. Priscilla raise her eyes to the chef. His eyebrows went up. He went to make tea.

Priscilla said, "I think you're supposed to be home resting, Martha. Where's your mother?"

"Mother! Dragon Lady is stuck at home. I have her keys!" Martha held up the keys to her mother's Cadillac. "She hid mine!"

"Dear God," said Priscilla. "Did you drive here?"

"Ha ha. Yep. Yep. I did. Escaped the Dragon Lady. Yep. I got her goat. Flushed her pills. Ha ha ha ha!"

Ho boy, thought Priscilla.

"Ah, Martha," she said, "here's a cup of tea from Henry. Let's just have tea while we wait for MeiMei to find Smooch for you."

She said to the wait staff, "Everyone, just keep setting tables. We have about half an hour to complete this task."

Hector, coming in from the garden with a basket of flowers, saw Martha at the table. She stood up and dashed toward him, frowning. "Hector, Hector, my friend Hector. How's it, Hector, Garden Boy?"

Hector backed away.

Marcus, Smooch and Pete Daltry came through the door together following MeiMei.

At the same time, Martha's mother was in the Villa Zanetta driveway getting out of a taxi and rummaging through her purse for some bills to pay the driver.

Mrs. Watts came into the room just in time to see Martha leap away from Hector and go after Smooch McGuinn.

"Thief! Thief!" she cried. "You stole him! You stole him. Now you stole my job. You b—" She pulled on Smooch's hair, prepared for a knockdown drag out girl fight. Martha punched her adversary in the face.

Too late, Smooch put her hands up in defense and backed into a waiter. Smooch, the waiter, and his tray full of silverware crashed to the floor.

Pete Daltry was there in a flash and pulled Martha away. Marcus came to Smooch's side and picked her up off the floor.

Mrs. Watts pushed her way through the throng of onlookers. Martha was hysterical, tying to get out of Pete Daltry's arms. He held her like a baby, close to his chest.

Mrs. Watts came up close to the fighting Martha and got right in the middle. She lightly smacked Martha's cheek and said, "Martha! Martha! Wake up. Look at me. Focus on my face. Just me. Don't pay any attention to these other people. Just me."

It took ten minutes to calm Martha down. Encouraged by one and all, Mrs. Watts finally relented and agreed to take her broken-spirited daughter to the doctor.

The last they saw of Martha was the red and white poodle skirt flipping up as it squeezed all its white petticoats through the door.

Hector stared at the departing Martha. His eyes were un-focusing, so he sat down on the nearest chair.

Priscilla stood up and said, "Okie dokie, then. Waiters, it looks like we need to wash some flatware."

And to the waiter in the middle of it, she said, "Denny, you're Denny, right? Will you come with me. I want to make sure you're OK." As they walked out the door, she was heard to say, "Were you hurt?"

Marcus said to Smooch, "Are you OK? What was she talking about?"

Smooch said, "I'm fine. But I might need some ice. I have absolutely no idea what she meant."

The Theaters at Villa Zanetta
50th Anniversary
Gala Dinner Menu

Bacon Crackers
Caprese Salad Skewers
Tiny Taco Salad Cups
Tiny Pepperoni Pizza Rolls
Cream of Curried Carrot Bisque
Beef Short Ribs with Mustard Shallot Sauce
Roquefort Soufflés with Greens
Molten Chocolate Cake

Chef Henry Samuels Nelson
From Jamaica to California

The Gala Dinner was a success! Before he began his remarks, Marcus called for Chef Henry. The Chef was appreciated by a standing ovation, no easy task for a group of 100 well-fed people sitting in comfortable chairs.

Henry, those beautiful dreads pulled back in a neat and professional ponytail stuffed into a net, had donned his clean chef coat, hoping for a bow. He came through his green baize door like he was appearing in *Upstairs Downstairs*. With a serious expression, he bowed low to his appreciative eaters, then stood up and flashed the grin of his lifetime.

Marcus thanked Henry from the bottom of his heart and Henry bowed again and left, no less theatrical than one of Diesel's most memorable moments on the stage.

Marcus said, "Henry and I have been around actors for a long time." His audience laughed.

"Tonight," Marcus continued, "we celebrate 50 years of music and shows and stories and dances and art and did I say music of every kind? We celebrate the two men who started it all, and we celebrate you, our faithful followers and fans."

Marcus spoke briefly about the Villa's history, and shared a few stories of the early shows, as told to him by Hayne Williams and Robert

W. Edwards. He mentioned the first weekend performance in 1958, The Tiny Little Theater in the Barn highlights, and the beginning of the new theater.

"The most significant thing about the new theater chapter," he said, "was an overheard comment. In 1968, after a sold out performance in what was then known as the Great Hall, here, this lovely room we are in, which caps at 100 people and back then had the low lighting of the brothel it had been..." Marcus paused for a laugh..."a wealthy fan of the Villa named Robert MacCurdy happened to sit near a potted palm in the Atrium. On the other side of that palm, Hayne Williams leaned back in his chair and said to his companions (Robert "Diesel" Edwards and Gabriel Michaels), 'What we need is a well lit theater.'

"Mr. MacCurdy parted the palm fronds and said, 'Mr. Edwards, I'll give you a million dollars for your Well Lit Theater if the community will match it.'

"And a community campaign raised another $1,000,000. In 1968, that was enough to build a theater with 400 seats. The Well Lit Theater was finished and launched in 1970 with Benjamin Britten's *Turn of the Screw.*"

Big applause made Marcus beam. He looked around the room.

There were the donors and the fans and the mayor! Hayne and Diesel looked content. And the staff! Oh my word—Grady and Patrick, in tuxes, sitting with MeiMei and LuLu, of all people. Chatting! He hadn't even noticed, he was so busy with the hoity toity. For some reason, it made him really happy.

"We would like to share with you now the six soloists in our *Cosi fan tutte* production, each of whom will sing their favorite aria, accompanied by our Music Director, Sampson Powers." Sampson looked up at Marcus from the piano. He felt a heart pumping, light flashing moment of joy. He wasn't sure, but he thought he'd just been given a new title.

SMOOCH AND KENDRA

Smooch and Kendra took their dinners from the kitchen and scurried over to the dorm to avoid the incoming well-dressed guests. They could have attended the Gala, but when invited, they preferred the quiet company of each other on that momentous evening. They had a plan:

to divest themselves of the dramas around them, talk out their hurts and drink to their health.

In addition to her dinner, Smooch carried an ice pack for her purpling shiner. Kendra had the wine and two glasses packed in a Gala swag bag.

When they arrived at Kendra's room, she slid open the door to the tiny patio and they spread their loot out on the little table. Kendra brought out a small water glass holding a single rose. She set it in the middle of the table.

The warm evening, cooled on Kendra's patio by the shade of an old white oak, suited their needs of peace, quiet and fresh air, free of the eyes, ears, mouths and fists of any others, friend or foe.

Kendra pulled out the loosened cork and poured two glasses of pinot noir. They left the stainless covers over their dinners for the moment and started their celebration of friendship with a toast.

Kendra said, "Thank you for showing up like you did. I admit you were my idea. Sorry you got pulled into such...pulled in. To you." She raised her glass and had a sip.

"Was I your idea? We hardly knew each other," said Smooch.

"True, but, other than your choice of husbands, you have a good reputation." They laughed.

Smooch said, "And to you, Kendra Masters. Welcome to the world backstage. How do you feel about being out of the limelight?"

They drank to that, too.

"Fine," said Kendra. "I'm over the limelight. It hurts my big toe."

They sipped for another moment.

"That's a nice shiner you've got there. I'm sorry I was occupied at the time. I could have helped pick you up off the floor."

Smooch said, "Ha! That girl came at me like a fury. What do you suppose she thinks I did? I didn't take her man. I hardly knew Falcon Jennings."

"I hear her mother got new drugs and took her home. Marcus says she's marginally compos mentis right now."

"Yeah, well, I don't care how compos mentis she is. Keep her away from me."

"Happy Friday the 13th," said Kendra.

SMOOCH AND MARCUS HAVE A CHAT

Smooch was in her own bed in the dorm by 10. When Marcus called, she pushed the button on her cell phone and said, "Please don't be the bearer of any more bad news."

Marcus said, "I'm not. I'm just checking in to make sure you're OK. How's your shiner?"

"Purpler and purpler," she said. "I'm fine. I'm glad I didn't have my glasses on."

"Lordy, I'm so sorry, Smooch. Were you alone tonight? You should be watched over for a few hours."

"I was with your girlfriend."

"She's not my girlfriend, Smooch."

"Well, she should be. But I'll shut up."

"I've heard from Mrs. Watts," Marcus said. "You'll be glad to know Martha has calmed down and is reasonably lucid. She apparently had her on the wrong drug. I don't know how long this will last, but I'm going over to Petaluma to see her tomorrow. If she's lucid, Grady and Patrick would like to talk to her again."

"Well, don't go alone. I'll be glad when this part is over. Between Willard and Martha, I don't know who's crazier. What's the latest on Lurch?"

"Still out of it. Not shaking anymore and his fever is over."

"OK."

Marcus said, "I'm sorry it's worked out this way. I had no idea this would turn into a cat fight."

Smooch laughed. "It's OK, Marcus. I'd do it again. I'm like you. And Kendra. And all the rest. I do it for the art. What else should I be doing?"

NIGHT BEFORE OPENING NIGHT

Marcus's ritual of "Night before Opening Night" conversations with Hayne and Diesel continued, even after their retirement last year. At first, Marcus considered it a necessary condition of the old gents' retirement, and not always a positive one. But now, Marcus reconsidered. He saw how lit up they were in their involvements. And how much the company loved them both and loved just having them around.

Marcus, pretty lit up himself this night, walked up the hill to Hayne and Diesel's home, excited about new possibilities.

He found Hayne and Diesel out on the deck, basking in moonlight. Hector had gone to bed. The old gents offered Marcus a sherry and he gladly took it. They toasted each other.

"Is Hector all right?" Marcus asked. "He didn't look well after Martha's little scene in the Old Hall."

Hayne said, "Hector went to bed early. You know he doesn't like Galas. 'Too noithy, hurtth my earth,' he says. Plus, he's got something on his mind to remember. When that happens, Hector tends to disappear for a while. But, he's fine."

A few minutes of poetic rambling about the evening's events led them to, of course, the future. Marcus thanked them for stepping in to save their artistic and professional behinds in this most egregious situation. Both Hayne and Diesel said they would be sad to see this week of rehearsals and puppets and creativity end. Silver linings, and all that.

"Well, that's just what I wanted to talk about tonight." Pause for dramatic effect.

"Uh oh," said Hayne, with a smile. "What next?"

Marcus smiled. "I don't want to disturb your retirement. I want to enhance it. I would like to revert to an old way, in a new way."

Marcus had heard so much about Hayne and Diesel's long time partnership with Gabriel Michaels. From Marcus's point of view after ten years of work with the Villa, rotating through a succession of outside talent—particularly stage and music directors—didn't work out so cohesively.

"So, here's my suggestion: We have new people who fit with the company vision. Sampson stepped in so beautifully, it almost makes me cry again to think about it. He is focused and professional and musically adept.

"And, Diesel, you say Kendra has potential as a stage director.

"We'd need an in-house art director, and I have an idea about that. But, the point is, I would like to ask you both to be Villa Mentors— you, Diesel to Kendra, and you, Hayne, to a new art director. I'd like the Villa to have its own team again—who know each other, work well together and have the same vision always in the forefront of their minds. Like you did in the beginning.

"But it won't work without you. If we can work out a plan that wouldn't tie you down, or wear you out, would you be willing to rejoin the Villa on emeritus levels and be our guides?"

CHAPTER TWELVE
SATURDAY, JUNE 14, 2008

Our peace shall stand as firm as rocky mountains.
Henry IV
~ Wm. Shakespeare

HECTOR TRIES TO REMEMBER

Hector woke up Saturday morning filled with agitation. He tossed and turned until he got out of bed and opened the window. He felt the breeze on his face and let it wake him, like a bird feather on his cheeks.

Hector closed his eyes to listen to the rustling sounds of the leaves. Madrone trees shed bark in thin strips in June, and when he listened really hard, he could hear the bark peeling off. When he *looked* really hard, he saw all the different colors as it shed its skin to reveal smooth, new, greenish bark that ripens into a deep, dark red. He could hear it turning red. Within a month, Hector might have six baskets filled with peeled madrone bark, useful faerie town building material.

Hector's biggest problem was hanging onto a thought once it arrived in his mind. He worried and worried until he forgot what he was worrying about and then worried about worrying. And forgetting. Immersing himself in garden chores helped.

This Saturday morning he planned to feed all the pumpkin plants in the patch. He picked up his shovel and bucket and went to shift some dirt around.

Hector moved methodically along the rows, careful not to step on any seedlings popping up in non-standard places. The pumpkin vines had early flowers to pinch back. He had his eye on one plant on which to pinch back all flowers except one, for a big giant gigantic huge "humoungeth" pumpkin.

Noodleth, he thought.

He shook his hands out like they were wet while he tried to remember the words. *Oodleth of Noodleth.*

Marcus and Priscilla Take a Drive to Petaluma on Saturday Morning

"About Martha," Marcus said. "Her mother said it's like dealing with two different people. She's had a couple of spells, and she is…remote… but *in there*, you know? But, kind of in and out."

Priscilla said, "OK. Yes. I saw that yesterday. I feared for her safety—well, everyone's, really. Driving her mother's big car. Flushing pills! Punching out Smooch! She's a loose cannon. Very dramatic woman."

"Yes. I asked you to come with me for two reasons. One, because I know I shouldn't go alone to these kinds of meetings. I need a witness, and all that. But, two, I heard you handled Martha well yesterday, and I thought she might remember that and feel more comfortable with you."

"Yes. Good idea."

"I want to take her emotional and mental pulse, see if she's really able to speak to Grady and Patrick. I know this is distressing for her, but they are pushing for it now. 'Get in there while she's lucid,' they said. We can assess that. She could be of some help if she can talk now. She might know more than she's been able to say, so far. Mrs. Watts is doing better, too. Calmed the EFF down, as you say."

Hector Saves the Day

"Oh, noooooo! I 'member, now. Oh, nooooo. It'th Oodleth of Poodleth. Poodleth on Noodleth. Oh, noooo."

Hector threw down the rake and ran like the wind to get to Haynie on the deck. He kept repeating, so he wouldn't forget, "Oodleth of poodleth…oodleth of poodleth…"

Hayne saw Hector coming. He stood up to great him.

"Ohhhh, Haynie, I'm tho thowwy, I'm tho thowwy. I am beaw'ing vewwy bad newth."

Hector's head kept moving and bouncing from side to side. He was so agitated, he'd lost every correction to his speech he'd ever learned and babbled incoherently. His face glistened with sweat and he panted a little. Hayne suggested they sit down on the bench.

"Now, why do you have bad news, Hector? Tell me what's happened."

206

Hector's eyes weren't focused. "It'th noodleth on poodleth, Haynie. Oodleth of poodleth. Oh dear, oh dear..."

Hector is remembering the red poodle skirt the day Falcon became D.E.A.D. "The r-r-ed poodle thkirt. Haynie, Maw'tha! Maw'tha'th thkirt! She wath there!"

"Where was Martha, Hector? Just breathe. Take your time."

"The red poodleth thkirt made me think about Maw'tha befo'. Befo' she changed to...I don't know. Changed. Oodleth of poodleth. I made a joke...about her thkirt, once, Haynie. Maw'tha laughed and laughed. She ith not laughing now. Anyway, oodleth..."

"Where was Martha on the day Falcon died, Hector?"

"In the busheth, Haynie. In her red and white poodle thkirt. I think she went to the thecret door."

Ten minutes later, Grady and Patrick sped their way to Petaluma.

MARTHA

Martha palavered a litany of complaints and whines about her mother. Whenever Marcus or Priscilla tried to mention Falcon, she changed the subject.

"I don't like her cooking, either. I think she puts extra meds in my food. I can't even go to the bathroom without her following me. She thinks..."

Marcus tried once more. "Martha, can you talk to us about what happened to Falcon? We need your help to solve this puzzle."

"Then," Martha said, ignoring Marcus's question, "then, she took me to the doctor yesterday. The doctor! As if that was what I needed. What I need is..."

Marcus was getting tired of being so conciliatory. He and Priscilla had finished Mrs. Watts's coffee and were about to give up when they heard a car in the driveway. Before you could say Jack Spratt, Grady and Patrick were in the room on either side of Martha Jennings with their guns drawn.

Martha froze in her chair. Her eyes grew wide and her face turned beet red.

"Patrick, Grady, what's this about," Marcus asked, jumping up from his chair. "What in blazes?"

"Martha Jennings, we have reason to believe you murdered your husband, Falcon Jennings." This was Grady, in his bluntest aspect.

Martha tried to get up but Grady restrained her. Marcus said later that he could hear and see Martha's body deflate, like she had been holding her breath for a week and could finally exhale.

Her long exhale breathed into, "Falcon asked me to do it."

Marcus practically fell back down in his chair. Mrs. Watts stood in the kitchen doorway, eyes wide.

Priscilla rose, went to Mrs. Watts and took her hand. Patrick put his gun away.

"Kill him? Falcon asked you to kill him?" asked Grady, putting his gun in its holster. He pulled up a chair and sat down next to Martha.

Turning cold, she said, "No...No...Kill Willard..." Martha paused for a very long time. Marcus saw the wheels turning inside her head. He saw her weigh the situation. He watched her face and in fact her whole countenance change when she realized she was completely defeated, and there was nowhere to hide. "I meant to kill Willard."

"What? And you missed?" asked Patrick.

"I miscalculated. I only had the tiny cable hole to see. I thought it was Willard...but their hair is the same...and they had brown jackets on...and they both look down at pennies."

"Pennies?"

Martha was silent.

Priscilla said, "Pennies. Slipping pennies in their shoes. For good luck. They had the same habit." Marcus looked at Priscilla. She raised her eyebrows and shrugged.

"OK, Martha. Go on," said Patrick.

"Willard was my first love, ever. My first lover. It was a secret I had to keep, always. Sorry, Mother, you never knew. I was very, very, very young. Ha ha! Then Willard up and married Smooch, that b—married Smooch McGuinn! She stole him right out from under my nose."

Martha suddenly stopped talking, like her battery went dead.

After 30 seconds of silence, Grady said, "Martha, we're not going anywhere until you finish your story. It's best if you stay with us here."

Thirty more seconds elapsed before a disjointed and fast-paced explanation poured out of Martha in a torrent, a pitcher full of troublesome information, like her motor was revved up so high it spun faster and faster until an explosion was imminent.

"I kept seeing Willard, even after I married Falcon, even after he married Smooch McGuinn. Willard is…kind of addicting. I don't know. Hard to leave. Willard promised me he'd love me forever. He found out, Falcon did. He found out, of course. Then they had even more reason to hate each other. They always hated each other. I didn't care. I wanted them both. I couldn't have them both. So, I finally chose Falcon, because Willard wanted me but didn't love me. I figured that one out. Falcon loved me. Falcon hated Willard. I wanted to make it up to Falcon, what I'd done with Willard.

"One day, after they'd fought about something, I heard Falcon say, 'Will no one rid me of this meddlesome priest?' and I thought, *Oh, perfect. Just like King Henry! I can make it up to Falcon by getting rid of Willard.*

"So, I set out to kill Willard for Falcon. I knew I could win him back that way. Falcon. I knew he wanted Willard dead. Isn't that what he meant?

"Willard was sure to leave the meeting at 5, he is exact about those things, and he'd stop to pick up a shiny penny if he saw one, so I placed one on the floor, and I'd be up there with the chandelier ready to slice through the cable, and Willard would probably die and I could get out unseen down the secret stairs.

"See, I knew about the secret door and I went up to the cupola once with Willard, just to see where the stairway went, and we had a good laugh about how easy it would be to drop that chandelier on someone you wanted to get rid of. It was a joke, of course, it was a joke, but then it sounded plausible, and I thought, hah, hoist by your own petard, except this time the petard was the chandelier dropping on the victim, but the victim was the wrong guy, the wrong guy."

Then, Martha began to cry and beat her fists on the arms of her chair, still talking a mile a minute. "I thought it was Willard. I thought it was Willard. I didn't know until you told me, Marcus, that I had killed Falcon and not Willard. I was so sure I was free of him. Free of it. I was so excited to be meeting Falcon for dinner. Now Falcon is gone and Willard is still here. Still maddeningly alive!

"I was very thorough, though," she sniffed as the torrent of words continue to spill. "Wasn't I thorough, for a crazy person? I know you think I'm crazy. But, I thought of everything, you have to admit. Even my petticoats dusted the secret stairs behind me! No one would know it was me. Only Willard and I and Hector knew about the door, and Hector's memory...well, he doesn't remember anything, and Willard would be dead, so it was a pretty safe secret. And now, Willard is still alive. I was only worried once, when the door slammed behind me." Martha snarled this last, like in shock about being discovered. "You must have found out about my secret. How?"

Grady looked around the room and looked back at Martha and said, "You don't know Hector as well as you think you do."

"Hector?" she said.

Patrick asked, "Martha, who was the blonde with Willard when he discovered the secret door and stairs?"

"Well, me, of course. I have a wig for every occasion, you know, just like a petticoat for every skirt. I would not be caught dead without my wigs, or my petticoats."

HAYNE REMEMBERS

After Martha's confession, Marcus called Hayne and Diesel. Hayne went to find Hector. Hector blinked his eyes, not knowing whether he was happy or sad at the news.

For a few moments of beauty to balance the unpleasant truth, the threesome slipped into the full and final rehearsal of *Cosi fan tutte*. They took their favorite seats in the last row—in the dark, to sit and be quiet and absorb the sounds without disturbing the performers. Hector sat between his best friends in the world, thinking about Martha and Falcon and Willard and wondering what made people do the things they do.

Now, Willard and Martha were both in hospitals and Falcon Jennings was still D.E.A.D. Hector shook his head until Hayne put his hand on his. Then Hector closed his eyes and let the pretty music wrap him in a blanket of beauty.

Kendra sat down in the seat next to Diesel, who whispered the morning's events in her ear. From then on, it was hard to keep her mind on the rehearsal. She wondered about Marcus and how this news affected his fragile decisions.

Diesel patted Kendra's hand and whispered, "We did a good job, Kendra." She smiled and tried to focus on Sampson's back and the regular movements of his baton.

Hayne held Hector's hand and let the music take him away. He, too, was exhaling deeply after the week's events. He tried to think of any other major disturbance in all their 50 years of occupation in The Theaters at Villa Zanetta. But every blooper or disaster or event was nothing compared to this.

There was the time the power went out during the last act of Macbeth *and the actors completed the performance with flashlights. But it just added to the general spookiness and the audience thought we meant to do it!*

Or, how about the final duet in Don Pasquale *where the tenor had to sing both parts because the soprano missed her entrance? Ha ha! That was tenor Daniel Greebs, the best Mighty Mouse of all performers.*

He filled in several times at the last minute, and I think he was the one who sang in the pit for the tenor when he had laryngitis and there was no time to learn the staging, so Daniel sang in the pit and the sick tenor completed his roll by mouthing the words and syncing his lips with Daniel.

After the rehearsal, the foursome met on the patio at the big table. To lighten their load of dark thoughts, Hayne said, "Remember when the windmill scenery fell on Don Quixote in *Man of La Mancha*?" Everyone laughed. Soon, they were engaged in a full trip down memory lane.

Diesel remembered the 80s, when the recorded wind and storm sounds for *Hamlet* suddenly turned into disco music during the show.

"The last time we ever had candles on stage," Hayne said, "was in *Lady Windermere's Fan*, when the curtains ignited and the crew put out the fire with extinguishers."

Hector enjoyed this immensely. He said, "'Member the pizza boy?" And everyone laughed, thinking of the unlocked stage door and the lost and wandering deliverer arriving on the stage with three pepperoni pizzas in the middle of the last act of *Evita*.

There were so many memories, bloopers and scenery disasters, like the night the singer tripped, fell into the pit and landed on the kettle drum, or...

But, wait, Hayne thought. *I should be writing these down. What shall I call my book?*

In an inspired pre-concert lecture, Sampson spent some time on the genesis of *Cosi fan tutte*, those early stories, like *The Deceived Women*, that led to the libretto and the creation of the opera.

He described the plot of *Cosi* and discussed its relative silliness and what else Mozart was up to at the time of its creation.

"So as you can see," he said to his attentive audience, "it's much too easy to belittle *Cosi fan tutte* simply because its plot is quaint, outmoded, and preposterous. But *Cosi* was never meant to be real-life any more than were its predecessors, the commedia dell'arte players of the 16th and 17th centuries.

"*Cosi* is a farce, pure and simple, an entertainment. But, it is ennobled by some of the most divine music Mozart ever wrote. Mozart's music takes us into the world of imagination, far beyond disguises and mere comedy. It elevates and inspires us with its beauty.

"As an Austrian poet wrote long ago, let's allow this music to 'bear us away to a better world.'"

THE WELL LIT THEATER
WELCOME AND PRE-CONCERT ANNOUNCEMENT
BY MARCUS BROWN

"Welcome to the 50th anniversary of Villa Zanetta. I loathe pre-concert speeches, but due to the chaos and sadness of the last week, we thought you might like to hear some good news.

"We have been thrown together, the musicians, the staff, the soloists, the leadership and all the supporting members of our artistic community—we have been thrown into a cauldron of change. Much to our amazement, the main ingredient in this pot of soup was the tragedy which caused the death of our *Cosi fan tutte* stage director, Falcon Jennings.

"To be honest, we have been struggling with the constant need to find the right mix of artistic leadership for every show. We need more than musicianship in a music director, more than stagecraft in a stage director, more than a good keen eye, a sense of the ridiculous as well as the sublime in an artistic director. We want to know that these key ingredients to a good performance and an enjoyable production will blend together with the entire company to create the perfection we seek, on our stage, in the pit, in the presentation.

"We are so fortunate to have our former Associate Conductor, Sampson Powers join the team as Music Director of Villa Zanetta. He has taken the podium with grace, humor and focus, and we are grateful.

"The founders of The Theaters at Villa Zanetta, Hayne Williams and Robert 'Diesel' Edwards, have stepped up to the challenging tasks of this summer and are assisting the Villa Zanetta company in bringing you beautiful art, in every way, and we thank them for that. Mr. Edwards has assumed the duties of Stage Director for this production of *Cosi fan tutte* with our able Assistant Director, Kendra Masters, and Mr. Williams is back in The Tiny Little Theater in the Barn, with his arms full of puppets.

"But, even more exciting is the news that they will allow us to disturb their retirement further. Beginning immediately, Mr. Edwards and Mr. Williams will join us as Mentors to our new Director Fellowship Training Program at Villa Zanetta.

"And so, we present to you, our first participants in the Director Fellowship. Please join me in welcoming Kendra Masters, our first Stage Director Fellow, and Samantha Margaret 'Smooch' McGuinn as Artistic Director Fellow."

When the two women walked onto the stage, the audience erupted in approval.

"Thank you for the opportunity to make this announcement before the concert. We can all relax into the music now. An die Musik. To music."

SUCCESS

The backstage area at The Well Lit Theater at Villa Zanetta almost split its sides with exuberant people: musicians, supporters, staff, audience members and well-wishers of all sorts.

"What an amazing production!" was the buzz.

Sampson Powers found himself surrounded by fans. The soloists basked in adulation. Bette Belle held court with a bevy of adoring men.

Kendra Masters stood between Diesel and Hayne, shaking hands with practically everyone. Even Hector, who normally left immediately after seeing a show from backstage, stood proudly by his people and clapped every time he heard an appreciative comment. Hector was still confused by all the disturbing happenings of the last week, but, well, everyone seemed so happy, he let it wash over him, like a warm rain. He said to Hayne, "Show bithneth ith tho fun."

But, it is more than fun. It is essential.

Marcus Brown stood off to the side. This moment was for the creators of this event, and he wanted these folks to have the glory. They deserved it.

Look at them, he thought. *A week ago we were poleaxed in shock and sadness, involved in a company-wide case of PTSD. Tonight, they have proven themselves true thespians, true artists. Each and every one of our people stepped up, stayed professional, helped each other, and made this production one of the best in our history. Even Diesel, our fiercest critic, agreed.*

Marcus was understandably still rattled by, not only the morning's discoveries, but the lingering effects of his brush with death. *Perhaps we can put Falcon to rest now,* he thought; *the "culprit," Martha, is in custody and under the protection of the Gateway nurses, Willard is emerging from his delirium, Opening Night is over, and I am not retiring to Point Reyes, with or without a dog.*

Martha disturbed him greatly. What kind of crazy mind would take a comment ("Who will rid me of this meddlesome priest?") from a famous play (*Beckett*) about an event that happened in 1170 and hear it as a request or an order and be motivated to kill someone? And, in Martha's case, her own lover!

He remembered the term "stochastic violence" from a recent article he read about rhetoric. Did King Henry II really mean to have his minions kill Thomas Becket, Archbishop of Canterbury? Or was it hyperbole and completely misunderstood? We'll never know.

But in 1170, following the murder, Becket was venerated and Henry, vilified. There were demands that the king be excommunicated. Pope Alexander made Henry do public penance before he would let him hear a Mass. The four knights got themselves excommunicated by the

Pope and had to go on "penitentiary pilgrimages" to the Holy Land for fourteen years.

Did Falcon mean it? Of course not. Did he? No. What will happen to Martha? And Willard?

MARCUS AND KENDRA

Relieved of its evening's full audience, the theater darkened, and the revelers moved from backstage to the Old Hall, where a cast party was in full motion. Drinks were poured, finger foods gobbled, tears and laughter and joy and relief and all kind of other emotions bloomed fully in the glow of a successful event.

Marcus and Kendra caught each other's eyes from across the crowded Old Hall. Marcus excused himself from a throng of admirers and began to walk her way. Kendra, just accepting a glass of Sonoma Cutrer from a waiter, took a second glass and walked toward Marcus.

When they met, she handed him a glass of his favorite chardonnay and they moved to Marcus's quiet and always reserved table in the back of the room. For the moment, neither Marcus nor Kendra had words. Oh, believe me, myriad thoughts, but no words could express those thoughts adequately, so they remained blissfully silent.

They sat down across from each other and clicked glasses. For a few minutes, they listened to the roar of the crowd. The roar was chirpy, full of exclamations and excitement. It filled them with gladness, on many levels.

Marcus, who began the week's events with the scare of his life and a longing to escape, felt at peace with all his decisions except one, which he would take care of now.

Kendra, who a week ago thought her new career was over, was blown away by the actual events. Although her grief about Falcon still hovered, and her deep embarrassment over that impulsive declaration to Marcus still lingered, Kendra felt good inside, like something had healed, or at least had begun to heal.

She made herself look at Marcus.

He said, "After closing night, would you go to Point Reyes with me to see my new cabin?"

Standing Ovation

Marcus felt the need to address the revelers before the adrenaline began to fade. He said to Kendra, "Don't go away." He walked to the stage and boosted himself up to sit on its edge. When the partiers saw him there, someone started to clap, and soon, all stood up and gave Marcus a three minute standing ovation. He knew not why. He kept shaking his head and laughing, like, *What are ya'll doing?*

Smooch McGuinn approached Marcus with a large rolled paper in her hand. As the din died down, she said to him, "Thanks for coming up here so I didn't have to go looking for you."

Marcus had a big question mark visible in his face. "I came up to give some sort of thank you speech. What's this?"

Smooch half addressed Marcus and half the group of 60. She was elated to have been singled out for this honor, and gave it her best. Somehow, her life, too, had turned around, and she wanted him to know it.

"Marcus, we know what you did this week to keep us together. We know it was not easy, with you're having been so…uhm…close to the 'incident.' But, we all have been affected in some way by the events happening here at Villa Zanetta, and we want you to know that we appreciate you, that we see the good you have created out of a bad situation. We have nothing give you but our love, so here it is. It is signed by everyone in this room."

Smooch handed Marcus a scroll. When he unrolled it, he found a hand painted red heart and the signatures of his 60 companions on this ride.

Marcus took off his glasses and cried. There would be no speech.

Midnight
Hayne Diesel and John Eagle and Hector Chat

Hayne said, "John Eagle, I invited you over tonight because I am vibrating with this book idea and I just want to say one thing about it so I can sleep tonight. I want you to help me. But I also want you to finish the book if I die before it's done. And, I want to write it as kind of a memoir. Almost like a novel."

John Eagle smiled, nodded, and accepted the job. Of course he did. John Eagle was dedicated to telling the Villa Zanetta story.

Hector, lying in his beanbag chair with Furry Bells, started to mumble. "No, no, no, no, no, no, no..."

Hayne, Diesel, and John Eagle looked over at Hector. Again, he mumbled, "No, no, no..."

Hayne stood up from his chair and went to Hector. He got down on the floor. "Hector, look at me. What is troubling you? Look at me, honey."

"Bad. I made it bad fo' Mawtha. Mawtha in twouble. Go to jail. They make her D.E.A.D."

"No, Hector. Martha will get help. She is in hospital. Not jail. Martha is not a bad person, Hector. She's sick."

"The nurtheth and doctorth can help Mawtha?" Hector wiped his tears.

"Yes, honey. They will help Martha. You can let it go, now. You helped everyone, Hector. You did a good job."

Hector settled right down and held onto Hayne's hand. He sighed a big "letting go" sigh.

"OK, Haynie. If you thay tho."

Epilogue

Love all, trust a few, do wrong to none.
All's Well That Ends Well
~ Wm. Shakespeare

Over the last fifty years, much has happened on the brick patio in front of Villa Zanetta; plans schemed, parties reveled, ceremonies performed and tears cried. But this…

It was late. Closing nights are always late nights. Hayne and Diesel were often ensconced in their living room by now, or with their heads on pillows, falling asleep. But, even they were up, and jazzed, ready to party. The lights were lit, the drinks flowing, the snacks passed around. A successful festival after all, and all hearts, minds, and souls on that patio were cheering each other and beaming with joy and not just a little adrenalin.

Falcon was not forgotten, but he was put to rest, at last. Hayne felt they could relax a bit, now that Martha was corralled and Willard getting the help he needed. Poor Willard. When he heard the reason the penny he slipped in his shoe was on the Lobby floor, he broke down and cried.

The Wrap Party on closing night of the 2008 Summer Opera Festival signified so much more than the end of a run. It was a landmark moment, when Hayne and Diesel, after 53 years of partnership, held hands in front of their Villa Zanetta family and declared their commitment. John Eagle, of course, presided.

During the marriage ceremony (legalized in California for same-gender couples on June 16 of that year), Hayne and Diesel's best man, Hector Farmdale, put his arms around them both and felt he was every bit a part of this "getting mawwied bithneth." He only asked once if they hadn't "awweady been mawwied fo' fifty yearth?" Hayne smiled and said, "This is just something more official," and explained how and why he, Hector, was their Best Man. Hayne said, "Remember when we officially adopted you? It's kind of like that."

Hector said, "OK. Thoundth good."

218

When the vows of Hayne and Diesel were spoken before the group of supporters and loved ones, the room was as silent as a monastery.

John Eagle said, "Hayne, do you have something to say to Robert?"

And Hayne said, "D, you have been my companion for life, and there has been no other. You have been at my side, my helpmate and best friend. You have been my world within this world. I thank you for all that. Our time together has been a true marriage, and I give you the rest of my life to see it through."

John Eagle said, "Robert, what words do you have for Hayne?"

And Diesel said, "My best friend and companion, Hayne. I asked you to marry me in 1957, right here on this spot on this patio, when we found Villa Zanetta together on a sunny day in May, and here we are. I cherish our time together, and I give you the rest of my life to see it through." The crystals trimming Hector's tuxedo glimmered in the light.

Among the guests were other couples and revelers, brought together by several creative declarations. Here were the sheriffs, in jeans and plaid shirts, getting to know MeiMei and LuLu Chinn. There were Marcus and Kendra, planning a getaway to the coast. After the ceremony, Hayne watched John Eagle head toward Priscilla with two glasses of champagne. Even Smooch and Sampson looked to be enjoying each other's company.

Hayne took a glass from Diesel and sat back in his chair. Diesel sat down beside him. There was so much to be grateful for, and so much joy to embrace in the future.

"*An die Musik*," Diesel said, raising his glass to Hayne. "To Music."

"To Music," said Hayne, and they touched glasses, looked into each other's eyes and felt deep and complete contentment.

– END –

CODA

An die Musik

"ahn dee moozeek"

(To Music)

Du holde Kunst, in wieviel grauen Stunden,
Wo mich des Lebens wilder Kreis umstrickt,
Hast du mein Herz zu warmer Lieb' entzunden,
Hast mich in eine beßre Welt entrückt!

Oft hat ein Seufzer, deiner Harf' entflossen,
Ein süßer, heiliger Akkord von dir,
Den Himmel beßrer Zeiten mir erschlossen,
Du holde Kunst, ich danke dir dafür.

You lovely art, in so many gloomy hours,
While the turmoil of life swirled around me,
Have you kindled the warmth of love in my heart
And borne me away to a better world.

Often a sigh, flowing from your harp,
A sweet and holy harmony from you,
Has revealed to me a heaven of happier times.
You lovely art, I thank you for this.

This poem was written in 1817 by the Austrian poet Franz von Schober. He gave a handwritten copy to his good friend, Franz Schubert, who set the words to music in Vienna that year. Schober was 21, Schubert was 20.

Schober's poem was never published and the original copy he gave to Schubert was lost. The poem survives today only as the lyrics in one of Schubert's most beloved songs.

(English version of the poem by David Gordon)

Author's Note

In 2014, my husband, David Gordon, wrote and published *Carmel Impresarios*, a cultural biography of the two women who, among other creative endeavors, founded Carmel Music Society and the Carmel Bach Festival in the early 1900s. For two years, while David researched and wrote about Dene Denny and Hazel Watrous, we joked that these two marvelous beings were always with us—at breakfast, at dinner, all day and long into the night. Fascinated by their ultra productive and creative lives, we discussed them thoroughly and regularly.

Dene and Hazel met in the 1920s and were together until Hazel's death in 1956. They built an artistic empire worth reading about and lived lives worthy of emulation. Their commitment to the arts, to the communities they served, and to each other inspired us. They lived as examples of two besties being more than the sum of their parts.

Read David's *Carmel Impresarios* for the full story of what Dene and Hazel accomplished.

Part of the fascination was that in all the historical material from newspapers, microfilms, memoirs, history books and letters, there were no mentions of their sexual preferences, gender identities, or partnership choices. They were simply Dene and Hazel, who touched many lives and built lasting organizations centered on music, art and ideas. They opened art galleries. They built their own home with their own four hands. They sponsored other artists. Dene was a brilliant avant-garde pianist. Hazel created everything from typefaces to house plans to paintings and unique printed programs for concerts. They were truly a dynamic duo with fire in their veins. They are buried in the same crypt in Monterey, California.

Our discussions about Dene and Hazel began in late 2011. David—historian and researcher—unearthed their library cards, birth certificates, various addresses, and the many contributions they made to the society in their purview. They became our friends, post mortem.

Fast forward to sometime in 2016, when the ongoing conversation turned to, "What was it like for them to live, work and play? Did they hide their love, or was it just accepted? Did they start with a big plan, or did they start out small and blossom into the leaders they became?" And then, one day, one of us asked, "What if two people came together, bonded for life, and started a performing arts colony? What would that be like?"

We created two characters: Hayne Williams and Diesel Edwards. The "ha ha" turn in their first names is one eeny weeny reference honoring Dene and Hazel. This is *not* a story about the Carmel Bach Festival. *Bear Me Away to a Better World* is about love, creativity and community, and how two people can make the world a better place.

One of my favorite scenes in *The King and I* finds His Highness, King Mongkut of Siam, dictating a letter to Anna Leonowens in the middle of the night.

The King, getting sleepy now, waves his hand. He says, "You fix up," and goes to his bed to sleep.

David's and my writing partnership goes something like that. After four years of notes, research and character development, he looked at me and said, "You're the fiction writer. You fix up."

I could not have written this book without David Gordon. His memories of show business, spontaneously imagined situations, responses to my questions (which usually began with, "What would happen if…?"), and encouragement have made *Bear Me Away* a reality. He is my story reality checker, my editor, my esteemed Happy Hour mate.

Thank you, David Gordon.

~ Ginna BB Gordon

FURTHER
ACKNOWLEDGEMENTS

A heartfelt thank you to my early (beta) readers, who pondered fragments, parts and full story readings as *Bear Me Away to a Better World* came together: Dennis Britten (author of *Men Shake Hands*), Dr. Frank DeLuca (author of *Humans: Enriching Relationships Through the Enneagram*), Ken Gregg, Gene Leutkemeyer (author of *Penitentiary Tales* and more), Anne Brooke, Nan Heflin, Barbara Rose Shuler, Marilyn Power Scott, and Melissa Lofton. Their notes and comments were in essence, "Write on!" which gave me heart.

Katherine Edison, my developmental editor, colleague and good friend, walked word-wise with me every step of the way, from Hayne and Diesel's first art class encounter to the final moments in the Epilogue. Katherine read *Bear Me Away* multiple times, made perfect suggestions and, in the kindest way possible, told me the truth when the story confounded or confused her, with brilliant fixes.

Dene Denny and Hazel Watrous started it. During the two years David researched and wrote *Carmel Impresarios*, their energies lived with us, 24/7/365. I thank these two impresarios and muses for the inspiration, dedication and resolution to keep writing.

I am eternally grateful to Franz von Schober for writing a poem called *An die Musik* in early-19th-century Vienna.

And I am grateful to Wolfgang Amadeus Mozart for writing *Cosi fan tutte* and *Ave verum corpus*.

My homage of appreciation for David Gordon is large and everlasting.

~ Ginna

About the Author

Ginna BB Gordon's life has been surrounded by music and the arts. Her father, Richard, was a musician, composer and conductor, her mother, Virginia, an actor, architect and accomplished artist in several mediums. While Ginna was in her mother's womb, Richard composed hymns and played them on the piano to ease Virginia's dreams. Morning reveille blasted through the household intercom at 6am and usually included a Sousa march.

After moving to California as a teenager, Ginna experienced 14 years on the stages of community theaters, with occasional bits in film and TV.

Ginna's passion for organic growing and cooking beautiful food led her to myriad venues where she reigned as chef, from a small conference center in Calistoga to the Chopra Center for Well Being in La Jolla, and a few cafes and restaurants in between.

Ginna began her writing career at age nine with *How to be Obnoxious in 25 Easy Lessons* (written at the suggestion of her irritated big brother). Now lost to history, *Obnoxious* is remembered as a small comic book with stick figure cartoons, stapled in the middle.

Ginna's first book was *A Simple Celebration, the Nutritional Program for the Chopra Center for Well Being*, published by Random House in 1997.

While honing her writing skills, Ginna served for eight years as Operations Director and Event Planner for Carmel Music Society, the oldest performing arts non-profit west of the Mississippi. Following that, for another seven years she planned and managed major events for the Carmel Bach Festival and other West Coast organizations.

Ginna has written five cookbooks, including *The Soup Kit*, a comprehensive guide to making gourmet broths and soups; *Bonnebrook* and *The Gingerbread Farm*, the first two volumes in her cooking memoir series; *First You Grow the Pumpkin*, about growing, making, and preserving culinary treats; and her latest, *Once a Baker: 100 Bakery Favorites*.

Ginna's previous novels are *Looking for John Steinbeck, Deke Interrupted* and *Humming in Spanish*, the first three volumes in her ongoing Lavandula Series, a saga about coming of age in California in the 1960s.

Ginna lives on the Pacific Rim with her husband, David Gordon, musician, book designer, and author of two non-fiction books. Together Ginna and David run Lucky Valley Press, a boutique book design and pre-press company serving independent authors throughout the US.

Bear Me Away to a Better World is Ginna's 11th book.

Learn more about Ginna at **www.luckyvalleypress.com**

ABOUT THE WITH

D avid Gordon was deeply involved in the development and creation of *Bear Me Away to a Better World*. He served as a reality check, advisor, a source of background information, a provider of show-biz color and details, and a constant and faithful supporter of the author.

After conservatory training in Montreal and Chicago, David made his operatic debut with the Lyric Opera of Chicago in 1973. In the following decades he forged a distinguished international career as opera and concert tenor, voice teacher, lecturer, and author.

David has appeared as tenor soloist with virtually every major North American symphony orchestra, and with other prestigious orchestras and music festivals on four continents. His classical repertoire spans eight centuries of music and eight languages.

"*A virtuoso singer and actor*," (Salzburg *Nachrichten*), David has portrayed 60 principal roles on the stages of the Chicago Lyric Opera; San Francisco Opera; Houston Grand Opera; Metropolitan Opera; Washington National Opera; Hamburg Staatsoper (Germany), and other opera companies in North America, Europe, and Japan.

David's classical discography includes eight centuries of music on CDs for RCA Red Seal, Decca, London, Telarc, Naxos, Delos, and Vox.

The music of J.S. Bach has a special place in David's career as singer, lecturer, and author. The Chicago *Tribune* described him as "*one of the world's great Bach tenors*," and the St. Louis Post-Dispatch called him "*One of the greatest interpreters of the Evangelist of our time*." He has sung Bach's music in hundreds of concerts in North and South America, Europe, and Japan.

David's fascination with Bach and daily life in historical times led him to write *The Little Bach Book*, his eclectic and unique study of the everyday world in Bach's time.

Learn more about David at **www.spiritsound.com**